Bing and Bucky and the Galaxy Orb

Pete Cleary

Galaxy Journeys LLC

1st edition 2024

To Aydan: You are the best reader I've ever known. I hope someday you can read this book to your children.

Growing up, the car ride to school was a daily occurrence that spanned up to two hours. Our family of five kids—comprising two girls and three boys—at that time were untouched by the distractions of cell phones, leaving vast stretches of time unfilled on our commutes. It was during these moments that my father's vivid imagination came to life, transforming mundane car rides into epic tales of adventure and intrigue.

My father, a master storyteller, introduced us to Bing and Bucky, characters who became as familiar to us as members of our own family. He spun tales of Bing and Bucky battling the ethereal Light People and their perilous encounters with the formidable Razor Man. These stories, rich with creativity and suspense, captivated us completely, making the miles pass quickly. I was particularly mesmerized by my father's ability to weave these narratives effortlessly, his imagination painting scenes more vivid than any landscape we passed by. My siblings and I hung on his every word, the stories making our journeys together not just bearable, but eagerly anticipated.

More than three decades have passed since my father's departure from this world, yet his stories—especially those of Bing and Bucky—remain a cherished memory within our family.

During holiday gatherings, reminiscences of those car rides and the fantastical worlds our father conjured would often surface, rekindling the warmth and wonder of those times.

It was a promise made in those moments of reflection—a vow to someday bring Bing and Bucky's adventures to life on the page, not only as a tribute to my father's extraordinary imagination but as a testament to the bond it fostered among us siblings.

This book, therefore, is dedicated to my dad, whose stories enchanted our childhood journeys and sparked our own imaginations. It serves as a homage to his creativity and a memento for my brothers and sisters, reminding us of the indelible mark those shared moments have left on our hearts. Through these pages, I hope to extend the legacy of Bing and Bucky, immortalizing the spirit of adventure and familial love that my father so brilliantly instilled in us.

Prologue

Out of all the stars and galaxies, we're bound by our simple minds to discover the endless possibilities that lie ahead. Is it truly fair to leave such a burden upon ourselves?

One wonders as the universe continues to live on, still untouched, still unknown, and still uncertain. Perhaps it is this very possibility of being simple-minded humans that pushes us to uniqueness, to greatness. Maybe our simple minds were made to explore these wonders, these mysteries. And maybe one day we will.

But that day is far away because the possibilities are endless, and the universe too.

***

"When you seek love with all your heart, you shall find its echo in the universe." – Rumi

***

" I don't think it's very useful to speculate on what God might or might not be able to do, rather we should examine what he actually does with the universe we live in. All our observations suggest that it operates according to well- defined laws. These laws may have been ordained by God, but it seems he does not intervene in the universe to break the laws, at least once he set the universe going." – Stephen Hawking.

***

After weeks at sea, the female Emperor penguin returned to the sprawling colony that painted the stark white ice with splotches of jet-black feathers. Her belly was full, her spirit alight with the rush of the hunt, but now her focus shifted—a primal, urgent need to reunite with her mate and their chick.

The ice echoed with the chorus of thousands of penguins, each uttering their own signature vibration. To any other creature, the sounds were indistinguishable from one another, a mere cacophony of nature. But to this mother, and to her kind, each vibration was as distinct as color, as individual as the very essence of the soul itself. Penguins vibrated their unique frequencies through the dense air, creating a tapestry of longing, duty, and recognition. It was through these vibrations that they found their families among the multitudes, the sound a direct resonance of their innermost selves—the very sound of their souls.

She positioned herself firmly on the ice, feeling the solid cold beneath her feet. She gathered a deep breath into her chest and released it, her throat and upper chest vibrating meticulously to emit her soul's signature. This vibration was not just a sound but a beacon crafted by nature, modulated by tiny muscles and air sacs to carry her unique essence. It traveled across the ice, an invisible thread seeking its other end.

Far from the sea's edge, nestled in a hollow carved into the snow, her mate stood guard over their fluffy, wide-eyed chick. His head was tilted, ever attentive to the symphony of sounds. Amidst the homogeneous calls, a thread of vibration struck him—a familiar, heart-stirring sequence that surged through his body. It was his mate's vibration, her soul calling to his, a melody woven into the fabric of his being. He responded instinctively, his own body mirroring the action, sending out a complementary vibration, rich and deep, a testament of his presence and their enduring bond.

Guided by this intimate exchange of vibrations, she navigated through the maze of black and white bodies, each step bringing her closer to the source of the reply. The vibrational path was clear and strong, drawing her with an almost magnetic pull. As she approached, his form became distinct, and their chick, sensing the nearing vibration of its mother, chirped excitedly.

The moment she arrived, the three of them huddled closely, their bodies touching, sharing warmth. The vibrations ceased, their purpose fulfilled. They stood together in the silent assurance of reunion, their connection a private language understood only by them, amidst the chaotic orchestra of the colony. The sound of their souls had guided them back to each other, a miracle of nature played out on the endless ice.

Chapter One

Something Big Is Happening Out There

Miranda, bathed in the soft glow of bedside lamps, sat amidst a sea of papers and folders strewn across her bed. The dim light cast shadows around her room, highlighting the intensity in her eyes as she pored over the documents. The coming day's presentation loomed over her—a presentation that could redefine their understanding of the universe.

Dr. Miranda Richards, director of the Laser Interferometer Gravitational-Wave Observatory (LIGO) in Hanford, Washington, was a prodigy in the realm of astrophysics. At thirty-eight, her achievements were nothing short of remarkable, with an academic lineage tracing back to MIT and Stanford University. Yet, it wasn't her credentials that set her apart tonight; it was the fervor with which she tackled the challenge before her.

Miranda, with her shoulder-length blonde hair and striking blue eyes, had a presence that was both commanding and charismatic. Her peers often joked about her multifaceted talents, suggesting she could excel in anything she set her mind to—be it leading groundbreaking research or inspiring the next generation of scientists with her dedication and passion.

Her journey started as a spirited, lone girl in a family with four brothers. Growing up in Colorado, hiking and skiing in the nearby mountains instilled in her a resilience that now defined her professional life. Her endless summer days traveling back to the northeast were spent exploring the campuses of MIT and the shores of Cape Cod, which nurtured a dream of adventure that had become her reality. Yet, as she sat there, her mind occasionally drifted to her nephews and nieces, whose pictures smiled back at her from the bedside table, a silent reminder of the world outside her scientific endeavors.

LIGO had two observatories, one in Hanford in southeastern Washington State, where Miranda lived, and the other in Livingston, tucked away in a pine forest east of Baton Rouge, Louisiana. It had the world's largest gravitational wave observatory, comprising two enormous laser interferometers located 3000 kilometers apart.

These observatories, more sensitive than any instrument ever conceived, listen for the faint ripples in the fabric of spacetime—gravitational waves. These waves, once just theoretical predictions, were now the key to unlocking some of the most profound secrets of the universe. Gravitational waves are created from some of the most violent and energetic processes in the universe. So powerful, so extreme, that their echoes bend the very essence of reality.

She scribbled in the margins as she turned the pages of her notes. The end of her pen found its way to her lips, where she chewed on it, deep in thought.

The LIGO observatory had been detecting gravitational waves for the past several years, and her latest presentation to the LIGO engineers was to reconfigure the detectors for the newest set of observations and data collection.

Miranda was no stranger to the late-night shifts as they bore their inspiration from her profound love for science and cosmology. It was her driving force, and while she had worked hard to attain her current role, she often felt tremendous pressure to meet the expectations of the funding organizations.

Miranda's heart always found its way back to the laughter and warmth of her oldest brother's home in the Colorado mountains, where her nieces and nephews filled the rooms with joy. Each birthday and Christmas, she was there, her gifts often blending education with fun, a testament to her love for both family and science. These moments, precious and too infrequent, reminded her of roads not taken, of whispers of a different life amidst the clamor of her achievements.

Her romantic endeavors, though earnest, had wilted under the unyielding demand of her dedication to her work. Relationships, it seemed, were another experiment in balancing forces she had yet to master. The gentle ribbing from her family about finding someone who shared her unwavering commitment to the cosmos was met with laughter, yet behind her jest about being "married to work" lay an unspoken yearning for a partner who understood the stars that captivated her mind and the dreams that fueled her soul.

Miranda's heart skipped as the sudden ring of her cell phone shattered the night's silence, its vibration a harsh contrast to the stillness of her bedroom. She cast a bewildered glance at the device as it persisted with its insistent melody. "Who could possibly need me at this hour?" she wondered aloud, the annoyance tinged with a trace of concern.

Leaning over, her eyes narrowed on the caller ID illuminating the screen. "The lab?" she whispered to herself, a mix of surprise and intrigue coloring her voice. Without hesitation, she grabbed the phone as it beckoned her once more.

"This is Miranda," she answered, her voice steady despite the unexpected call.

"Dr. Richards, my apologies for the late call," came the earnest voice from the other end, tinged with urgency. '"James, what's up?" Miranda questioned, recognizing his voice.

"We've encountered something... extraordinary with the detectors over the past couple of hours. We all agreed it was important we reach you immediately," he said with a hint of excitement in his voice.

"Extraordinary? What's happening, Dr. Spellman?" Miranda pressed, her initial irritation now replaced with a growing curiosity and concern.

Dr. Spellman's reply was measured, yet Miranda could detect the undercurrent of excitement in his voice. "We've conducted thorough diagnostics to rule out any anomalies. The equipment is functioning perfectly, but the signals we're receiving are unprecedented. The amplitudes are unlike anything we've ever recorded. And it's consistent across both here and Livingston."

A surge of adrenaline coursed through Miranda as she scribbled down the details Spellman provided, her mind racing with the implications of his words. "And the source? Have we pinpointed where these waves are coming from?" she asked, her voice barely concealing her anticipation.

"The team is finalizing the calculations as we speak," he assured her.

Without a moment's hesitation, Miranda's decision was made. "I'm on my way," she declared, a mixture of determination and excitement in her voice.

Miranda efficiently gathered her papers into her briefcase and switched her bedclothes for more suitable attire for the lab. The drive from her home to the laboratory, a 12-mile journey, was swift and uneventful. Upon her arrival, she greeted the security guard at the entrance gate with her badge.

"Working late again, Dr. Richards?" he asked, a familiar routine between them.

"Maybe something big, George," Miranda responded with a brief smile and nod in response before proceeding through the gate. After parking in her usual spot, she paused for a moment before entering the building, taking a moment to gaze at the star-filled sky—a habit born from her lifelong fascination with the cosmos.

"What do you have for me tonight?" she said quietly to herself, always curious about the unknown forces shaping the universe.

Inside the main LIGO operations center was somewhat reminiscent of NASA's control rooms, though on a smaller scale. Screens displayed an array of graphs and data, including some alerts and messages Miranda hadn't seen before, indicating something unusual was happening.

A technician came up and handed her a tablet, its display echoing the information shown on the larger screens. She scrutinized the data, her expression one of focused concern as she began to piece together the unusual signals they were receiving.

Looking at the tablet, she said, "A broad range of wave frequencies, some fluctuating or modulating in patterns. I have not seen this before. The signal is intermittent, with bursts of gravitational waves. Very unusual harmonics," she said, interpreting the data.

Doctor James Spellman, a young astrophysicist who had been working at the observatory for the past year, approached Miranda and said, "Notice the low-frequency wave overlaid with various higher-frequency components and intermittent amplitude spikes. We've never seen anything like this."

As he explained, Miranda's eyes darted back and forth across her tablet again.

"The gravitational wave's polarization exhibits unusual characteristics not seen in waves from any conventional astrophysical events we've observed," Doctor Spellman continued. "Like a noisy signal."

Miranda couldn't hide her frustration and skepticism. She turned to Doctor Spellman and asked, "This doesn't make any sense. Are you absolutely certain the detectors are functioning properly?"

"Doctor Richards, Livingston recorded the same signal signatures, the same frequency, and amplitude," Doctor Spellman responded. "They also said the source is very close, given the strength and wavelength of the signal."

"How close?" Miranda asked.

"We should know shortly. Bob is running the telemetry models now, but Livingston gave an estimate of approximately six billion kilometers," the technician responded.

"Kilometers? Not light years?" Miranda said incredulously. "That's impossible! That's just outside our solar system, about 1 billion kilometers from Pluto, I believe."

Suddenly, a cacophony of alarms shattered the routine hum of the control room, signaling a departure far from their typical observations. These were not the alerts the team was accustomed to; they signified something extraordinary—a profound deviation in the laser's behavior or a failure in the machinery that veered sharply from the known and expected. The monitors burst into life, their screens awash with urgent, flashing messages, capturing the attention of everyone present.

The Gravitational Wave monitor then translated the wave frequencies of space itself into sound—a sound that, for a moment, bridged the cosmic expanse. Initially, there was a subtle hum, so deep and resonant that it seemed to vibrate in their very bodies. This was not the characteristic chirp associated with black hole mergers, but rather a continuous, undulating tone, rich with complexity. Layered upon this bass were transient, varied pitches; some tones soared high and brief, while others stretched out, low and haunting.

In an instant, the room plunged into a dense silence, the auditory window into the cosmos abruptly closed.

The team in the LIGO control room froze, enveloped in a collective, breathless anticipation. The data on the monitors confirmed it—the gravitational wave detections from both Livingston and Hanford mirrored each other perfectly, dispelling any notion of error or anomaly.

"I just got the distance calculation of the wave source," Bob spoke loud enough for the entire control room to hear. "It's approximately six billion kilometers, the same as the Livingston calculation."

"What in God's name is going on out there?" Miranda said softly.

Several of the physicists who had been in the operations room watching the event gathered around Miranda. They stood close, their eyes fixed on her, silently awaiting her insights.

"Well," Miranda began, "since we observed the same signals from Livingston, we have to assume that we just witnessed some kind of real gravitational wave event."

Miranda looked over their concerned faces.

"Let's talk about these observations, starting with your insights, Bob." Miranda turned towards Bob, the observatory's sage, whose wisdom was as evident as the years etched in the lines of his face and the untamed, thinning hair that spoke of countless nights spent under the stars.

Bob had long been the cornerstone of their team, his knack for navigating the labyrinth of complex calculations and machinery adjustments revered by all. Yet, even he seemed momentarily adrift in the sea of the unknown.

"Truthfully, Dr. Richards," Bob admitted, his voice laced with a rare uncertainty, "the phenomena we're observing are unprecedented in my experience. Fluctuating amplitudes of this nature? They're not accounted for in any of our models. This is uncharted territory for us."

As the conversation made its way around the room, a chorus of perplexity echoed Bob's sentiments. Each physicist, in turn, confessed their bewilderment, underscoring the anomaly's deviation from the expected and known.

Miranda's gaze then shifted to Lori, the newest addition to their constellation of minds. "Lori, what's your perspective?"

Lori Johnson, barely two months into her tenure at the observatory, stood on the precipice of theory and discovery. Her arrival was fresh with the latest insights from the scientific academic community.

Lori began, her voice laced with hesitation, "Last year, at a conference... I sat in on a session where..." She trailed off, her gaze sweeping across the room, meeting the eyes of her colleagues who awaited her next words. "They discussed the theoretical signatures of gravitational waves emanating from something... um.. a wormhole," she finally declared, the word 'wormhole' hanging in the air like a revelation.

The room instantly buzzed with a mix of skepticism and intrigue. The mere mention of a wormhole sparked a flurry of voices, each physicist eager to contribute their thoughts, theories, and speculations to the unfolding mystery.

Miranda's hand sliced through the cacophony, restoring order. "Continue, Lori. What specifics did the paper outline?" she encouraged, signaling for Lori to elaborate on her ground-breaking proposition.

Regaining her composure, Lori spoke with renewed confidence, "The presentation detailed how a wormhole's formation would emit gravitational waves with distinctive characteristics—intensely powerful and unmistakably unique. Such spacetime disturbances would dwarf the signals of conventional cosmic events, making our current findings not just plausible but indicative of something like a wormhole's emergence."

The room fell into a contemplative silence, every mind grappling with the implications of Lori's insights. It was Miranda who broke the stillness, her voice steady yet filled with awe. "A wormhole... Created just outside our solar system, manifesting gravitational waves that just reached us at the speed of light. This means whatever happened out there, happened roughly six hours ago. But this raises questions far more profound than mere technicalities—what, or perhaps who, could generate such a phenomenon? And even more unsettling, what might this gateway introduce into our solar system and potentially earth?"

Chapter Two

About Bucky

Bucky Adams lay awake, his mind buzzing with the remnants of the day's upheaval. The move to yet another new town had left him and his mother exhausted, settling into a house that was "new" only in its novelty to them. Their latest residence bore the familiar marks of modest living, its worn edges and slightly shabby appearance echoing the many homes they had transiently called theirs. Their belongings, a collection of essentials worn from travel, bore testament to their nomadic life, each scuff and scratch a story of resilience.

At sixteen, Bucky found refuge in the quiet corners of his mind, a sanctuary for his introverted nature. He was a young man of few words but vast thoughts, particularly drawn to the mysteries of space and the intricate dance of celestial bodies. His room, a chaotic canvas of unpacked boxes and scattered belongings, held one constant amidst the change: a solar system mobile. This delicate artifact, safeguarded through every move, hung as a silent ode to his passion for astronomy and the scattered memories of his former school.

As the clock's luminescent hands marked the early hours of the morning, he felt an irresistible pull towards the night sky. He quietly opened his window, welcoming the cool, gentle breeze and the expansive view it offered. The stars, scattered across the velvety darkness, beckoned with their ancient light, inviting him to lose himself in contemplation.

A particular memory surfaced, vivid and warm—a night when he was five, and the world seemed a vast, unexplored frontier. His father, then a constant figure in his life, had presented him with a small telescope. The excitement of that evening was etched in Bucky's heart, as his father patiently guided his first celestial explorations. "See that, Bucky?" his father's voice echoed in his memory, a comforting presence in the chill of the night. "With this telescope, you can explore the universe from right here."

That moment, shared in the quiet of a long-gone night, had sparked Bucky's enduring fascination with the cosmos. It was a passion that remained a beacon of hope and curiosity, lighting his path through the uncertainty of constant change and the absence of his father.

"Mom would be furious if she caught me awake at this hour," he mused softly. He silently closed the window and retraced his steps back to bed, longing for dreams to guide him into a more hopeful tomorrow.

As the alarm shattered the morning calm, he awoke to face his first day at a new school. Rubbing the sleep from his eyes, he found himself surrounded by unfamiliarity. There was a fleeting sense of being lost. He took several startled breaths before realizing this was his bedroom, in his new, but unfamiliar home. These moments happened often due to their nomadic life, which prevented him from forming lasting friendships and a reassuring sense of home.

Bucky deeply appreciated his mother's unwavering commitment, recognizing the immense effort she put forth to provide for them amidst their ongoing challenges. He made a silent vow never to burden her with complaints, choosing instead to extend his support in whatever way he could. Yet, the prospect of adapting to another new school weighed heavily on him, this challenge magnified by their recent move to a quaint town in upstate New York.

With his sleek black hair catching the early morning light and his piercing blue eyes reflecting a hopeful yet apprehensive spirit, Bucky set out with a lunch packed by his mother, Helena. Helena, a single mother, exemplified resilience and dedication, balancing two jobs to maintain their modest way of life. Her love for Bucky was boundless, a force strong enough to shield him from the brunt of their reality. She carried the weight of their world on her shoulders, all the while nurturing Bucky's well-being and dreams.

As he made his way to the bus, he skillfully stepped around the cracks in the sidewalk, noting they were in need of repair. He was the only student at this particular stop. When the bus finally arrived, he stepped inside and instinctively gravitated towards an unoccupied seat near the back, yearning for solitude. Laughter and chatter reverberated within the yellow vehicle, the boisterous conversations recounting the past summer's adventures. These were unfamiliar faces, reminding him he was starting over yet again.

As he approached some empty seats near the back, he caught sight of a large boy staring at him in an all too familiar way, sitting midway down the bus. The boy had dull-brown eyes, crooked teeth, and a menacing smirk. Bucky quickly looked away, but he knew it was too late. He could feel the boy's stare as he walked past. He made sure not to look at him again.

"Hey Newbie," the voice cut through the din of the school bus from the boy he just passed, catching him off guard. It was clear from the way the boy sized him up that Bucky's status as the new kid was unmistakable. Being on the smaller side for his age often made him a target for such unwelcome attention.

"That seat is taken, newbie," announced the dull-faced kid. Wishing to avoid any trouble, Bucky retreated further back, hoping for a quieter spot. Just as he thought he'd secured a seat, another voice cut in, "Taken too," snickered yet another kid from a couple of rows ahead. Bucky's heart dropped; he found himself standing awkwardly at the back, the empty seats now only in the front, past the unwelcoming stares.

The large boy sitting mid-way up the bus twisted in his seat, legs blocking the aisle in a silent challenge. Bucky's anxiety mounted as the bus driver, catching his eye in the mirror, barked, "We're not moving until you sit down!" The weight of the bus's collective gaze fell heavy on Bucky, some students suppressing laughs, others indifferent to his dilemma. Just as he considered fleeing the scene altogether, a surprising gesture—a gentle tap on his arm—offered a reprieve.

He turned to find a girl with a compassionate smile, her eyes meeting his in quiet solidarity. Beside her sat a friendly-looking large African-American kid, both signaling him to join their space. Gratefully, Bucky squeezed into the seat alongside them, their shared smiles a silent reassurance to him.

The bus journey resumed, the encountered bullies falling silent as other students filled the seats without protest. Arriving at the school, the students filed out, a mix of excitement and lethargy marking the start of a new school year. Bucky lingered, taking a moment at the entrance to steel himself against the vast, unknown halls of his new school. "Just make it through," he whispered to himself, stepping forward with a mix of apprehension and a flicker of hope, the bustling corridors swallowing him into the day's routine.

He retrieved his schedule, quickly scanning it to find his first class: English Literature. It wasn't a subject that excited him, as it didn't ignite his scientific passion. Aiming for just passing grades mostly, he excelled in certain subjects but struggled to summon the dedication required for other, non-science classes.

As the class began, the teacher dove enthusiastically into a lecture on Shakespeare, seemingly oblivious to the varying degrees of student engagement. While some students found ways to entertain themselves quietly amidst the perceived irrelevance of the lesson, Bucky found himself the unwelcome focus of attention from a group of boys at the back of the room. With the teacher's attention elsewhere, they targeted him with a series of spit wads, their snickers barely masked under the guise of attentiveness.

Bucky, determined not to let them see how deeply it affected him, chose to remain silent, even through the sting of embarrassment. He couldn't help but question what had made him the object of their derision. Stoically, he weathered the undercurrent of mockery and taunts, a test of endurance that lasted the entirety of the lesson.

As the class concluded with the shrill ring of the bell, Bucky frantically scooped up his books, his heart pounding in anticipation of what awaited him outside. No sooner had he stepped into the hallway than he found himself face-to-face with the trio that had made it their mission to make his day miserable. The leader of the pack, he knew now from his class, was named Tony because the teacher was calling his name several times to settle down. He was a hulking figure with a sneer that seemed permanently etched on his face. He was blocking Bucky's path with an intimidating stance.

"What's your problem, newbie?" he jeered, leaning in so close Bucky could feel his not so great breath. Bucky attempted a feeble dodge, seeking a way past this human barrier, but a forceful push pinned him against the locker-lined wall.

"I don't like your face," the bully taunted, his voice dripping with derision. Bucky thought it was ironic because this kid was pretty ugly himself. The others with Tony, nearly as menacing though lacking the leader's sheer bulk, crowded in. One jabbed a finger into Bucky's chest, the other swatted his books from his grasp, scattering them across the floor. Their laughter was harsh as his face flushed red from humiliation.

This was a pattern Bucky knew all too well. At each new school, it seemed a fresh set of bullies lay in wait, keen to stake their claim over someone deemed an easy target. His smaller stature did him no favors, marking him as prey in the unforgiving social hierarchy of adolescence.

As Bucky bent to retrieve his scattered belongings, a vicious kick sent his books skittering further away, and he himself tumbled to the ground. The pain from a book corner jabbing into his side was sharp, but the embarrassment and helplessness he felt were far deeper wounds. The bullies' laughter echoed off the corridor walls, a stark reminder of Bucky's isolation in this latest battleground of his turbulent school life.

As the bullies receded, their laughter echoing mockingly down the corridor, Bucky began to push himself up from the floor, each movement sharp with the bite of both physical discomfort and the deeper, more insidious pain of humiliation. It was then that a voice, warm and unexpectedly kind, cut through the residual echoes of mockery. "Let me help you with that."

Looking through the haze of his discomfort, Bucky's eyes met with the teen from the bus who'd offered him a seat when no one else would. He stood tall above him, his presence commanding yet reassuring. He was clad in a Letterman jacket, the gold football pin glinting under the hallway lights, paired with a track athlete insignia that spoke volumes of his versatility and athleticism. His hands, confident and steady, reached out to gather Bucky's scattered notebooks.

"Sorry about those guys. They don't know any better," he said, his voice carrying a note of disapproval that hinted at his own disdain for such mindless cruelty. "I'm Marcus Denson," he introduced himself, standing up straight, his demeanor exuding a natural leadership that seemed to effortlessly command respect.

Bucky, still kneeling and clutching his now-rescued books, felt a wave of gratitude wash over him. “I’m Bucky Adams. It’s... well, it’s been a rough first day,” he admitted, his voice trailing off with a sigh that bore the weight of his ongoing struggle to fit in.

“Nice to meet you Bucky,” Marcus said, offering Bucky a hand to help him to his feet. Marcus then offered a parting nod, his eyes reflecting an understanding that went beyond mere sympathy. “Hang in there, Bucky Adams. First days can be brutal, but it gets better,” he assured with a smile. “I’ve got to head to my next class, but I’ll catch you later.” With that, Marcus turned and strode away, leaving Bucky with a lingering sense of solace. In that brief encounter, Marcus had not only offered assistance but had also given Bucky a fleeting glimpse of hope—a reassurance that amidst the unknowns of a new school, kindness could still be found.

Chapter Three

Bucky's Buddies

Bucky took out his folded schedule from his back pocket and looked for his next class. He felt a surge of anticipation as he read: Physics. Energized by the prospect of delving into a subject that always sparked his interest, he navigated the hallways toward the science wing. Along the way, something caught his attention. It was a poster taped to the wall, featuring a now familiar face. It was Marcus, smiling confidently with a the bold caption 'Marcus Denson for Class President.' His picture showed handsome features marked by a bright, engaging smile and expressive eyes that added a charismatic touch to his youthful appearance. Bucky paused, struck by the thought that someone so popular had paid any attention to him.

Entering the Physics classroom and looking around for an open desk, Bucky's eyes immediately found Marcus, who was seated comfortably near the back. Next to him was the girl who had offered him a seat on the bus. Their faces lit up with welcoming smiles as they caught sight of him, and they gestured invitingly for him to join them. Grateful for this small oasis of friendship, Bucky navigated through the rows of desks, his books held tightly under his arm, until he reached Marcus and the girl. As he began to set his belongings down, an unpleasantly familiar voice cut through the air, dripping with menace. "That seat is taken, newbie," sneered one of the bullies who had tormented him on the bus and earlier in the day. He stood alone this time, without his cronies to back him up.

Marcus was up in an instant, a protective barrier between Bucky and the aggressor. His fists were clenched, but it was the unwavering confidence in his stance that spoke volumes. "This seat belongs to my friend Bucky," he stated firmly, his voice carrying a quiet threat. "If you have a problem with that, we can discuss it outside. Your choice, buddy."

The bully hesitated, the certainty in Marcus's voice and demeanor unbalancing him. He retreated, his threat sounding weaker than intended as he slunk away. "Stay out of our business, Marcus," he said, not sounding so tough now.

Marcus flinched toward the would-be bully causing him to recoil further. Gratitude washed over Bucky as he settled into his seat, turning to thank Marcus. It was then that the girl leaned closer, her hand outstretched in a gesture of friendship. "Hi, I'm Jen. Jen Williams," she introduced herself with a warm smile. "We were happy to help on the bus," she added, looking at Marcus smiling. As Bucky shook her hand, a sense of belonging began to take root. Perhaps, he mused, this new school held more promise than he had dared to hope.

Jen's brilliance shone brightly in the classroom, her hand frequently raised in a dance of inquiry and insight. Her heritage hinted at distant shores, her dark hair elegantly captured in a high tie, framing a face lit by strikingly vivid green eyes. Her smile, effortlessly warm and inviting, mirrored that of Marcus, making it all too easy for Bucky to feel drawn to them.

As Mr. Ronald, affectionately dubbed Dr. Ronald by his students, wove through the intricacies of physics, Bucky found himself captivated. Dr. Ronald, with his light brown hair thinning gracefully and clad in a sleeveless sweater atop a well-worn white shirt, embodied a passion for teaching, but suggested a simple lifestyle outside of school. During the class, Dr. Ronald responded generously to several of Bucky's space-oriented queries. The professor's encouragement, reflected in his kind smile, signaled not just an acceptance of curiosity but a celebration of it.

The lecture neared its end with Dr. Ronald's customary 'quote of the day,' a moment some students met with mild exasperation. Yet, Bucky leaned in, recognizing the value in the teacher's words, as if they were a personal guide. "To leave a mark that outlasts our departure," Dr. Ronald mused, "we must embrace bravery, confront challenges with boldness, yet anchor ourselves in kindness and politeness. For in elevating ourselves above the lowest standards, we find our greatness when it's most needed." These words resonated deeply with Bucky, a beacon of wisdom in the sea of academic rigor.

"One more thing, students," Dr. Ronald said as the class was about to end. He announced the upcoming science fair, with its promise of a scholarship for the winner. "No more than three students per team," he added.

This ignited a spark within Bucky. The thought of the scholarship, a tangible aid in his academic journey, filled him with a mix of excitement and resolve. Glancing towards Marcus and Jen, their shared smiles and unspoken support, embodied in Marcus's raised hand for a high five and Jen's affirmative nod, solidified their newfound alliance. The challenge of the science fair didn't just represent a competition; it was an opportunity to forge deeper bonds, to collaborate and work together toward a shared vision.

***

"You know the maximum time to keep a book is four weeks," Miss Cathy, the librarian, reminded Bucky as he checked out several books on astrophysics and astronomy at the school library. Lacking a computer and internet service at home due to financial constraints, Bucky relied on the library for his research needs.

The librarian was intrigued by his selection and couldn't help but inquire, "My goodness, what are you doing with such advanced science books?"

Bucky's eyes lit up as he replied, "I'm researching for a project we're planning to submit to the science fair next month."

Curious, she leaned forward. "And what is your topic?" she asked.

With a hint of pride, Bucky answered, "Black holes. We're exploring how they consume stars, affect time, and their role in the universe. Did you know there's a supermassive black hole at the center of our galaxy, and likely at the center of most galaxies?"

She was taken aback by the depth of his question, responded, "No, Bucky, I wasn't aware." It was clear she was not accustomed to such detailed scientific inquiries from students. With a supportive nod, she concluded, "Well, best of luck, young man. And remember, return the books within a month."

Eager to share his vision, Bucky discussed the black hole concept for the science fair with Marcus and Jen after their next physics class.

"That's awesome," Marcus exclaimed, his interest piqued despite admitting, "I don't know much about black holes, but they sound fascinating."

Jen shared in the excitement, added, "That's a fantastic idea, Bucky. I've read a bit about black holes myself. Working on them for our project will be fun."

In the days that followed, the trio dedicated their after-school hours to the black hole science project. With Marcus and Jen having access to computers and the internet at home, they could delve into black hole details that was beyond the reach of library books, sharing their findings with Bucky for further discussion.

They alternated meetings between Jen and Marcus's houses, both of which were situated in an upper-middle class, urbanized neighborhood—a stark contrast to Bucky's more neglected area.

While in Marcus's room, Bucky observed an array of shiny trophies, evidence of his athletic prowess, positioned alongside his electronic projects that featured cool, blinking lights. Conscious of his words, he carefully avoided saying anything awkward or appearing nervous around them.

Despite his efforts to remain calm, Bucky felt a surge of nerves, as this was the first time he had been invited into a friend's home. Glancing over at Jen, he could easily picture her as the high school homecoming queen or even a fashion model, given her poise and grace. She was kind to him and appeared very close to Marcus. For the first time in his life, Bucky felt genuinely happy to have true friends like them. Remarkably, they even acknowledged him at school, despite usually being surrounded by the popular crowd.

When the frequent rotational visits for the project called for Bucky's home, he became agitated and overly embarrassed to invite them over. But Bucky's home had its own unique resource—a vast area of woods behind his house, complete with an old, sturdy treehouse discovered by the property's owner. The owner, upon showing it to Bucky and his mother, mentioned he didn't know its origins but assured them it was well-constructed and abandoned. He encouraged Bucky to use it, though he cautioned him to be mindful of safety, a concern visibly shared by Bucky's mother. This treehouse, nestled in the tranquil woods, became a haven for creativity and exploration for Bucky and his friends as they embarked on their ambitious project.

When Bucky introduced Marcus and Jen to the treehouse, they walked through the thick foliage with anticipation of progress on their black hole project. Once inside the treehouse, they settled into their normal routine, spreading out their materials and notes across the worn wooden floor.

In the midst of their preparations, Jen, her curiosity piqued, turned to Bucky with a question. "Bucky, why are you so fascinated by black holes?" she inquired, her notebook paused mid-flip.

With a playful grin, Marcus leaned in. "Yeah, Bucky, what's the deal. You sure ask a lot of questions in Physics?"

Bucky leaned back against a sturdy beam, his gaze drifting out through the trees above the treehouse as if he could see beyond the stars. "Well," he began, his voice tinged with wonder, "I had a telescope when I was young I used to look at the moon and stars. But I really got into it when my mom took me to an observatory. They had this presentation under a dome that projected stars and constellations. When they talked about the supermassive black hole at the center of our galaxy... its power, its mysteries... I was hooked."

Jen nodded, a smile of encouragement on her face. "That's pretty cool, Bucky."

The conversation shifted, and Bucky, curious about his friends' passions, turned to Jen. "And what about you, Jen? What drives your curiosity?"

Jen exchanged a knowing glance with Marcus before answering. "Languages," she declared, her eyes lighting up. "I'm fascinated by how we create structures to communicate, from the sounds we make to the way we arrange words to convey meaning."

Marcus jumped in, his admiration for Jen evident. "She's incredible, Bucky. Knows more languages than anyone I know."

Jen blushed slightly but continued, warming to the topic. "It's not just about knowing different languages. It's understanding the structure—phonology, morphology, syntax... How we use sounds, form words, and build sentences."

"Come on, girl, you know you're smart. I always make sure I'm in her class when I take foreign languages. I couldn't pass without her," Marcus said in a playful tone.

"You know, when my relatives first arrived here from China," Jen continued smiling at Marcus. "It was like stepping into a whole new world for them. Not just the place, but the language. They were used to the sound of our own language, with its tones and characters painting pictures. I remember how they'd practice every day, trying new words so unfamiliar to them. They were determined to learn, to adapt. It was inspiring, really. They'd laugh at their own mistakes, but never let them become obstacles. Instead, those mistakes were stepping stones, each one a victory in its own right."

Marcus looked at Jen with amazement. "You're beautiful and smart girl. Will you marry me?" he said, laughing, but Bucky sensed a tiny hint of truth.

"What about you, Marcus?" Bucky began. "What are you interested in? I saw all those sports trophies in your room."

"Yeah, I'm pretty good at sports. My mom and dad pushed me from when I was a little kid. I guess to keep me out of trouble. But I really love technology," Marcus said with a smile. "You've seen some of the projects in my room. My mom and dad also keep buying me those at-home science projects for my birthday and Christmas. My dad is an engineer. He's always lecturing me about technology."

"What type of technology?" Bucky asked.

"Marcus can do anything that requires a technical solution," Jen said, interrupting Marcus as he was about to speak.

"Well," Marcus spoke, looking at Jen and placing his hand on her arm. "I enjoy anything that requires a mechanical or logical challenge. That's why I'm pretty good at computer programming and solving tough problems that require thinking your way through them," he said releasing his hand from Jen's arm. "My dad would take me to work with him sometimes when he worked weekends. Jen and Bucky exchanged glances, "With your dad?" Jen echoed. "You mean at his office?"

"More like his lab," Marcus corrected. "He's an aerospace engineer. He's working on this experiment for the space station."

Bucky's eyes widened. "The space station? Seriously?"

"Yeah," Marcus nodded. "So, we get there, and it's like stepping into a sci-fi movie. There's all this high-tech equipment everywhere. My dad was showing me this new experiment they're working on. It's supposed to study how microgravity affects plant growth. They're trying to figure out how to grow food in space."

Jen's interest was piqued. "That's incredible. What did you get to do?"

Marcus grinned, clearly enjoying the attention. "At first, I just watched and asked a lot of questions. But then my dad let me help with some of the simpler tasks. I got to handle some of the equipment and take measurements. It was so precise, like, even the slightest mistake could mess up the whole experiment."

"Wow," Bucky said, genuinely impressed. "That sounds intense."

"It was," Marcus admitted. "But it was also amazing. Seeing how everything works, how much detail goes into every little part of the project, it gave me a whole new appreciation for what my dad does. And the coolest part? They're planning to send the experiment up to the space station in a few months. My dad said if everything goes well, he might even take me to the launch."

"That would be epic," Jen said, her eyes wide with excitement. "Can you imagine seeing a rocket launch in person?"

Marcus nodded. “Yeah, it’s like a dream come true. I never really understood how awesome my dad’s job was until now. It’s inspired me to think about what I want to do in the future.”

“You mean, like, become an aerospace engineer too?” Bucky asked.

“Maybe,” Marcus replied thoughtfully. “Or something else in science. I just know I want to be part of something that makes a difference, you know?”

Jen smiled. “That’s really cool, Marcus. I’m glad you got to see that side of your dad’s work.”

“Me too,” Marcus said, his voice filled with newfound determination.

Bucky felt a little sad at the mention of Marcus’s father and the time they spent together. He missed his father at that moment, but he quickly returned his focused to his new friends. This was a new experience for him and brought him joy and hope for the new school year.

The three friends continued their time together in the tree house, with Bucky taking the lead in explaining their project. He described the concept, which involved creating a representation of a black hole eating a star. He discussed how they could build something to represent the event horizon since black holes did not give off any light. They discussed what materials they would need to build the model.

Their conversation highlighted the diverse talents within their group, each bringing a unique strength to their collaborative efforts. As they turned their attention back to the project at hand—a model of a black hole consuming a star—they brainstormed materials and designs, their camaraderie a testament to the bonds formed in the pursuit of knowledge.

***

Several days before the science fair, again meeting at the treehouse, Bucky, Jen, and Marcus stood back to admire their finished project, their makeshift workshop brimming with the fruits of their labor and creativity. Marcus had ingeniously crafted the event horizon of the black hole using stiffened white mesh around a black spray-painted tennis ball fixed on a sturdy metal frame that did not distract from the visual effects. A salvaged circular lamp, found by Marcus at a thrift store, served as the halo of light of the black hole event horizon, cleverly illuminated by a battery-powered setup he had built together.

Jen and Bucky had focused on depicting a star being consumed by the black hole. They chose a smaller ball, enveloped in cotton and spray-painted yellow to resemble a sun, with streams of cotton stretching towards the event horizon held up by a sturdy thin metal rod bent and cut to size, simulating the material being devoured by the black hole. The entire assembly, held aloft by the metal frame painted black and set upon a rotating disk engineered by Marcus, completed their ambitious representation.

Standing around their creation, the sense of accomplishment was palpable. Marcus couldn't help but express his admiration. "Damn, that looks good," he said, unable to hide his pride.

"It's beautiful, Bucky. Thank you for dreaming this up." Jen added, her voice warm with gratitude,

"I should be thanking you both. I couldn't have done this without you," Bucky said with some emotion. He was clearly moved by their shared achievement and the bond they had formed.

Chapter Four

School Confrontation

With their project in tow, Bucky and Jen met at the school's entrance, ready to present their hard work to Professor Ronald for his final review before the fair. Their anticipation was cut short by an unwelcome encounter with Tony and his cronies.

"Let us through, Tony," Jen said, her voice steady but filled with defiance.

"Oh, what do we have here? The genius club and their masterpiece?" Tony said, reveling in the discomfort he caused, mocking them as he reached out to grab their hard work.

Bucky and Jen pulled the project back from Tony's reach, which only enraged him. The other bullies quickly moved in and grabbed Bucky and Jen by the arms while Tony walked over and pulled the science project from their grasp. He dropped it with a sarcastic "oops," expecting it to break into many pieces.

Despite the durability of their project, Tony wasn't satisfied until he had exerted every ounce of his strength to destroy it. The resilience of the model only fueled his determination, resulting in a heartbreaking scene for Bucky and Jen as they witnessed the culmination of their efforts being reduced to rubble.

Bucky knew he had to do something, to defend himself and Jen. He found he couldn't move or speak as these bullies smashed his creation. More humiliation, embarrassment in front of his new friend. What would she think of him, he thought. He felt like running, but he didn't.

"There, now it's real trash," Tony declared, his voice heavy with exertion. With a final taunt, he and his cronies made a hasty retreat, leaving Jen and Bucky amidst the remnants of their project.

The devastation was palpable as Jen, fighting back tears, stooped to salvage what remained. "I'm so sorry, Bucky," she expressed, her voice a mixture of sorrow and rage. "Marcus needs to hear about this."

Finally finding the strength to speak, Bucky's voice was tinged with regret as he urged Jen, "No, don't tell Marcus. He'll just end up in trouble for going after them. I'm sorry I couldn't stand up to them."

Jen, her voice soft with understanding, reassured him, "It's alright. Standing up to them might have made things worse. You did what you thought was best." *Nothing* Bucky thought to himself.

Marcus came running up to them, his initial enthusiasm dimming instantly as his eyes fell on the remnants of their project. "What's this? What happened?" he demanded, his breath short from the rush.

Jen, unable to hide her distress, feigned responsibility through her tears. "It... it was an accident. I dropped it."

Marcus's gaze shifted between Bucky and Jen, searching for the truth. "Bucky, what really happened? If those bullies were behind this..."

"It was an accident, Marcus. We just... lost our grip on it." Bucky said, trying to maintain their fabricated story.

Marcus's skepticism was clear, but he bit back his initial response, his frustration evident. "Unbelievable," he said sounding angry. With a final deep sigh he said "Well, there's nothing we can do right now. We still need to get to class," he conceded, though the fight hadn't quite left his eyes.

Bucky looked at the scattered pieces, then at his friends, then made a decision. "Go ahead to class. I'll try to salvage what I can and follow you."

“You’re sure you’ll be okay?” Jen said, still visibly upset but nodding in agreement.

“Yeah, I’ll be fine. Don’t worry about me,” Bucky reassured her, his tone firmer than he felt.

With a lingering look of concern, Jen and Marcus headed towards the school, leaving Bucky alone with the debris of their hard work.

After they left, Bucky gathered the pieces of their project, each fragment a reminder of their efforts and aspirations. He stood motionless for a moment, the weight of the day heavy on his shoulders, then turned and headed home, not ready to face the classroom.

The walk back home was long. Several times he dropped parts of their shattered project, but he wasn't going to leave anything behind. Bucky watched as cars passed by with people going about their daily routine, completely unaware of the pain he felt. When he finally arrived home, his mother immediately sensed his distress as he entered the kitchen. He saw the familiar silent support expression from her. She didn’t ask why he was home early or why the project was in pieces. Instead, she embraced him, her presence a comforting distraction.

“It’s okay, Bucky. You’ve put so much into this,” she said, her voice soft and understanding. “Tell me what you need.”

He sighed, the fight drained from him. "I think I need some time alone. Maybe in the treehouse."

She nodded, her smile warm and understanding. "Let me get you something to eat, and you take all the time you need."

In that moment, Bucky felt a profound gratitude for his mother's unwavering support, a silver lining in a day marred by disappointment and frustration.

As Bucky inhaled deeply, the comforting scent of his mother, a blend of clean laundry and her subtle perfume, enveloped him. This scent, so familiar and grounding, immediately transported him to a sense of security and warmth, a feeling that was distinctly "home," regardless of their actual location.

"Thanks, Mom. It looks like there's no way to salvage the project now. Too late to start over," Bucky admitted, his voice heavy with resignation. "I think I'll head to the treehouse. Maybe even spend the night there, especially since there's no school tomorrow."

She responded with a nod, her expression filled with empathy. She understood her son's need for solitude, a trait he had shown since he was little. With a gentle smile, she began to prepare for his retreat, gathering a blanket and a pillow for comfort, and making his favorite sandwich, packing it alongside a bottle of water into a small brown plastic grocery bag. Bucky also grabbed one of the astrophysics books he'd borrowed from the library, seeking not just escape but perhaps, in the pages, finding solace in the constellations and cosmic phenomena he loved so much.

The walk to the treehouse, set deep within the woods behind their home, was a journey he had made countless times, yet each step now felt like a move towards reclaiming a piece of himself. He navigated the familiar path with ease, the stream and the rocks beneath his feet marking the way to his sanctuary.

Climbing up into the treehouse, he pushed the trap door open and settled his belongings inside. This place, suspended among the trees, was more than just a childhood construct; it was a refuge from the world's chaos, a space where he could be alone with his thoughts and the stars.

The anger that had fueled his steps dissipated as he settled into the treehouse. Instead, a profound weariness took hold, a physical manifestation of his mental and emotional exhaustion. He lay back, the blanket beneath him a small comfort, and opened his book, immersing himself in the cosmos through the written word.

Eventually, the book lay forgotten beside him as he gazed upwards through the open hatch at the cloudless morning sky, a vast canvas of infinite possibilities. It was here, amidst the quiet of the forest and the majesty of the universe above, that Bucky found his peace, if only for a moment. As sleep finally claimed him, he allowed himself to drift, hoping to dream of distant galaxies and the mysteries they held, a welcome escape from the trials of his earthbound existence.

***

Suddenly, a voice cut through the silence, waking him, calling out his name.

"Bucky! Bucky!"

He stirred and slowly opened his eyes. He had no idea how much time had passed since he fell asleep. Jen was kneeling next to him, gently touching his shoulder. Marcus stood beside her, looking concerned.

"Wake up," Jen softly said as she gently poked. "We missed you in Professor Ronald's class, and you were nowhere at school."

"Sorry, guys, I just couldn't. We worked so hard." He rubbed his eyes. Sadness was evident in his voice.

It was late afternoon. The sun was low in the sky, and the cool September breeze eased through the treehouse as the three friends sat in a circle, discussing what could have been with their project.

"You know, I read that our universe was created by a black hole from another universe. It spewed matter and energy to create our expanding universe at the Big Bang," he said, holding up the library book he was reading and looking up through the trees at the faintly emerging stars in the late afternoon.

"Bro, do you ever think of anything else besides space? You're just not normal, Bucky, no offense," Marcus quipped, lightly laughing.

"I know," he admitted. "I don't completely understand it myself. It's in my dreams, a part of me as long as I can remember."

With a playful tease, Jen joined, "You are definitely an old soul."

"Well," Marcus said, looking at his watch, "I have a game tonight, and I have to get home to get my stuff."

"Oh, Bucky," Jen excitedly said. "Do you want to go to the football game with me tonight? It will help get your mind off the project."

He was suddenly startled at the idea of actually attending a High School sporting event. He had never been before and no one ever asked him to go.

"Yes," he replied, trying not to sound too excited.

"Great!" she said. "I'll pick you up at seven. My mom said I could take the car tonight."

Jen and Marcus left the treehouse while he stayed behind for a little while, trying to get used to the idea that his life was so different now. He had friends. Cool ones. Maybe he was a little cool after all.

Chapter Five

Friday Night Light

Bucky, charged with an unexpected burst of energy and anticipation, made his way back home from his secluded retreat in the treehouse. The reason for his newfound enthusiasm? A decision to step out of his comfort zone and attend the high school football game that evening—a decision that brought with it a mix of excitement and apprehension.

As he entered the kitchen, his mother was in the midst of dinner preparations, her hands busy and her focus unwavering until Bucky's announcement caught her attention.

"Mom, guess what? I got invited to go to the football game tonight," Bucky announced, barely containing his excitement.

She paused, her expression a mixture of surprise and mild concern. This was uncharted territory for both of them, given Bucky's usual preference for quieter evenings at home or in his treehouse.

"That's wonderful, Bucky," she replied, her voice warm but cautious. She reached for her purse on the counter, pulling out a few dollars to give to him. "Here, I hope this helps. Have a good time."

"Thanks, Mom," Bucky said, accepting the money with a smile. He could see the worry etching lines on her face and sought to reassure her. "Really, it's going to be fine."

He then retreated to his room to change, selecting the best outfit he could muster, though he knew it hardly measured up to the typical high school fashion scene. Standing by the front window as the clock neared seven, he watched for Jen's car, dreading the thought of a formal introduction at the door. As soon as he saw the car pull up, Bucky didn't hesitate. He bolted outside, making it to the passenger seat before Jen could even think to get out.

"Let's head out," he urged, perhaps a bit too eagerly.

Jen looked over at him, a hint of amusement in her eyes. "I was actually looking forward to meeting your mom tonight."

Bucky shifted uncomfortably in his seat, the idea of blending his school life with his home life still feeling foreign to him.

"Maybe next time," he replied quickly, his gaze fixed ahead, signaling his readiness to leave the safety of his known world behind, if only for an evening.

As they drove away, Bucky couldn't help but glance back at his mother standing in the doorway. Her wave, full of love yet tinged with a subtle hint of concern, stayed with him as they headed towards the high school stadium. The excitement of the evening lay ahead, but her expression lingered in his mind, a reminder of the small, protective bubble of his world stretching just a bit.

The stadium loomed large and vibrant, its lights piercing the evening sky, transforming the night into a spectacle of high school sports fervor. They parked and walked through the grassy lot towards the sounds and lights, the anticipation building with every step.

At the entrance, after handing their tickets to a cheerful parent volunteer, Bucky stepped into a world so familiar yet so distant. The marching band's rhythms throbbed through the air, a heartbeat of high school spirit that Bucky felt reverberate through his own chest. The air was thick with the scent of popcorn and the chatter of excited fans, a mosaic of school colors everywhere he looked.

Jen moved with a confidence that Bucky admired, greeting people with a casual ease that made him acutely aware of his own discomfort. Their curious glances made him feel even more like an outsider, but Jen's presence was a comforting anchor in this sea of new experiences.

He followed Jen up the bleacher stairs about halfway up the student section. Sitting down, he felt the cool metal of the seat pressed against his legs through his jeans. Jen turned to introduce Bucky to her circle – a group of four girls sitting to her right. "Everyone, this is Bucky Adams," she said with a welcoming smile.

The group of girls, clearly key figures in the school's social landscape, gave Bucky a once-over. Their assessment, unspoken yet evident, made him self-conscious, but Jen's unwavering friendliness eased the moment. "Hi, nice to meet you all," Bucky said, trying to match Jen's ease, his voice nearly lost in the surrounding noise.

Jen's laughter at his tentative greeting, rather than adding to his discomfort, somehow made him feel more at ease. She nudged him gently, directing his attention to the field where the teams were warming up, a wordless reminder that tonight was about more than fitting in—it was about experiencing the moment, together with Marcus.

During the game, Jen's enthusiasm for football—and specifically for Marcus's performance—was infectious. As she pointed out Marcus on the field, her pride in her friend was evident.

"Look, there's Marcus, number 24," she said, her eyes sparkling with excitement as Marcus caught a football with impressive skill.

Bucky watched Marcus in action, and couldn't help but be impressed. "He's really good," he remarked, his voice carrying a mix of surprise and admiration. Clearly football was a tough sport. The sounds of collision between the players shook him.

As the game progressed, Jen took it upon herself to explain the intricacies of the sport to Bucky, pointing out key plays and strategies. The atmosphere in the stadium was electric, with the crowd's energy palpable. Bucky, while new to the sport, found himself drawn into the excitement, cheering alongside Jen.

The clear, starlit sky offered a stark contrast to the bright stadium lights and the intensity on the field. Bucky, ever the stargazer, found his attention divided between the game and the heavens above. It was during one of these moments, his eyes scanning the night sky, that he spotted something extraordinary—a glowing object moving at an incredible speed across the sky.

Suddenly, there were two very loud bangs, like thunder after a lightning strike. It shook the stands and rattled the glass in the press booth behind them. Now, everyone in the stadium noticed. Many in the stands started pointing at the bright light in the sky. Even from a great distance it appeared like an object with a rectangular shape. In no time, it streaked across the sky and disappeared. Jen looked over at him and asked, "What was that?"

"I don't know," was all he could answer. He thought hard about all the possibilities. He remembered a video he had seen of the Space Shuttle returning through the atmosphere. It made two loud thunder sounds that were sonic booms created as it was slowed by the Earth's atmosphere. He turned towards her to explain but noticed that she, like all the others, had her attention occupied with the game again.

The game ended and Bucky and Jen met Marcus in the parking lot as he was getting on the bus to return to the high school.

"Did you enjoy the game?" Marcus asked Bucky.

"That was my first football game. Thanks you guys," Bucky responded with a little emotion in his voice. "You were great Marcus," he added.

"We're heading over to Charlie's," Marcus said to Jen, then looked over at Bucky and smiled. He hesitated slightly before saying to Bucky "do you want to come with us?"

Bucky knew the hesitation was Marcus thinking about Bucky fitting into the popular high school crowd. He quickly said "no thanks. I have to get home."

"Ok," Marcus said. "See you over there Jen," he continued as he turned to get on the school bus.

Jen drove Bucky back to his house. The excitement of the game lingering, fueled by the crowd's roaring cheers, the bright lights illuminating the field, and the relentless, heart-pounding action of the game. He experienced a sense of belonging, a connection to his peers that had previously eluded him in his simple life s of solitary interests. Amidst the noise and celebration, he found a moment of clear insight. He realized that life, much like the game, was unpredictable and full of challenges but also rich with opportunities for connection, growth, and self-discovery. He knew he had to go slow with his new friends, he didn't want them to tire of him.

Then there was that object in the sky. That's what he remembered most about the night. *A mystery to be solved* he thought as Jen pulled up to his house.

Bucky found his mother asleep on the couch with the crochet normally folded over the back covering her. He scribbled a quick note explaining his plan to spend the night in the treehouse. He gathered his things and headed out into the peaceful embrace of the night. In the solitude of his treehouse, surrounded by the gentle sounds of the forest, Bucky pondered the day's experiences. The football game, his burgeoning friendship with Jen and Marcus, and the mysterious object in the sky—all swirled in his mind as he lay back, staring into the vastness of the universe. The day had been full of new discoveries and emotions, but it was the enigmatic sight in the sky that held his thoughts captive as he drifted off to sleep.

Chapter Six

The Galaxy Orb

Bucky awoke abruptly, heart pounding and breaths coming in sharp gasps. Surrounded by darkness, he lay disoriented in the depths of the night, unsure of the hour. Had a nightmare stirred him from sleep? He couldn't remember, but an unsettling feeling gnawed at him. His skin prickled with goosebumps, a primal alert to an unseen threat lurking nearby. This bizarre sensation left him on edge, despite attempts to soothe his alarmed senses.

Before he could see it, he sensed it—a presence, undefined yet palpably close, unlike anything he'd ever encountered. A mysterious void unfolded before him, a patch of reality seemingly erased, leaving a deep, resonant emptiness. The surrounding air hummed, charged with an energy that created a stark contrast against the soft moonlight.

What captivated him was the void's effect before him on the moon's glow. The void seemed to devour the light, casting an eerie shadow over the forest and his treehouse sanctuary. It felt as if reality itself had been hollowed out.

Gradually, Bucky realized the void, disrupting the space a short distance before him, was moving, inching closer with an almost purposeful intent. His heart raced with a mix of awe and apprehension as he observed its silent approach, a phenomenon that felt both alien and oddly personal.

Caught between his instinct to flee and his insatiable curiosity, Bucky stood frozen, watching as the void drew closer. The sensation of being pulled towards it intensified, a silent call to step into the unknown. In that moment, the boundaries between the known and the unimaginable blurred, leaving Bucky on the precipice of a discovery that would challenge his understanding of reality itself.

As the object pulsed ever closer to him, his fascination overcame his fear. Like it was something natural to him and the universe, he watched, entranced, as the void continued its methodical approach, irresistibly drawn toward him. He gasped in fascination as it entered his body right above his heart through his chest.

In that bizarre moment, he felt and heard many things. He had an overwhelming sense of energy, of power connected directly through him to the universe, as if the infinite expanse of the universe was now an intrinsic part of him. He felt distant stars, nebulae, all parts of the galaxy within his consciousness. He was overwhelmed with a sense of the vast expanse of the galaxy, the ebb and flow of celestial tides resonating within him. A weightless sensation engulfed him.

At that exact moment, he heard what sounded like millions of musical notes, a rhythmic pleasure, all playing simultaneously. But each was so unique, like hearing a single violin playing unique notes in an orchestra of uncountable violins. It was music unlike his ears had ever heard. Millions of unique vibrations originated through all of space, from every direction he sensed life. These were vibrations from sources that were alive, a part of this same spacetime.

He also felt a strange physical sensation. His arms started quivering as if he was being electrocuted by a high-voltage live power line. The hairs on his arms took an upright position again, like they were being pushed from within his skin. Just as quickly, he felt the hairs reverse and press against his skin like a strong magnet. His arms were vibrating with energy. As he brought them up and moved his hands closer to each other, he noticed a very powerful attracting force, like placing oppositely charged ends of two very large magnets together.

And then, as suddenly as it had begun, the phenomenon ceased. The void, and the connection it had established, vanished, leaving Bucky alone in the night, grappling with the reality of what had just occurred. He was himself again, yet irrevocably changed by the encounter. The sensations had faded, leaving only a memory of the profound connection he had felt to the universe.

For a long while, Bucky stood in silence, trying to comprehend the inexplicable. He examined his arms, half-expecting to find some physical evidence of the encounter, but there was nothing—only the lingering memory of that powerful energy.

He questioned whether it had all been a dream, a figment of his imagination fueled by his deep-seated passion for the stars. But just as he began to doubt the reality of his experience, the next thing happened, something that would change his life and his perception of the universe forever.

Chapter Seven

Bing And Bucky

Bucky's attention was captured by a bright light maneuvering across the sky, eerily similar of the object he'd observed at the football game. It steadily grew brighter and seemed to be on a direct course towards him, sparking a surge of apprehension. "What is going on?" he voiced his confusion, rushing to the window of the tree fort. The mysterious object was now alarmingly close and considerably larger, yet utterly silent. Shaking his head in disbelief, Bucky struggled to discern reality from nightmare, the rapid beat of his heart confirming the frightening truth of his situation.

He ducked down, hoping to remain unseen, his body tensed in anticipation. Peeking again cautiously, he saw the object a short distance away descend gracefully through the trees, landing with a muted thud that sent a slight tremor through the treehouse. The impact, surprisingly gentle for its apparent size, suggested a deliberate control that was unlike anything man-made.

Despite his instinct screaming for him to flee, curiosity anchored him to the spot. Through the moonlit foliage, he discerned the silhouette of the craft, now settled on the ground. "Could this be a flying saucer?" he pondered, yet it bore no resemblance to the stereotypical images he'd seen. From what he could make out through the moonlit trees the craft looked square on each end and about the size and height of a school bus.

A sudden hiss snapped him from his thoughts, signaling a large opening materializing on the craft's side he could just make out through the trees. Within the opening, illuminated by a soft interior light, stood a large figure—vast and imposing. It had the shape of a human, with arms and legs, but even from this distance he could see an oddly shaped cylinder-like head. Even from this distance, he could see this figure was much taller then any human he had seen.

Frozen in place, Bucky's heart hammered against his ribs, each beat echoing the fear and awe wrestling within him. The spaceship's door had revealed an entity so foreign, so imposing, that Bucky's mind raced to make sense of the sight. The figure, had stepped out into the night, the door sealing behind it with a definitive hiss, plunging the area back into darkness save for the occasional glint of moonlight off its surface.

He now heard the distinct sound of slow, deliberate footsteps approaching with the familiar sounds of leaves and twigs crushed underfoot. The figure's progress through the woods, intermittently revealed by moonlight, was for sure, moving toward him.

"What is happening?" Bucky whispered to the emptiness of the tree fort, as he crawled away from the window, he heard the sounds of footsteps. Deliberate and measured, they grew louder, each step a solid thud against the earth, the sounds of the natural world beneath its weight. Bucky, overwhelmed by a mix of curiosity and terror, pressed himself against the floor, his eyes wide as he dared not to peek, yet unable to resist the urge to understand what approached.

Minutes passed, or perhaps it was seconds—time had lost all meaning in the intensity of the moment. Slowly, with a caution borne of primal fear, he began to crawl back towards the window, compelled by a desperate need to see, to understand, even as every instinct screamed for him to hide.

Suddenly, the wooden ladder leading up to his treehouse creaked under the unknown creatures' weight. This thing was climbing up the ladder. With that realization he felt an electric-like surge start in his stomach and wash over his head making his face flush with heat. The sequential groaning of each rung echoed like a countdown, each step bringing the thing closer to his makeshift sanctuary. Then, as abruptly as it began, the creaking ceased, signaling the creature's arrival at the treehouse's entrance.

The brief silence that followed was shattered by the appearance of a light, probing through the cracks in the floorboards, sweeping across the entrance in a deliberate search. Bucky's heart pounded in his chest as he watched, petrified, the beam of light extinguishing suddenly, replaced by the sound of something metallic scraping against the door.

He took in a quick, deep breath as the door to the treehouse creaked open on it's single squeaky hinge. Bucky pressed his back against the wall, clutching his flashlight, the weight of his decision to hide or reveal himself.

The silhouette of the thing filled the doorway, its form obscured by darkness but outlined by the faint moonlight. As it maneuvered its way inside, the details of its appearance began to materialize—cylindrical head, large metallic hands, and an imposing stature that dwarfed the small confines of the treehouse.

Once fully inside, the creature stood, unfolding to its full height between the tree branches above the roofless treehouse platform and walls. Bucky estimated it towered at least seven feet tall. The absurdity of focusing on its height struck him, a bizarre moment of clarity amidst the fear. *Why am I thinking about how tall it is?* he wondered silently, his mind grappling with the surreal situation.

The creature paused, as if acclimating to its new surroundings, giving Bucky a moment to observe it in silence. The tension in the air was extreme, a standoff between the unknown and the all-too-familiar fear of the dark and what it conceals.

As the creature very slowly advanced, each small step seemed to echo through the small confines of the treehouse, a reminder of the precarious situation Bucky found himself in. The weight of the being caused the wooden boards beneath its feet to protest audibly, amplifying Bucky's fear that the structure might not withstand the encounter and they would all simply crash to the ground. Amid his fear, Bucky's curiosity couldn't be quelled—a part of him marveled at the the experience and wondered discoveries this could lead to, if he survived for the next seconds and minutes. He thought about what Professor Ronald might say or do in the face of such an unprecedented scientific marvel.

With a trembling hand, Bucky clicked on his flashlight, directing the beam towards the entity. The light revealed a head, initially cylinder-shaped and featureless, resembling nothing living he had ever seen. But then, before his eyes, it began to change. The surface that seemed metallic and inanimate started to morph, adopting features that were unmistakably human. Eyes, a nose, and a mouth emerged from the previously flat surface, crafting the visage of a man where none had been.

As the transformation completed, Bucky found himself staring into the face of a young man who, despite the extraordinary circumstances, appeared remarkably handsome. His hair, dark and straight, framed his face, lending him an almost familiar air.

The silence that had enveloped the treehouse was broken by the stranger's voice, a curious blend of mechanical and human tones, "I have found you, my brother, after a thousand years since you were taken from us. I heard your song, I knew it was you."

Chapter Eight

Brothers Reunited

Bucky's flashlight shifted from the face to the intricate armor that encased the robot man's towering frame. The metallic exterior gleamed, reflecting his flashlight. Its surface etched with an array of mysterious symbols and patterns lining the arms and legs. The armor appeared both formidable and elegant, a fusion of technology and an aesthetic that was clearly alien.

Returning the flashlight to the robot's head he looked upon a fascinating blend of human and machine. His facial features had a lifelike quality, with expressive eyes that radiated intelligence and a hint of emotion. The artificial skin covering his face was so intricately designed that it almost mimicked the imperfections of real skin, creating a captivating illusion of humanity. As he spoke, his lips moved with an uncannily natural fluidity, his voice transitioning from a mechanical cadence to a more human-like tone.

Bucky could only stare as the human-looking head atop a robot's body before him smiled, a gesture so human it belied the incredible journey that must have led him here. Bucky's initial fear began to ebb as curiosity took hold. The robot man standing before him, so startling at first, now sparked a multitude of questions about its origins, his journey, and the connection he claimed to share with Bucky.

"Who are you?" Bucky managed to ask, his voice steadier now.

"I am called Bing," he said in a voice that still sounded more machine-like than human. "I am from a place far beyond your understanding of distance and time. My journey here was not by choice, but by necessity. For a millennium, I have been lost, manipulated by forces beyond my control. But finding you has awakened something within me—memories of a life that was lost to me," he explained, his voice becoming more humanlike, more familiar.

"Bing? That's your name. Bing? I don't remember you. You look like a machine to me. How can you be a machine and be my brother?"

"I was not always like this. I will explain, my brother. My complete memories are not clear to me yet." He said as he took a slight step back from Bucky. "It was so long ago, another lifetime for you. For me, I have existed like this since we were together, imprisoned." Bing hesitated before continuing.

"This planet has so much life energy, so many songs. Among all those songs, I experienced yours. I knew the Orb would seek you as it did so long ago. I released it and followed. As before, it found you. It meant to join with you again."

"The Orb?' Bucky questioned. "Is that the thing that... that went into me?"

"Yes," Bing replied.

"What is it?" Bucky stammered.

"The Orb was forged at the center of this galaxy. It draws its energy from a great force that was once an immense sun, but now only takes in light, matter, and energy. The object you call a supermassive black hole," Bing explained.

Bucky listened awestruck, with a sense of unreality he said "I don't understand. How did you use it to find me?"

"There is a connection between the black hole and every unique sentient life energy in this galaxy," Bing explained. "The black hole has a memory, a record of the unique sentient life energy vibrations. The Orb was forged from the black hole and contains the record of all the life energies that currently exist in this galaxy. It was integrated into this machine, to use as a sensor to discover life energies across this galaxy," Bing continued. "I have heard so many... so much destruction. The Orb vibrated with the frequency of your life energy. It is like a song. So familiar to me, like your voice. It changed me. I remembered who I was. I had to find you."

"Destruction? What do you mean?" Bucky asked as a chill of fear shook him.

"There is a very powerful entity in this galaxy that seeks the life energy of sentient beings," Bing continued solemnly. "I was not aware. I was not myself. I was programmed to use the Orb to discover life energy for the Collectors. They come to discovered worlds and harvest the life energy of sentient beings for the Entity that created the Orb."

Bucky's realization dawned with a cold shiver, the concept of 'life energy' making the distant threat suddenly intimate and terrifying. "You mean souls? They collect souls?" he repeated. The notion that something so fundamentally human could be harvested like a crop for some malevolent entity's evil purpose was both unfathomable and horrifying.

"Why?" Is all Bucky could say barely above a whisper.

"Sentient life is the most unique energy in the universe," Bing continue. "It endures beyond the boundary of time and space. It animates biological units such as yours, and me, when I had a biological form, and even now trapped in this machine. Life energy allows us to be sentient, to experience consciousness, to interact with free will in this space-time, to dream, and to create.

This energy is the essence of existence. The entity has found a way to extract and store it. It has created armies of machines like this," he said pointing to himself. "It has found a way to control free will."

Bucky listened, a mix of awe and horror washing over him as Bing's words sank in. After a moment of silence, he finally spoke, his voice a whisper against the enormity of what he'd just learned. "So, this entity... it harvests what makes us *us*—our souls, our will, everything that life means?"

"There are two Collectors, controlled by the entity, that will come to your planet and harvest all sentient life. Unless we can stop them. The Orb you now possess has great powers. It may be the only thing that can save your world." Bing's words hung heavy in the night air.

Bucky reeled, his knees weakened, almost giving out from beneath him. He rubbed his chest and then his arms remembering the sensations and power of the Orb that entered him. He could not feel it now. He looked up at this alien thinking, *how could any of this be true.* He wanted to run, to wake up from this nightmare.

"Brothers?" Bucky finally said, trying to focus, grappling with the revelations. The flashlight, still aimed at Bing, trembled slightly in his hand, mirroring the turmoil of emotions he felt.

"So, you're telling me that we're... brothers? And that this Orb, this thing, led you to me?" His voice was a mix of skepticism and fear.

Bing nodded, the artificial skin of his face mimicking the somber expression of someone burdened with untold loss. "Yes, Bucky. We were together once. We grew up with our mother and father, before the Collectors came."

Bucky absorbed Bing's words, each sentence adding layers to a narrative so fantastical it challenged his understanding of reality. Bing's explanation of the Orb, its origins, and its purpose painted a picture of a universe interconnected in ways Bucky could never imagined.

"The Orb went into me. Right here," Bucky said pointing to his chest just above his heart. "I heard music. Like millions of violins. It came from out there," he said pointing up towards the stars.

Bing knelt and bent over to be at eye level with Bucky, placed a reassuring hand on Bucky's shoulder. His touch, though metallic, conveyed a warmth and sincerity that surprised Bucky. "Exactly, my brother. The Orb allows you to perceive the life energy that exists throughout our galaxy. Each entity, each being has a unique 'song.' With practice, you'll learn to distinguish these songs, to understand their essence. Even the location of individual life energies."

Bucky's mind reeled at the concept. "And it's... part of me now? This Orb and its power?" he asked, his voice steadier, a sign of his growing acceptance of his new reality.

"Yes, you and the Orb are now connected. Its created purpose by the entity who seeks to control and harvest, can now be guided by your inherent goodness. Your life's energy is key to wielding the Orb's power with wisdom," Bing explained, his voice imbued with a gentle confidence.

The mention of Collectors harvesting life energy sent a shiver down Bucky's spine. "That's... terrifying. Who would ever think something like that was possible, harvesting life like it's... it's just a resource," he said.

Bing's demeanor shifted, the weight of his past actions and their implications evident in his posture. "I was unaware of the suffering I enabled. My awakening, the Orb's connection with you, has freed me from that purpose. I now see the value and sanctity of life."

Bucky observed the anguish in Bing's expression, the struggle of a being caught between its programming and a newfound conscience. Despite the surreal circumstances, a bond, inexplicable yet undeniable, began to form between them. "I believe you," Bucky affirmed, his empathy for Bing's plight clear. "Feeling connected, it's not something you can fake. It's like family, right? You feel it in your heart."

Bing lifted his head, meeting Bucky's gaze. "Yes, Bucky. Despite the changes I've undergone, the essence of who I am remains. Our reunion, our connection, it transcends the physical. We are family."

Chapter Nine

1000 Years Ago

Bing stood up and placed his large metallic hand on Bucky's shoulder. "Bucky," he began, "let me explain what I do know about the Orb and the energy that animates all living things. Life energy is unique in the whole universe. Like other energies, it vibrates. The vibration has a unique frequency that can be heard as a song using the Orb. Your life energy is tuned to the Orb. You have the ability to control its power completely, like the creator of the Orb. I do not think it ever intended to have any other life energy control it the way you can."

Bucky stared at Bing bewildered. "I still don't understand any of this. I didn't know I had a unique song. We talk about souls at church, but I didn't think there was something like that as a part of me," he said.

Bing looked lost in thought for a moment before responding, "I can share some of my memories with you and show you images and sounds from your past through my memories. You will see with your mind, not your eyes. You will hear, but not with your ears."

"Will it hurt?" he asked.

"No, Bucky, it won't hurt. Close your eyes and try to clear your thoughts," Bing instructed. Then, he stepped closer to him and placed both his large robotic hands around his head. Initially, the contact shocked him, and he wanted to pull away but decided to stand still.

"I'm scared," Bucky shared, trembling a bit. He tried to clear his mind, but the sights and sounds from the last hour overwhelmed him.

"Breathe slowly," Bing guided. "It will help your biological mechanisms to slow down."

He remembered his mother telling him to breathe slowly, in and out, when he was afraid. Nothing from his past could really prepare him for this. Still, he knew he had to try to learn what Bing needed to show him. He managed to slow his breathing and could feel his heart rate ease from his initial jolt. There was a slight shock from Bing's large metallic robot hands. Bucky remembered the same effect when he sometimes shuffled his feet over a carpet in the winter, then got a shock touching something metal. He then heard Bing say,

"Bucky, my long-lost brother, can you hear me?"

With his eyes still closed, he began to open his mouth to respond when he heard Bing say, "You don't have to speak for me to hear you."

He opened his eyes and looked up at Bing through the large metallic hands against his head. He heard Bing's voice as though he was speaking, yet Bing's human mouth was not moving. In fact, Bing was smiling. It was these smiles that made Bing feel so much more human to him.

He smiled back and said to Bing in his mind, "Cool."

"Now, I will try to share some of my memories with you. Show you some fragments of your past, our past" Bing spoke in his mind. "These memories are broken and incomplete, but it is the best I can do with this technology combined with my life energy. Close your eyes and clear your mind again."

He obeyed and shut his eyes, wondering if this would look like one of his video games. Again, he felt the light electrical shock on his head. Suddenly, he could see faint images and blurred movement, and slowly, he could hear sounds he knew did not come from his ears. He began to smell something, like freshly cooked food. He could see and hear what looked like a family sitting at a large wood-like table with some plates holding what was clearly exotic-looking food.

He realized this was Bing's memory, and as Bing looked around the scene, he saw what must be a mother and a father because they looked older, very much like human parents. The clothes were strange and colorful. He could hear faint voices but could not understand the language. He then saw what looked like a young boy sitting across the table from Bing's view: long dark hair, bright eyes, and an easy smile.

Bing's voice spoke to him in his mind. "Yes, Bucky, that was you, your life, my brother, with our parents."

He gasped and opened his eyes wide, causing the scene in his mind to dissolve into nothing. He opened his mouth and attempted to ask the first of many questions, but could only manage a trembling mumble. "And those were your, I mean, our... parents?" he asked.

"Yes," Bing answered aloud now.

Bucky lowered his gaze, a whirlwind of confusion and disbelief swirling within him. He inhaled deeply, trying to steady his racing heart, and confessed, "I don't remember any of that. It's like you're showing me someone else's life, not mine, ever."

Bing responded with a tone of understanding, yet tinged with regret. "I wish I could offer you more clarity," he admitted. "All I possess are my memories within this form and my experiences, the same as you experience within this time, your biology containing your life energy. Your soul." He paused, the weight of his words hanging in the air. "As to why your essence is reborn in this time, in this form, I do not know. But even confined within this mechanical structure, I have come to recognize the capacity for love. Your soul's melody, unchanged by the eons, confirmed your identity to me."

Bucky, grappling with the notion, pressed further. "But how? How could you be so certain of who I am?" He asked, almost desperate, trying to make sense of his current situation.

Bing's explanation was gentle, yet firm. "Yes, my brother. When the Orb reflected the signature of your life energy in this galaxy, it was as though a light shone through the darkness of time. It wasn't just a sensation but a recognition of shared experiences, of a bond that transcends lifetimes. That's how I knew—it was you."

Bucky closed his eyes and took in a deep breath to try and calm himself. He recalled the scene Bing shared with him at their home so long ago. He remembered how he felt looking at the boy from Bing's memory. He somehow knew deep inside that Bing was telling the truth, and that was his former self from another lifetime.

Bing put his large machine hand on his shoulder and bent down on one knee again. He looked Bucky in the eyes, and, with an expression of pain, he spoke. "There is more I must show you, memories of your fate so long ago. A fate that will befall all the people, the souls on this planet, if we do not do something to stop it."

"We?" asked Bucky. "If we don't stop it?" he stammered.

"Let me share more of my memories, our experiences, it will help explain," Bing said.

Bucky closed his eyes again and tried to calm himself. He shook and tried to hold back tears. He balled his fists and grimaced as though he was about to be struck. What terrible images would he see now? Bing again placed his robot hands on his head. Once again, a blurry image formed in his mind. Slowly, the sound emerged. This time, it was screaming and what looked like fire and smoke. The strange language returned, but it sounded like shouts of terror this time. No matter the language, Bucky could recognize these people were terrified and running away from something emerging from the nearby smoke and flames.

He could now make out what they were running from. They were fleeing from other people like themselves, except something was wrong with the pursuers. The look on their faces was empty and malignant. They were running awkwardly as if controlled like puppets.

He could hear popping sounds, like an electrical spark, when the pursuing creatures touched one of the fleeing. The touched immediately fell lifeless, but very quickly regained their feet. However, now they had changed like the pursuing creatures.

Looking around briefly, then joining the chase of the others not yet affected by the touch.

Bucky knew this was Bing's memory because he saw himself, his former self, standing close to Bing. His former self was holding some sort of weapon aimed at the attackers. He was not using the weapon. He knew in the confusion of the horrible scene; their people had been turned into some kind of zombie, but they were still his people.

The memory then focused on a figure walking behind the attacking creatures, reminiscent of Bing, but not quite the same. This robot had a large, mechanical form with a cylinder head lacking definition. Its robotic body adorned in armor that suggested a military purpose, contrasting with Bing's appearance. The presence of this mechanized being among the attackers hinted at its role as orchestrator or enforcer of the chaos.

"Is that a Collector?" Bucky asked Bing in his mind.

"Yes," Bing responded in Bucky's mind.

Suddenly, the Collector guiding the attackers clutched at its chest, collapsing to its knees in an almost human gesture of distress. From its chest emerged what Bucky knew was the Galaxy Orb. It pulsed with the now familiar inner darkness that seemed to swallow light. The attackers, as if commanded by an unseen signal, ceased their assault, turning their attention to the spectacle.

Bucky, through the lens of Bing's memory, watched as the Galaxy Orb drifted towards the Bucky from so long ago. The familiarity of the scene struck him; the orb was unmistakably drawn to him then, as now, a beacon to his life energy. Just as earlier that night, the Orb entered the past Bucky. The same astonished look on the face. As the robot that had held the Orb rose, it issued a booming command, pointing at Bing and Bucky. The transformed beings charged towards them, moving with an eerie coordination that reflected their puppet-like existence.

As the attackers grew closer, he could see his former self drop the weapon and run to stand in front of Bing. He held his arms up, palms outstretched as if to try and stop the attacking horde. Suddenly, the nearest attackers were launched into the air and quickly went out of sight.

He could see his former self, as he turned to look at his brother with a shocked expression. The Bucky from so long ago was able to easily hold the attackers back with some kind of force using the Orb that had become part of him.

"My brother, you were able to stop not just those attackers but many more, including Collectors," Bing said in his mind.

A string of partial images and sounds passed through his mind—images of strange spacecraft and an army of robots attacking his people. He saw the enemy robots crushed and the alien spacecraft flung into the sky with very unnatural violence. And he was causing it with complex motions of his hands and body, as seen through Bing's memories. He was also wearing some kind of military uniform.

"The creator of the Orb came to our world to retrieve its creation," Bing said.

In his mind, Bucky saw a blurry image of a gigantic dark cloud with many tentacles of smoke extending from the center hovering in front of an army of robots. He once again saw himself step in front of Bing and hold his hands out as if to stop the attackers, but this time, the large dark figure held up a tentacle of ethereal black smoke and pointed at the Bucky from the distant past. He saw a very bright light shoot from the tentacle and hit the past Bucky with a shower of sparks, and the past Bucky fell lifeless.

The Orb left the body and returned to the dark figure. Bucky, viewing the scene through Bing's eyes, saw him fall to his knees next to the lifeless body and held it in his arms. Through Bing's memories, he saw the large cloud-like figure ascend into the air. Then, in that scene, the robots descended upon Bing.

The horrible sounds subsided to distant echoes. The images faded in his mind. He opened his eyes and saw he was still in the tree house. He felt unsteady, and his mind reeled from the experience. He noticed Bing kneeling with his robot hands now covering his human face.

"My brother," Bing said with a sobbing voice. "They killed my brother. I have been so lost. I have done terrible things. I have helped the Collectors and the dark Entity destroy so many civilizations. Taking the life energy of so many sentient beings in this galaxy. This memory is the most difficult for me," Bing continued. "I lost you, and I was taken and made into what you see before you now. I have no memory after that day until I detected your soul song. When I found you again, those memories returned to me. I remembered love and hope again." Bing spoke in a tone that he had not heard from him before now. He looked a little less of a machine and more like someone he knew, someone human, broken and imperfect.

"There is so much the Entity does not understand," Bing said in an angry voice. "It has a mindless pursuit of power and disregard for the essence of life, the natural order, and the purpose of sentient organic forms animated by the energy of life. I remember now, Bucky. I feel again because I have found you. You have saved me and perhaps your planet now that the Orb has been reunited with its only other true master in this galaxy."

Bucky sat down heavily, trying to process everything. "So, those attackers, the Collector, they were being controlled? Like puppets?" he asked, trying to piece together the scenes of chaos and violence.

"Yes," Bing confirmed. "The Collectors transform the collected into creatures that continue the harvest of life energies. They corrupt and control, turning beings against their own. They consume for the Entity, until nothing remains but shadows of life. That's what they did to our world, and that's what they plan to do here. The scene you witnessed, it was an invasion, a harvesting. But you stopped it, even if just for a moment."

The revelation hit Bucky like a tidal wave. He opened his eyes, meeting Bing's gaze. "And you think I can stop them? With the Orb?"

"Yes, Bucky. The Orb chose you for a reason. You have the power to influence its energies, to protect instead of destroy," Bing explained, his tone imbued with a mixture of hope and desperation.

Bucky struggled to comprehend the enormity of his role. "But I'm just a kid. I... I don't even understand any of this," he protested, the fear and uncertainty clear in his voice.

Bing stood up, his posture one of determination. "You're much more than you realize, Bucky. I've seen it. The day you repelled the attackers, you did it instinctively, without understanding the Orb or your connection to it. That's your strength—the innate ability to control and direct the Orb's power."

The scenes of destruction and terror lingered in Bucky's mind, a stark contrast to the quiet of the treehouse. "So, what do we do? How do we even begin to fight something like the Collectors?" Bucky asked, the weight of their task dawning on him.

"We start by understanding the Orb, by unlocking its secrets and your connection to it. We train, we prepare, and when the time comes, we stand together against the Collectors," Bing said, his voice firm, leaving no room for doubt.

As the reality of their situation settled in, Bucky realized that his life had changed forever. No longer just a teenager from Earth, he was now a key player in a cosmic struggle spanning the galaxy. With Bing by his side, he faced an uncertain future, armed with the unknown power of the Orb and the evolving bond of brotherhood.

Chapter Ten

Bucky's Buddies

"I must leave you now, my Brother," Bing said as he placed his large metallic hand on Bucky's shoulder. "I must do what I can to slow the Collectors. I will return tomorrow." With that, Bing carefully started climbing down the ladder leading to the treehouse. Just when his head was all that remained in the entrance, he turned to Bucky and said,

"I love you brother."

He then climbed down and returned through the woods to his spacecraft where he entered, and in minutes disappeared into the night.

Bucky, still reeling from the night's revelations and watching Bing's departure, still in a state of unreality, sat down on the treehouse floor. Time seemed to stretch and warp as he sat there, his mind continuously replaying the night's events, like scenes from a vivid yet intangible dream. He felt so overwhelmed with the experience. He laid down on his back and looked up through the branches of the great tree to the star filled night sky. The gentle breeze teased the early autumn leaves, causing them to dance and drift into his sanctuary, each leaf a silent witness to the passage of time. He imagined all the life that must exist in the galaxy, maybe all galaxies. With those overwhelming thoughts, and exhaustion overtaking him, he drifted off to sleep where the boundaries of reality and imagination blurred.

***

"Bucky, you up there?" Bucky heard, as if from a great distance. Perhaps he was still dreaming.

"Hey Bucky," He heard again, shaking off sleep and sitting up now. The air was cool and the sun indicated it was early morning. He moved over the window and leaned out to see Marcus and Jen looking up at him, their presence a sudden return to normalcy. The transition from the cosmic scale of his experiences back to the familiar faces of his friends was jarring.

"Your mom said you were out here. Can we come up?" Marcus asked, shouting to be heard from the ground below.

"Yeah, come on up," Bucky called down, trying to mask the turmoil of emotions with a appearance of normalcy and the idea that they had met his mom. As he heard the familiar creaks of the ladder under Marcus and Jen's weight, he realized just how much had changed for him in one night. The knowledge he now carried, the secrets of the universe and the impending danger, felt like a such a heavy responsibility.

As Jen and Marcus made their way into the treehouse, their concern was evident. "You okay, Bucky? You look like you haven't slept," Jen observed, her voice laced with worry.

Marcus chimed in, "Yeah, man, is everything alright?"

Bucky sighed, realizing the enormity of what he had to explain to them. "It was just a long night," he offered, knowing how inadequate the explanation sounded.

"You sure? You know you can talk to us about anything, right?" Jen insisted, sitting down next to him, her expression earnest.

Bucky nodded, appreciating their concern but feeling the isolation his unique burden imposed. "I know, and I appreciate it. It's just... family stuff, you know?" he hinted, trying to think of the best way to explain to them what happened. He thought hard about how to explain the events of the night. It was still so fantastic to him.

"Marcus, Jen, you cannot imagine what has happened," he said, almost breathless, his heart beginning to race with apprehension.

Bucky spent the next many minutes describing every detail about what had happened. When he got to the part of his past life through Bing's memories, he paused, looked down, and put his hands over his face.

He lifted his head and looked at his friends. "You guys, I... I don't know how to describe what Bing showed me through his memories. His... our planet was attacked, and the people were turned into some sort of zombie. They began attacking each other. It was horrible. I saw my former self from the past through Bing's eyes. I was some kind of warrior. The Orb came to me back then, the same as it did last night. I was able to make the attackers fly into the sky," he demonstrated with his hands, raising them as if he were lifting something heavy. "It was like gravity no longer held them down, and they went into the sky."

"That's crazy, Bucky," Marcus said. "Are you sure that wasn't just part of your dream?"

Bucky looked down again and said, "That thing came into me last night. It was a sensation like I'd never felt before. I could sort of sense the planets and life in our galaxy."

"Life in our galaxy? Really? That's also pretty crazy," Marcus said with a note of disbelief.

Bucky continued describing his encounter with Bing and concluded with Bing's departure in his spaceship.

"That was some dream you had there. What an imagination you have. A mini black hole? And now it's part of you?" Marcus said, frowning in disbelief.

"Marcus, it's the truth!" Bucky shouted.

Marcus looked over at Jen. "Do you believe this story?" Jen's eyes darted between Marcus and Bucky, her expression torn as she struggled to decide who to believe.

Bucky exhaled with a note of frustration and gave Marcus an 'I don't understand why you don't believe me' look. He then carried on with his recounting of the events.

Jen looked at Marcus and finally spoke. "You're right. That was an amazing dream. What an imagination you have, Bucky."

"That's what I said," Marcus laughed.

"Do you have any proof, Bucky?" Jen asked. "Maybe you could show us this... ' Orb'?"

"It's right here, inside me," he said as he pointed to his chest. "Maybe I can lift something." He held his arms out and began to wave his hands in random patterns, hoping to coax some response. Marcus and Jen started laughing when nothing mysterious happened. Watching them laugh at him, he realized he must look quite silly.

"I swear to you, guys," he said as he knew his story did sound quite crazy. Marcus and Jen got up and hugged Bucky when they could see he was frustrated with them by the look on his face.

"Try to get some rest, Bucky. You look exhausted," Jen said. "We can talk some more about your dream later." She placed her hands on his shoulders. "We'll stay with you for a while," she added, looking over at Marcus, who nodded in agreement. He gave one more sigh of frustration and nodded as he returned to the corner of the tree house. He lay down and pulled his blanket almost over his head. He placed his hand over his chest and wondered if it all wasn't a dream after all.

As he succumbed to the embrace of sleep, his dreams unfolded into a vision of a colossal black hole, a maw in the fabric of space, surrounded by an armada of minute objects. Together, they seemed to orchestrated the construction of an immense structure, a colossal edifice that seemed to surround the black hole itself. As the unimaginable site unfolded in his dream. an inexorable force began to exert its pull on him, an irresistible call drawing him toward the event horizon of the black hole. This force, relentless and unyielding, dragged him ever closer, accelerating his descent into the void, past the luminous halo of light ensnared in the black hole's gravitational pull. In the dream he tried to resist this pull, his arms raised in a futile gesture of defiance against the engulfing darkness.

Amidst this descent, a sound pierced the silence of his dream-world—a cacophony unlike any he had known. Voiceless, he attempted to cry out, but his pleas were swallowed by the void. The sound intensified as he plummeted, a discordant symphony of shattered melodies, the lament of a thousand broken musical instruments. On the precipice of oblivion, as he teetered on the edge of the abyss, the shriek of millions of tormented screams. Abruptly, he was torn from the grips of this nightmare, awakening with a sharp intake of breath and a stifled cry, his heart pounding.

"Bucky! Are you ok?" Jen and Marcus said almost together. They rushed over to him and knelt next to him. He sat up with sweat covering his face, and he trembled, looking terrified.

"I saw it. I saw the black hole," he said in a faraway voice. He then tried to tell them all that he could remember about the dream. What he remembered most was the great fear and overwhelming sense of evil and the shrill, penetrating sounds.

"Marcus. Jen. I think I'm supposed to help Bing save the people here on Earth. We are all in great danger, and I need you two to help me," Bucky said, sounding very ominous and serious.

Marcus and Jen looked at each other and were no longer smiling, hearing the tone in Bucky's voice.

Bucky looked around and realized it was late morning. The sun was bright, and he could feel the cool morning breeze on his face. He knew nothing would ever be the same again. At least he was not alone.

Chapter Eleven

The Bullies

Lying in bed the following Sunday evening, Bucky's mind raced with the new revelations and the responsibilities that now lay upon him. The solar system mobile above him, once a simple project, now seemed like a mocking reminder of his newfound connection to the vast cosmos. He recalled the vivid sensations from his encounter with the Orb—the overwhelming sense of being linked to the very fabric of the universe, to life energies spanning across the galaxy. Yet, alongside this awe-inspiring connection, lurked the dark shadow of the dream, the menacing black hole, and the cryptic construction encircling it, symbols of an impending threat of unimaginable scale.

As he pondered the significance of his dream, his mother's voice brought him back to the reality of his bedroom. "Try to get some sleep now, sweetheart," she said, her voice a comforting presence in the whirlwind of his thoughts.

Looking up at her, Bucky felt a surge of determination. Bing's warning about the danger facing Earth wasn't just a distant problem; it was deeply personal. The thought of his mother, his friends, and the world he called home being in peril ignited a resolve within him. "I will, Mom. Goodnight," he responded, forcing a smile to hide the tumult within.

As his mother closed the door, leaving him in the semi-darkness, the reality of his situation set in. The fantastical idea of "Bucky Adams saves the Earth" felt both exhilarating and terrifying. For a moment, he allowed himself to entertain the heroic notion, but it quickly gave way to the weight of what failure could mean—he could lose everything, everyone he cared about and loved.

With a heavy heart, he placed his hand over his chest, searching for the inexplicable presence of the Orb within him. It was a constant reminder of the extraordinary journey ahead and the monumental task of safeguarding not just those he loved, but the entire planet. As sleep finally claimed him, Bucky drifted off with a mix of fear and courage, knowing that the path ahead was fraught with danger but also filled with the potential for unparalleled heroism.

***

Bucky, Marcus, and Jen met on the school bus the following morning, the air between them heavy with the revelations from Bucky. Jen reached out, with a warm embrace she inquired with genuine concern, "How are you feeling? That experience you described... it sounded quite intense. To be honest, the whole thing was a bit frightening."

"We can talk more at school," Marcus said looking around at the other students on the bus as their conversation dwindled to silence. Despite their support, Bucky sensed a level of skepticism, a silent question of belief in his experience that remained unspoken. The bus arrived at its destination, and the three of them walked to the side of the school, where they knew they could spend a few minutes in relative privacy before their first class.

"You guys have no idea what it felt like," Bucky started. "The sensation of things in our galaxy, especially the life energies. It was amazing and terrifying at the same time. I still don't understand any of it. It all felt too real to be a dream." He thought hard about how much he should tell them, not wanting to scare them until he knew more. But he decided it was important for them to learn as much as he did so maybe they could make sense of it and help him in a way he couldn't.

"There were other things Bing showed me," he continued. "He told me that the Earth was in grave danger. Other aliens will come here and..." He paused, trying to think of the right way to describe beings that harvested souls. The thought of it was horrifying to him. "They will attack us," he finally revealed.

"Bucky, that sounds terrible," Jen said, trying to empathize but not sounding quite convinced.

"Man, that sounds like a horror science fiction," Marcus added, still suspicious of the story. "Are you sure that's not from a movie you've seen?"

Bucky looked at his friends and again realized this was far too incomprehensible for them to just take his word for it. He even had some doubts in his own mind. Just then, the bullies turned the corner and approached them. Like always, they looked menacing. This time, there were three others, six in total. Marcus instinctively stepped forward, positioning himself as a protective barrier between the bullies and Jen and Bucky. His stance was firm, fists clenched with resolve.

Tony towered above the rest, stepped forward with a swagger that spoke volumes of his intent. "Well, look what we have here. Nerd central," he taunted, his voice dripping with disdain. His words hung in the air, a challenge and an insult all at once. The others, emboldened by their leader's bravado, echoed his mockery.

Marcus met Antonio's gaze and snarled, "what're you going to do, punks?"

"We just want to teach you a lesson, Marcus. You think you're such a big shot around here. Big man on the football team. Now you're hanging out with the newbie?" Antonio sneered.

Marcus laughed. Antonio balled his fists and started moving in on Marcus. Just then, Bucky moved quickly to stand in front of Marcus and Jen. "Just leave us alone, or I'll... I'll do something," he warned.

The bullies all laughed in unison. Tony, laughing along with the others, said "Do something? Huh Newbie? Let's see". Tony, along with the other bullies then charged Bucky and his friends, fists raised.

Several things happened at once. Bucky finally sensed the Orb. He heard the life energy vibrations of the bullies, their soul songs. They were weak and harsh sounding, not even at the level of music, like something broken. The next instant, he once again became aware of all the planets and life energies in the galaxy. He sensed the immense power of gravity and energy of the planets and suns, even the ultimate force at the center of the galaxy. He thrust his hands in front of him, palms up, towards the oncoming bullies and willed in his mind for them to stop. Some unknown energy vibrated through his arms and hands like an electrical shock. Suddenly, all the bullies were stopped in their tracks, and a look of bewilderment came over their faces. He flicked his palms up instinctively. There was a rush of air around the bullies; dirt and rocks began flying up where they stood. Then all the boys shot into the air and immediately disappeared into the clouds. The dirt, leaves, and rocks followed them.

Marcus and Jen immediately let out a startled cry.

"What! What was that? What did you do, Bucky?" Jen screamed in a terrified voice.

He turned to face his friends with his arms still outstretched toward the clouds. Marcus and Jen both stepped back from him, both with a shocked expression.

"Don't kill them, Bucky! Bring them back, now!" Jen shouted.

He was aware he had to keep his concentration. So, he slowly lowered his hands raised toward the sky. The bullies descended back through the clouds at very high speed. With subtle hand gestures, he slowed them until they landed back on the ground in front of him, exactly where they had stood. The bullies each immediately fell to the ground, unable to stay on their feet. Each of them had, what appeared to be, frost in their hair and eyebrows and a look of absolute terror on their faces. They scrambled clumsily to their feet and ran as fast as they could away, stumbling and falling as they went.

Jen and Marcus stood looking at Bucky in astonishment and subsiding fear. After a few moments Marcus said calmly,

"That was crazy. So, I guess it wasn't a dream, huh, Bucky? Were you using... what did you call it? The Galaxy Orb?"

"Yes," he replied.

"How did you know how to do that?" Jen asked.

"I don't know. It just felt natural," he said in a far-off voice. "I felt and sensed the same things when it first came to me, but only for a moment," he continued. "I can't feel it or sense the Orb right now. I still don't understand what it is or the power. Bing didn't explain much about it, just that it was forged inside the black hole at the center of our galaxy."

"Forged at the center of our galaxy?" Jen questioned. "How is that possible? That black hole is tens of thousands of light-years away. How is it that part of it is here, and inside you?"

"Bucky, I want you to tell us again exactly what happened in the treehouse with Bing, starting from the beginning, in as much detail as you can remember," Marcus requested, his tone serious.

As Bucky took in a breath to recount the events in the treehouse, their second-period teacher, Miss Boson, came from around the corner of the building and walked toward the three of them. They all stopped and turned to look at the teacher, only now realizing that the bullies might have told her what had happened. What would they say? How could something like that be explained?

Miss Boson clapped her hands two times and, in a very cheery voice and a smile, said, “Come on, you three, run along to class. You don’t want to be late.”

With a great sigh of relief, the three friends turned and walked slowly toward the school entrance. Marcus and Jen both put an arm around Bucky as they walked.

“We’ll figure this out together, Bucky. We have to,” Jen said. Marcus nodded in agreement.

Chapter Twelve

Bing Returns

The three met back at the treehouse that night, around the time Bucky first saw Bing. Bucky led them to the clearing where Bing had landed his spaceship. It was a cool, mostly clear night, typical for early fall. The almost full moon provided enough light so that they didn't need a flashlight to move through the trees to the clearing.

"Are you sure this was the place he landed, Bucky?" Jen asked nervously.

"Yes, this is the spot," he replied.

"Has he, uh, Bing, spoken to you since we were at school?" Marcus asked, appearing to search for a conversation to ease the nervous tension.

"No," he answered.

"Are you sure it's ok with Bing that we are with you?" Jen asked again with a slight quiver in her voice.

"Yes, Jen. I'm sure it's fine," he said, trying to reassure her, recognizing her apprehension.

They all entered the clearing not far from the treehouse and stood looking up at the night sky. Jen stayed close to Marcus. He smiled when she held on to his arm. Marcus gestured toward a log at the edge of the clearing, and they both walked over and sat down, still looking up toward the sky.

In what seemed like an hour passed without any of the three saying anything. Bucky paced slowly around the clearing while Jen and Marcus sat close together on the log. They all looked up occasionally, still expectant, at the vast expanse of stars that were periodically covered by blue-gray clouds moving slowly through the sky. Marcus removed his jacket and put it over Jen's shoulders when she began to shake a little from the cool night.

Bucky began to feel something stir inside him. A warm, pleasant sensation overtook him. He began to 'hear' a beautiful song in his head. It only had a few notes, but the smooth rise and fall between the notes was captivating and somehow familiar. He knew in that moment that this was Bing's soul song. *I hear you, Bing,* he thought to himself.

Just then, Marcus said, "Look! What's that?" pointing to the sky. Bucky and Jen looked up where Marcus was pointing. At first, it looked like just another star. But this star was moving. It gradually looked bigger as it appeared to move directly toward them. The school bus-sized spacecraft lowered from the sky and hovered noiselessly just above the trees before gently landing in the middle of the clearing. Jen was still holding on to Marcus as they stood and took several steps, backing away from the direction of the spacecraft.

Bucky approached his friends, positioning himself before them with Bing's spacecraft as their backdrop. The hull of the ship began to deform, a shape pressing outward as if a colossal force from within sought escape. It was Bing, his form distorting the spacecraft's exterior as he emerged. Standing beneath the silvery glow of the moonlight, he towered nearly seven feet tall, his stature accentuated by what appeared to be military-style armor in shades of gray and white.

Jen gasped and clutched at Marcus, taking refuge behind him as Bing advanced. His head, initially a featureless metallic cylinder reminiscent of their first encounter, halted after a mere ten feet. Then, it began to transform, contours shifting and details emerging until it settled into the familiar visage of a young man. Bing's face, now fully human, broke into a warm, recognizing smile as he locked eyes with Bucky.

Acting on impulse, Bucky sprinted towards Bing and embraced him, managing only to wrap his arms just above Bing's robotic hips.

Bing looked down at Bucky and gently wrapped his arms around his head. "So good to see you again, my brother," he said softly.

At that moment, Jen looked up at Marcus and began to smile. Marcus smiled back and nodded, remarking, "That's some unbelievably crazy family."

Bucky stepped back from Bing's embrace and said. "Let me introduce you to my best friends." He gestured for Jen and Marcus to come closer. They approached cautiously, their expressions a mix of curiosity and uncertainty. "This is Jen Williams," he said, pointing to Jen, "and this is Marcus Denson."

Both Jen and Marcus nodded, still unsure of what to say.

"I am called Bing, friends of my brother," Bing responded, echoing their nods. He then turned to Bucky, his smile fading as he spoke with gravity. "My brother, I must speak with you about the danger to your planet. The Collectors are coming. We must prepare. You must learn to use the Orb to defend your planet."

Under the late evening moonlight, Bucky paled, his face a mask of fear at Bing's words and solemn tone. Bing stepped forward and placed his large mechanical hands on Bucky's shoulders, kneeling to bring his face level with Bucky's. "My brother, you are not alone. I am your biggest supporter. I will help you learn the power of the Orb within my programmed knowledge. Together, we have great power yet to be discovered."

"Can't you fight them, Bing? Can't you use your spaceship to fight the Collectors?" Bucky asked, his voice tinged with desperation.

"The Collector's ship possesses weapons this craft does not," Bing answered, gesturing to his spacecraft. "They have the weaponry to threaten all life on this planet. Only by working together, with the power of the Orb, can we hope to defend against them."

Bucly turned to look at his friends. Their faces mirrored his fear; Jen covered her mouth with her hands, her eyes wide with shock. Marcus walked over and stood next to him, a solid presence in the face of looming danger.

"What is he talking about? What are Collectors?" Marcus asked, then turned to Bing, seeking an explanation.

"There is a force at work in this galaxy. A dark Entity that believes only in power and destruction," Bing began to explain. "It seeks a very special energy throughout this galaxy that is collected and used to create great armies of androids like me. It also uses collected energy to contain the greatest forces known in this universe. The Collectors are servants of this Entity. They come to planets where the special life energy is discovered by scouts, who are also controlled by the dark Entity."

Bing paused, looking around at Bucky and his friends. "I am a scout," he added with a sense of despair in his voice.

Jen and Marcus gasped together and stepped back from Bing. Bucky looked up at Bing with a bewildered look.

"You led them to earth?" Bucky questioned desperately.

Bing looked between Bucky and his friends and said, "I was not myself. I have not been myself for so long. That changed when I discovered you," Bing said in a softer voice.

"I know you didn't mean to, but you told them about earth, our home?" Bucky responded.

"Yes," Bing answered softly. "I was following my programming before I found you. Before I regained awareness of myself."

"Can't you tell them not to come? Can't you do something to protect us?" Bucky pleaded.

"I cannot. I attempted to change the instructions the Collectors use to travel to this world, but I failed. I was discovered before I could complete the change and only just escaped to return here to warn you and help you prepare," Bing explained. "They will also be coming for me now."

Bucky and his friends stood staring at Bing.

"We fought together before, my brother, against this evil. We can do it again. You have the Orb now. Once you learn how to control its powers, we can fight them," Bing said.

"And if I fail, the earth will be destroyed?" Bucky said with a note of desperation.

"We won't fail" Bing assured with confidence. "You are not alone. I will be with you, training you. We don't have much time before the Collectors come."

Jen and Marcus walked over to Bucky and stood with him. "We are here for you, Bucky," Jen said.

"Yeah" Marcus added. "I don't understand any of this, but I do know friends stick together no matter what."

Just then, the Orb reasserted itself, and Bucky was overwhelmed with the amazing sounds of the song from the surrounding souls. He felt the love, the life energies. He understood a little better the nature of his existence and his place in the universe. He was as much a part of this universe as the Orb and the black hole from where it came.

Bing waited for a moment, allowing a hushed anticipation to settle over the group before he began addressing them. "We have a great challenge before us," he started. "We must prepare for the attack of the Collectors. There are two that will come in a transport like the one you see here." He gestured again to his spaceship.

"They will use the people of your planet to spread the collection virus. The physical touch extracts the life energy. It is collected and stored in a device within the Collector spacecraft. Human life energy is replaced with a synthetic energy that only animates the host biology and controls it to continue the spread of the virus. Once all the life energy is collected on your planet, the synthetic energy is withdrawn, and all the biological units will cease to function."

"Cease to function? You mean to die?" questioned Marcus, clearly startled.

Bucky shook his head and said, "Bing, why can I control the Orb? Why me?"

"I do not know why your life energy binds so completely with the Orb," Bing responded. "It was created by the Entity, which is the only other life form in this galaxy that can completely control it."

"That's just crazy. It's unbelievable," Bucky said.

"How did you get here?" Marcus asked. "I mean, the black hole is like, 26,000,000 light years away," he asked looking at Bucky and smiling, a nod to their research on black holes.

"The negative energy extracted from the black hole is used to create the transit portals. We use them to move throughout this galaxy," Bing responded.

"Are the transit portals wormholes?" Bucky asked.

"Yes. I believe the physics is the same," Bing responded. "My spacecraft also uses the negative energy extracted from the black hole. The negative energy from the spacecraft and the Orb can open and hold open a portal through space from the black hole at the center of this galaxy. A portal to anywhere, only within this galaxy. The portal must originate at the black hole. And transit is only to and from the black hole," Bing explained.

Bucky turned to his friends with an expression of awe and disbelief. He had read about these things but never imagined they could be true.

"I closed the portal to this solar system, so it will take them some time to rebuild it and traverse it to attack," Bing said. "Bucky, can you sense the Orb?" he continued turning to face Bucky.

Bucky turned back to Bing and again realized the seriousness of their situation.

"Right now, I don't feel or have any sense of the Orb, Bing," he replied with a note of frustration. "I heard your soul song when you landed, and I sent those bullies from school into the sky. Both times, I don't remember doing anything special to make it happen."

"You must learn to sense the Orb before you can control it," advised Bing. "I had very limited access to its powers, but you can join with it. You can direct its powers in ways I could not."

"Why did they give you the Orb, and make you a Scout?" Bucky inquired.

"My memory of that time is vague. I was aware of my programming to use the Orb to detect life energies. I do not know when the Orb was joined with this machine. I do not know why life energy is needed to animate these machines. I believe it is a corruption against the natural order of sentient biological systems," Bing said in a voice that can only be described as anger.

"Natural order? What do you mean?" he asked.

"Life and death," Bing responded. "All biological systems are time limited from animation to the time the systems become aged and cease to function, when the life energy is released back into the universe. The Entity has interrupted that process when it imprisons life energy in these machines and other things," Bing explained, his voice trailing off into silence.

At that moment, Bing took a few steps back, gazed at his hands, and then gently touched the sides of his face. He stood still for several minutes. Bucky and his friends just looked at each other, not knowing what to expect.

A look of great fear came over Bing's synthetic face. Then he spoke in a voice that was slight and low. "I am trapped. This is not right. This is not right. What did they do to me?" He moved his metallic hand, rubbing it over his opposite arm. "I remember the feel of a touch. This is not feeling. This is not being."

Bucky moved closer to Bing, his hands reaching out as he tried to touch him. Bing stepped back, creating distance as he drew near. Bing initially spoke softly in a language that none of them could understand. Then, his voice grew louder, and he began to shout, also in his native language. He started to shake, his arms falling limp at his sides, and his head returned to its cylindrical shape. Finally, he fell silent.

Bucky and his friends stood in silence, their gazes fixed on Bing, not sure what to do or say. He reached up to hold Bing's large mechanical hand.

"Bing? Are you all right?" he said. Looking stunned, he turned to his friends and asked, "What do we do? Something is wrong with him."

Jen and Marcus joined him. "He was just talking about being trapped" Jen said. "Maybe he's just realizing what happened to him."

"What should we do?" asked Marcus.

Bucky knew he had to help. He knew he now possessed the Orb, but still had only a vague idea of how to use it. The enormity of the situation threatened to overwhelm him. At this moment, he knew his life would never be the same. He knew he needed his new-found brother if he had any chance to save the earth. He knew so many were depending on him. He had to be strong for his brother, for his friends, for his mother, and now all the lives on earth.

He took a deep breath and closed his eyes. He searched for the Orb, its presence within him. He took several more deep breaths, causing his muscles to ease. He began to hear very distant sounds which slowly became louder to him. Distinct music-like notes yet clearly part of a collective of unique sources. He knew this was the sound-like sensations of life energy vibrating close to him and farther away. He could sense the distance of each source.

With his eyes closed, he felt what had to be Jen and Marcus' hands on both his shoulders. He focused on finding their soul songs, searching with his mind through the Orb.

Then he found them. Two beautiful songs from their vibrating life energies. So clear, so unique, and pleasing to experience. Not heard with his ears but just as clear in his mind. Even with his eyes closed, he could sense them. He memorized their songs.

He knew if he ever needed to find them again, he could just search for their life energy, their soul songs.

Still standing there with his eyes closed, he searched for Bing's life energy. He remembered now what it felt like to him. Very quickly, he found Bing's life energy vibrations and focused his mind on the source. This time, the music-like sound was very faint and was slowly fading.

"Bing, he said in his mind. Bing, can you hear me? I'm right here." With that, he sensed Bing's life energy music get slightly louder in his mind.

"Bing, Are you all right? I need you. I need you to help me learn to fight, to save my mom and my friends from the Collectors. Please, Bing, my brother, help me," he thought.

He then felt Bing's song gradually becoming stronger in his mind. Then, he heard in his head a faint voice from Bing.

"My brother. Once again, you have saved me. I am here now. I remember myself. For now, I am trapped in this machine. I must accept this existence. It enables me to be with you again and help save you and your friends. I choose to be here, even like this."

Bucky opened his eyes. They all observed Bing's cylinder head morph into the young man's face they all recognized as Bing.

"I choose to be here with you all now," Bing said aloud. "I do not know if what has been done to me can be undone, but I can still fight. I will stand with you, my brother, and your friends and fight the Entity."

Marcus, Bucky, and Jen all gathered around Bing. They looked at each other and nodded in silence. Each understanding the immense challenge before them.

"We're a team!" Bucky exclaimed. "I've always wanted to be on a team! "

"This is not like any team I've been on," Marcus added. "Save the earth? Sure, no problem."

"We have work to do, my brother and friends of my brother," Bing proclaimed. "Now, you all must rest. Meet me back here at the same time tomorrow. We will start your training."

Bucky and his friends watched Bing return to his spaceship. Bing's head reformed to the cylinder, and he re-entered the spacecraft by moving slowly through the surface just as before. The spacecraft lifted off noiselessly and disappeared into the night sky. They all stood in silence, looking up at the departing spacecraft.

Bucky sensed Bing's soul energy again as the spacecraft disappeared among the stars. He noticed that Bing's soul song did not fade as the spaceship drew further away. He closed his eyes and sensed Bing's life energy even stronger as he felt the Orb responding to his thoughts, his own life energy.

"No one is going to believe this," Marcus said, jolting Bucky back to the moment.

Bing's song faded to silence as he stopped channeling the Orb. *Lesson one for this Orb and me*, he thought to himself.

Chapter Thirteen

Bucky Starts Training

At school the next day, it was hard for the three to concentrate, given the great responsibility they all now shared. Bucky walked through the school halls between classes, looking at all the other students going about their day, unaware of the dangers they all faced. Occasionally, he would come across one or more of the bullies in a hallway. They would always look away in fear and quickly move in a direction away from him. He and his friends sat by themselves at lunch and discussed the challenge before them.

"This is all still so hard to believe," Jen said, starting the conversation. "Is there anything else you can tell us that will help us understand what we're supposed to do?"

"Trust me, I feel completely overwhelmed with all of this," Bucky said. "I have this Orb thing inside of me that supposedly has so much power, and I only barely know how to use it. Wouldn't Professor Ronald be interested in this physics?"

"Maybe we can talk to him and explain some of what happened," Jen suggested.

"Not sure that's a good idea, Jen," Marcus interrupted. "If he didn't believe us or told someone else, it could distract us or worse, put Bing in danger."

"You're right, Marcus," Jen said.

"I agree with Marcus, too," Bucky said. "Bing said we didn't have a lot of time, so we need to spend it with him and do whatever he tells us to prepare for... the attack of the Collectors."

"How do you feel, Bucky?" Jen asked. "I mean, with this whole thing of having a brother, with the idea that you existed as another person before now. The implications are just unbelievable."

"I know, Jen. It is unbelievable, but you both saw Bing, his spaceship, what I did with those bullies. I think we also have to believe what Bing told us about being attacked... and our life energy. This is all so crazy," Bucky said, shaking his head and looking down.

"Just before Bing froze, he started speaking a different language," Jen added. "I wonder if maybe I can learn it from him. Maybe that way I could help in some way."

"That's a good idea," Bucky said, looking up.

"Yeah, and maybe Bing will teach me to fly that spaceship of his. How cool would that be?" Marcus added with a note of enthusiasm.

"We can talk to him tonight and ask," Bucky said. "Of course, I'm supposed to learn how to use the Orb. I have no idea what that involves."

"Are you scared, Bucky?" Jen asked, reaching out to him and placing her hand on his shoulder.

"Of course. How could I not be? How could either of you not be scared too?" he responded in a frustrated tone. "And all of them," he added, looking around at all the kids in the lunchroom laughing and having conversations about things that were not so important, not having even the slightest clue what danger was coming for them.

With that, the school bell rang, and the sounds of all the students pushing their chairs back and the chattering filled the cafeteria. The three stayed seated and just looked at each other with a sense of dread. Truly, this challenge would test them in ways they knew they were not prepared for.

That night, they returned to the clearing where, this time, Bing's spaceship had already landed. When they approached, Bing emerged from his spacecraft the same way he had before by moving through the surface.

"My brother and friends of my brother, we must prepare for the Collectors," Bing said after his cylinder head returned to its human-like shape.

Bucky and his friends approached Bing. Standing in front of Bing, Bucky said, "We're ready to do whatever you need. My friends also have skills they hope can help."

"Yes, we will need help," Bing replied.

Marcus and Jen glanced at each other with a look of anticipation mixed with apprehension.

"Well, Marcus is great with anything mechanical, and Jen is great at languages," Bucky said, smiling at his friends.

"That is good. Both skills can help," Bing said. "I will work with each of you. But now I will focus on Bucky." He turned to him. "The Orb has many powers. It can control the effects of gravity on specific objects also when directed."

"We saw that effect at school," Marcus said, smiling at Bucky, then Jen.

"Yes, it was very scary. He could have really hurt them, or worse," Jen said with concern in her voice and a stark look at Bucky.

"Maybe that's the idea, Jen. Maybe that power is what Mr. Bing is talking about," replied Marcus.

Marcus and Jen approached Bing and began a series of questions concerning the mechanics of the Orb and his language.

Bucky moved away from them to prepare himself for whatever Bing had in store for him. There was a cool breeze that provided a hint that Summer was giving way to Fall. Bucky loved the Fall. He thought about the years past and all the good memories. The colors, the cool evenings, pumpkins, and even the start of school. He remembered Halloween and the first snow before Christmas. Somehow, he knew it would never be the same again. He even wondered if they would all be alive the next Fall. Perhaps they would all be trapped in robot machines like his lost brother had endured.

He looked around at Bing, the great robot that was his brother from a prior life. *A previous life*, he thought to himself. *What a concept. I'm definitely going to have to do some research on that.*

He then looked over at his best friends. They were in deep conversation with Bing. He wondered what he had gotten them into. Would they all lose their lives when the Collectors came? He shuddered with fear of the unknown.

At the same time, the realization that there was other life in this galaxy. Perhaps all other galaxies. Millions of civilizations. That, which was now a fact, something he and his friends were probably the only ones on the entire planet who knew, gave him a sense of wonder and excitement. Perhaps they would live, and he could explore the galaxy with his brother. Maybe his friends could come along too. But now, he had to focus on the thing that would save him, his friends, and even the earth.

"Bucky, Bucky," Jen called, trying to get his attention.

He turned to face Jen and saw the other two facing him.

Bing approached Bucky and began, "We must begin your training with the Orb. It has many powers. I had very limited control accessing the Orb from this machine..." He pointed to himself and continued, "There are two powers you must learn. One, you have already experienced, and the second, much more powerful and dangerous."

"More dangerous?" Jen questioned, looking at Bing, then towards Bucky.

"Yes," Bing replied. "The Orb was forged from the black hole. It contains energy and capabilities of a black hole, including the ability to project a jet of very powerful energy."

Bucky put his hand to his chest and rubbed it slightly. "This thing... this Orb has that much power? How is that possible? How am I supposed to control it?" he looked toward his friends once again, a little confused and frightened.

Marcus walked over to Bucky and placed his hand on his shoulder. "We're with you. I know this is so much responsibility for you. We're all scared too. But all of us here now have a responsibility to each other, our families, and... crazy as it sounds, to all of humanity."

"You take the Orb, Marcus. You're much stronger and braver than me. I don't want this," he said on the verge of tears.

"That is not possible, my brother," Bing said. Yours is the only life energy that can join with the Orb. I would take the Orb and sacrifice myself if it would save you and your world, but I cannot."

There was a silence that lasted for several moments as Bucky sobbed, looking at the ground. He then looked up and took a deep breath while wiping the tears welling up in his eyes.

"By the way," Marcus started, apparently trying to break the awkward silence. "You can just call me Marcus. I think we all know by now that I am a friend of your brother."

Jen and Bucky laughed as Bing said, "Yes, I will call you Marcus."

"And you can just call me Jen," Jen said, still smiling.

"I still have much to learn," Bing replied with a smile on his young man's face.

"It's OK, Bing," Bucky said taking several deep breaths to calm himself. "This is new for all of us, too. Ok then. If it has to be me, then I need to learn how to control this thing, this Orb," Bucky said.

"First, we will start with the power of the Orb to project a negative energy field to work against gravity. You will use gestures to access, then channel the power of the Orb," Bing said.

"Yeah. We saw firsthand how that works," Marcus said with a smile.

Bucky quickly looked back at Bing, feeling a bit guilty. "But I really didn't know what I was doing."

Bing frowned, which was an interesting look for him. *It makes him look more human,* Bucky thought.

"You did not hurt anyone, my brother?" Bing asked. "No. It was OK. No one was hurt," he reassured.

"But they sure were scared, that's for sure," Marcus chimed in.

"You must be very careful. The Orb has great energy that can also be directed as a plasma jet. The Orb can be very dangerous and very destructive," Bing warned. "But it may be this capability you will need to defend the earth," he added in a very serious tone.

Bing continued, "The sequence to access the power of the Orb is first to connect with it and sense the negative energy, the energy that works against what you know as gravity." Bing raised his arms up in front of him and held them, pointing out. "Like this. You will direct the negative energy from the Orb inside you through your arms, then through your hands, at objects or anything you wish to resist the positive force of gravity. We will start on something small and then something much larger."

"Bucky, when I prepare to compete in sports," Marcus said, "I try to focus my mind on the challenge in front of me. I try to get into a zone where I don't think about anything other than applying myself to my objective. I visualize what I want to happen over and over in my mind. I put all other thoughts and distractions out of my mind. I close my eyes and see it very clearly. Then, when I'm on the field, it's automatic to me to execute exactly what I practiced in my mind."

"Marcus, I've never played sports before. I've never experienced the zone you're describing," he said with some frustration in his voice.

Jen walked over to Bucky. "When you were working on the science project, you were completely focused on the task in front of us. You were completely concentrating on the design and construction. In some way, I think that was a kind of zone that Marcus is talking about."

"Yes, Jen. I think I understand what you mean," he said. "When I was working on the science project, I always pictured the completed project in my head. It was like I knew exactly what it looked like completed. Let me give it a try."

Marcus bent down and looked around on the ground in the bright moonlight for something small for Bucky to practice on. He then found and picked up a stone about as big as a baseball.

"Here. Try this," Marcus said as he walked over and placed the rock on the ground in front of Bucky, then stepped back quickly as if he didn't know what to expect. Bucky looked a little bewildered as he turned toward Bing and said, "Now what?"

"Sense the Orb. Connect your life energy with it," Bing said.

He took a deep breath and focused his mind inward, trying to sense new things. He quickly picked up on the "soul songs" of those nearby. Then, he directed his concentration to the rock in front of him, guided by Bing's hand gestures.

Following Bing's lead, he straightened his arms with his fingers pointing at the rock. He felt a buzz of energy from the Orb, making the hairs on his arms stand up like when he rubbed a balloon on his arm. He then pointed his fists at the rock and opened his hands, sending a surge of energy through his arms to his fingertips. Suddenly, the rock, along with the dirt and leaves, shot into the air and disappeared from sight. He recoiled with shock at the effect. The objects fell back some distance away as he released his concentration.

"Whoa, cool," Marcus shouted. "Bucky, that was awesome!"

"Yes. That was amazing!" Jen exclaimed. She and Marcus ran over to him and patted him on the back.

He had a look of shock and surprise on his face, which changed to a smile as his friends congratulated him. "That was amazing!" he shouted, looking at his hands.

"Very good," Bing complimented with a smile. "You seem to be a natural at controlling the Orb," he added.

Bucky moved around the clearing and repeated the gestures on various other objects, like small rocks and branches. Marcus and Jen clapped with excitement each time.

"Very good," Bing said again. "Now you must learn to direct a stream of energy using the Orb."

Bucky and his friends walked over to Bing and listened intently.

"This is the most important and the most dangerous because you will need to use this power against those that will attack this planet. It may be the only way to fight them and the energy weapons they possess," Bing said in a very serious tone.

"To direct the Orb as a weapon, you will need to use the rotational power of the Orb to create a sphere of energy and project it at a target," Bing continued. "You can control the amount of energy by allowing the sphere to rotate to higher speeds before releasing the energy as a plasma jet," Bing added, using hand gestures to demonstrate the process to Bucky.

"How do I tell the difference between the gravity energy and the... the plasma jet energy?" he asked in a slightly trembling voice.

"It is the positive energy side of the Orb where the energy you used to disrupt the gravitational field was negative; this energy is positive," Bing answered.

"You will start by accessing the Orb and creating the rotating sphere of energy between your hands," Bing said, gesturing with his hands stretched in front of him, palms facing each other.

Bucky, still a little frightened, raised his arms and hands, mirroring Bing's movement. His hands were trembling. He closed his eyes and once again took a deep breath and searched for the Orb. Almost immediately, he sensed it. Instantly, he connected with its immense power. This time, he sought the positive aspect of the Orb and felt a force pushing outward from within. Concentrating, he directed this energy through his arms to his hands, feeling them grow warm as the energy flowed between them.

A small, glowing sphere began to form, rotating slowly between his palms. He realized he could control the release of the positive energy from the Orb into this sphere. As he allowed more energy to flow, the sphere rotated faster and faster and became very bright. The light from the sphere lit up the entire clearing and projected shadows behind the surrounding trees.

He opened his eyes and marveled at the tiny ball of radiant energy rotating between his hands. A smile spread across his face as he instinctively knew how to channel the energy to make it spin faster.

Marcus and Jen looked on with wide, astonished eyes and began to back away once again.

"I knew you would remember the Orb. It was a part of you so long ago as it is now," Bing said. "That is enough for now. Tomorrow, we will continue."

He stopped the flow of positive energy from the Orb to his hands, and the tiny sphere disappeared with a small popping sound. He felt extremely tired and slumped to his knees.

Jen and Marcus ran to Bucky and knelt by his side. They took each arm to hold him steady. He looked at both his friends. "Can you believe this? Did you see that? That was me. That Orb thing is a part of me. I could sense it. I felt both sides. It was almost easy," he said with a slight smile.

"Bucky, we saw it, and yes, it's very hard to believe," Jen said.

"Very cool. You're like a superhero now," Marcus said, almost laughing.

"Yeah. A superhero. Me. Imagine that," Bucky said in disbelief.

Chapter Fourteen

Black Hole Defined

The next day at school, the three met again at lunch, sitting by themselves so as not to be overheard by the other students. Jen was the first to speak.

"I'm really scared. I couldn't sleep last night, thinking about this whole thing with this alien robot that says he's your brother and the power of that Orb. I'm afraid for you. It has to be very dangerous."

"I agree with Jen," Marcus said. "We know nothing about these things."

"Haven't you ever wondered about other life in our galaxy, the universe?" Bucky asked, looking at Jen and Marcus. "I've been wondering about that my whole life. I look up at the stars and ask the question, are we alone? Now we know," he said firmly. "Of all the people on this planet, we alone are the ones who know. The idea that I lived before, the fact that's even possible, is amazing and profound."

"You don't sound like a 16-year-old, Bucky," Jen said.

He took a deep breath and sighed. "Yeah, I don't feel like one anymore, either."

"My grandmother used to describe what life and death mean in Chinese culture," Jen said. "We believe that the soul is an essential part of our being and continues to exist even after death. We believe in the importance of honoring and remembering our ancestors, as they have a profound influence on our lives and the world around us."

"That's cool, Jen," Marcus said. "For me, my mom and my grandmother also talked about life and death, but I think it has a lot to do with the church we go to. Death is not the end of a person's existence, they would say, but rather a transition to the afterlife where the soul will be judged by God. They believe that death is a natural part of life."

"I thought you said you didn't pay attention in church," Jen chided.

"Well, I don't really. But I hear my mom and my granny talk about it when we're having dinner sometimes," Marcus said. "Now I don't know what to believe."

There was a long silence before Marcus spoke. "I've been asking myself the same questions as you about our place in the universe since this thing started for all of us. I wonder if

I existed before now, too. Man, this is all so crazy." Jen and Bucky nodded in agreement.

Later that day, all three had science class with Dr. Ron. It was still hard for them to focus, given their recent experiences and discussions. The topic for the science lesson was about the sun.

"The sun is the star at the center of our solar system," Dr. Ron explained. "It's a giant, glowing ball of gas that is held together by its own gravity. It is made up mostly of hydrogen and helium, and it produces light and heat through a process called nuclear fusion."

The three of them started taking notes as Dr. Ron spoke.

"The sun is actually quite large," Dr. Ron continued. "If you were to compare it to the diameter of the earth, it would be about 109 times larger. And it is also very hot. The temperature on the surface of the sun can reach up to about 5500 degrees Celsius, or about 10,000 degrees Fahrenheit. But the sun is not just a giant ball of fire." His voice shifted to a more serious tone. "It is also the source of life on earth. Without the sun, there would be no plants, no animals, and no humans. We depend on the sun for everything, from the air we breathe to the food we eat."

Bucky sensed this was an opportunity to get Dr. Ron to explain some of the things they were experiencing. He raised his hand.

"Yes, Bucky. Do you have a question?" Dr. Ron asked.

"Yes. Um, I have a question about how a sun becomes a black hole, and is there negative energy at the center?" he asked. Jen and Marcus, seated on either side of him, both turned their heads to look at him, wearing expressions that clearly said, ' What are you doing?'

Dr. Ron considered the question for a moment before responding. "In theoretical physics, the concept of harnessing negative energy is fascinating. It's often discussed in the context of advanced propulsion systems or even time travel. However, it remains largely hypothetical. The energy scales required and the instability of such energies make practical application a daunting, if not impossible, challenge with our current understanding and technology."

"Well, Bucky, that's a good question," Dr. Ron said. "As you all know, a black hole is a region in space where the gravitational pull is so strong that nothing, not even light, can escape it. But what you may not know is that black holes also possess a property known as negative energy. Now, I know what you're thinking — how can energy be negative? But bear with me. In physics, energy is the ability to do work. Positive energy is the energy we typically think of — it's what powers our cars, our phones, and even our bodies. But negative energy is a bit more complex."

Bucky smiled at Jen and Marcus. He knew Dr. Ron might be able to explain at least some of what they've been experiencing.

"In order to understand negative energy," Dr. Ron continued, "we have to delve into the world of quantum mechanics. At the atomic level, particles are constantly popping in and out of existence. And when they do, they carry with them a tiny bit of energy. Now, normally, this energy is positive, but it can also be negative, and this is where black holes come in." Dr. Ron nodded in Bucky's direction.

Bucky leaned forward, listening intently.

"As matter falls into a black hole, it releases energy. However, this energy can be negative, meaning that it takes away from the overall energy of the system. In other words, the black hole is sucking in positive energy and replacing it with negative energy. This negative energy is what helps to keep the black hole stable. Without it, the black hole would collapse in on itself, resulting in a catastrophic explosion." Dr. Ronald concluded with a flourish of his hands, indicating an explosion.

Bucky smiled and nodded at Dr. Ron, expressing his understanding and appreciation for the information.

"That was a good question, Bucky," Dr. Ron said. "I'm glad to see you take so much interest in the physics of our galaxy."

"Thank you, Dr. Ron," he said. "I have one more question, though. "What is a black hole plasma jet?"

Marcus and Jen exchanged worried glances as they observed him. Sensing their concern, he made a reassuring gesture with his hand as if to say, "Don't worry."

"Well," Dr. Ron said, "at the center of a black hole, there is a theoretical singularity, a point where the density of matter potentially becomes infinite, if not for the presence of negative energy that I just spoke of. This is where the plasma jet comes into play."

A surge of excitement coursed through Bucky, his entire body was tingling with anticipation. He couldn't help but wonder if the Orb had anything to do with this sensation. The plasma jet is what Bing said he would be able to generate with the Orb. Now, Jen and Marcus were listening intently along with him as the teacher continued.

"A black hole plasma jet is a highly energetic outflow of charged particles, primarily electrons and protons. This plasma is accelerated to near the speed of light by the power of the black hole and forms a jet that shoots out. It is an incredible example of the power and mystery of the universe," Dr. Ron explained.

"What would happen if the jet hit a planet?" Bucky asked, hoping to get as much information as possible before the class ended.

Dr. Ron smiled and looked up at the clock. "Bucky, we only have time for this last question, but I'll try to answer," he said. "When these jets hit a planet or a star, the damage can be catastrophic. Imagine a beam of pure energy capable of destroying entire solar systems."

He glanced at Marcus and then Jen, pointing upward as if indicating the direction of the Entity described by Bing. Jen and Marcus both nodded solemnly, acknowledging the looming danger that threatened everything they held dear.

The bell rang indicating the end of the period. The three friends exchanged a look, each lost in thought over Dr. Ron's explanation. Bucky couldn't help but connect the lesson to their recent discoveries. After class, as they walked together in the hallway, Bucky shared his thoughts.

"Listening to Dr. Ron talk about the sun, I couldn't help but think about the power of the Orb and the energy it can unleash," Bucky mused, looking at Jen and Marcus. "It's like having a piece of the universe's power at my fingertips."

Jen nodded, her brow furrowed in thought. "It puts things into perspective, doesn't it? The vastness of the universe and our place in it. It's overwhelming but also incredibly fascinating."

As they reached their lockers, Bucky leaned against his, his gaze distant. "I keep thinking about what Bing said, about preparing to defend Earth. It's hard to wrap my head around the fact that we're going to be part of something so... monumental."

Jen placed a hand on his shoulder, offering a reassuring smile. "We're in this together, Bucky. We'll learn, and we'll help each other through it. And with Bing's guidance, we'll all prepare for what's to come."

Marcus punched Bucky lightly on the arm, a grin spreading across his face. "Plus, you've got superpowers now. If that doesn't boost your confidence, I don't know what will."

Bucky couldn't help but smile back, despite the heavy burden he felt. "Yeah, superpowers," he echoed softly, the reality of their situation sinking in. "It's just... I hope I'm ready when the time comes."

"You will be," Jen assured him. "And we'll be right there with you."

As the final bell rang, signaling the end of the school day, the three friends gathered their things and headed out together, united by a bond forged by extraordinary circumstances. They knew the challenges ahead would be unlike anything they had ever faced, but they also knew they had each other and the resolve to protect their world.

As they walked down the hallway, Bucky mused aloud, "Imagine what we could learn if we could really understand and use the Orb's powers."

Jen nodded, "And imagine the responsibility that comes with it."

"Guys, what we're dealing with... it's like something out of a sci-fi movie, but it's real," Marcus said.

Jen sighed deeply. "I keep thinking about what Dr. Ron said about the plasma jets. If Bing is right, and we're facing something capable of wielding that kind of power..."

"We'll need to be ready," Bucky interjected, determination settling in his voice. "Bing believes in us, and I believe in the Orb. We have to trust that we'll figure this out."

"Tonight, we train with Bing again. We're going to learn everything we can," Bucky said, closing his locker with a decisive thud.

"Right," Jen agreed, her usual optimism tinged with a hint of steel. "And we'll protect each other, no matter what."

Marcus put an arm around each of his friends, a determined look in his eyes. "Whatever comes, we'll face it together. Like Dr. Ron said, never stop asking questions. And never stop looking for answers."

With that, they stepped out of the school building, the setting sun casting long shadows behind them. The challenges ahead were daunting, but in this moment, they were united by a common purpose. As they walked home, their conversation turned to strategies and plans, their shared resolve growing stronger with every step.

Chapter Fifteen

To The Moon

Navigating the shadow-draped woods under the cloak of night, Bucky found his thoughts ensnared by Dr. Ron's revelations about the cosmos' forces. The concept of harnessing a plasma jet from a black hole loomed large in his mind. Questions of its creation, manipulation, and control spiraled within him, mirroring the cosmic phenomena he was now inexplicably linked to. Absently, his hand drifted to his chest, tracing the site of power that had become a part of his very essence.

Jen, keeping pace beside him, caught the gesture. "Are you okay?" she inquired, her voice laced with concern.

"I think so," Bucky replied, pausing to face his companions. His voice softened with gratitude. "Having you both by my side means more than I can say. Facing this alone... I can't even imagine."

A shared glance and a smile passed between Marcus and Jen, a silent acknowledgment of their unbreakable bond.

"Of course, Bucky. We know you'd do the same for us if we met our long-lost family stuck in a robot and had a chunk of a supermassive black hole jammed in our chest," Marcus joked.

Their laughter, though brief, was a welcome reprieve from the gravity of their mission. They resumed their walk toward the clearing, which served as the stage for their impending challenges. There, Bing awaited, a figure of calm assurance against the backdrop of his spacecraft, bathed in the amber hues of dusk. His attire, a seamless fusion of white and grey, highlighted his otherworldly origin, while his transformed visage bore a smile of genuine warmth as they approached.

"My brother, your presence brings me joy," Bing greeted, stepping forward. "And you, Marcus and Jen," he continued, his glance seeking Bucky's nod of affirmation to use their given names, "your courage is commendable. Tonight marks the beginning of our resistance."

Jen's response was to draw closer to Marcus, her action a wordless pledge of their collective resolve. "We're ready, Mr. Bing," she declared.

Marcus, buoyed by a mix of anticipation and resolve, added, "I'm ready to learn to fly," as he looked over Bing's spacecraft.

"Indeed, Marcus. However, before we fly, I have something for Jen," Bing announced, extending a spherical device toward her. "This will help bridge the gap between our languages." Jen accepted the device, about the size of a golf ball from Bing's outstretched palm.

"Remarkably light," Jen observed, elevating the device for closer examination. "What am I supposed to do?" she inquired, curiosity piqued by its simplicity yet apparent sophistication.

Bing gestured towards his ear in a way that mirrored human familiarity. "Press it gently against your ear, like so," he instructed. "It will adapt seamlessly to your ear's interior, enabling a bridge between our languages," he detailed further. "Understanding the Collectors, and potentially other entities we encounter, is crucial. Should I be incapacitated, this device will be invaluable for communication with others we may encounter."

With cautious optimism, Jen followed Bing's directions, affixing the device to her ear. It morphed with precision, aligning flawlessly with her ear's anatomy. Initial apprehension faded as she tentatively engaged with her surroundings, a look of anticipation in her eyes.

"Say something?" she prompted Marcus, her voice laced with a mix of excitement and disbelief. Her reaction was immediate, a blend of surprise and delight. "It's as though there's nothing there, yet my voice sounds crystal clear. It's really comfortable."

"And what should I say?" Marcus responded, intrigued by her reaction.

Jen's astonishment was evident as she touched her ear, marveling at the experience. "Incredible! I heard you, Marcus, and simultaneously, a foreign language echoed in my ear," she shared, attempting to mimic the unfamiliar sounds to Bing.

Bing responded with a smile of approval, "Excellent, Jen. Mastering the skill to comprehend both languages concurrently will require practice, but it's the most efficient method to learn."

"Ok, that time all I heard was English," Jen noted, slightly bemused.

The revelation sparked laughter from Marcus and Bucky, with Bucky clarifying, "Bing was communicating in his native language, which we couldn't understand a word."

Jen joined in the laughter, realizing the device's bidirectional effectiveness. "So, it works both ways," she concluded.

"Indeed," Bing affirmed. "It's vital to learn our shared language, especially if circumstances render the device unusable." He added, "Should you need to remove it, a gentle pinch will suffice, reverting it to its original form."

"I'll be careful, Mr. Bing," Jen said determined. "I want to do whatever I can to help."

Shifting focus to Marcus, Bing announced, "Now, for your preparation." He outlined his plan to adjust his ship's environment for their safety and introduce controls reminiscent of those familiar to human interfaces. "This will enable you to pilot the craft effectively." With that, Bing advanced towards his vessel, seamlessly merging with its structure as he entered, a testament to the wonders that awaited them.

The trio exchanged glances, a silent question hanging in the air as Bing vanished into the vessel. "How are we supposed to enter? Just walk through its walls?" Marcus asked with a measure of concern. "It seems this ship is made up of some kind of unique material, capable of altering its structure in response to its surroundings. I imagine it becomes incredibly resilient during space travel, softening to permit entry and exit. The technology must be like what powers Jen's translator device," he theorized.

Jen nodded in agreement, her smile reflecting her admiration for Marcus's insight.

Shortly after, a soft hissing sound broke the silence, indicating the opening of a square door along the spacecraft's side. As it slid open, revealing a passage about six feet tall and four feet wide, Bing's figure reappeared, slightly stooping to navigate through the doorway.

"I've adjusted the ship's atmosphere to ensure your comfort and safety, mimicking Earth's air composition and pressure. The artificial gravity has been set to Earth's standard, one G," Bing informed them.

Acknowledging Bing's efforts, Bucky exchanged a glance with Jen and Marcus, impressed.

Bing momentarily retreated into the ship, then extended his arm, inviting them inside. Marcus led the way, cautiously entering the spacecraft. Hand in hand, Jen and Bucky followed, stepping into the dimly lit interior. The ambient light seemed to radiate from the ship's very walls, devoid of discernible light fixtures. The vessel's interior, spacious yet intimate, resembled a school bus in size but with a more sophisticated, streamlined design. Its surfaces were bathed in shades of gray, devoid of any markings, maintaining an air of sleek functionality.

Bucky noted the ceiling's height, which allowed Bing to stand erect with room to spare, suggesting an interior clearance of about eight feet. The absence of conventional features such as seats, windows, or controls lent the space an otherworldly minimalism.

The craft's singular chamber extended some thirty feet in length, with the floor spanning ten feet across, flanked by smoothly curving walls that met a narrower ceiling strip. The structure tapered gently towards what Bucky assumed was the front, while the back was marked by a seamless wall uniting floor and ceiling.

As the entrance sealed shut with a quiet whoosh, a fleeting wave of claustrophobia washed over Bucky. The sudden realization of being enclosed—no visible exits or windows—briefly overwhelmed him. Sensing his discomfort, Bing assured, "It will be okay. Once I configure the interior further."

Bucky, still trying to calm himself, trusted Bing's demeanor, offering a measure of comfort amidst the unknown.

"Please, move towards the rear," Bing directed, his tone blending authority with an underlying warmth. The trio, moving as one, navigated to the specified area, great anticipation on their faces.

Bing, with a graceful pivot, faced the spacecraft's front. His hand, in a deliberate gesture, hovered above the floor. Moments later, a console emerged seamlessly from the floor, its expanse nearly matching the interior's width and projecting three feet forward. At its heart, a slender pillar anchored it firmly, a testament to the ship's advanced design.

The console, angling slightly towards Bing, came alive with a myriad of lights and displays, transforming into a command center befitting their celestial voyage. Simultaneously, two pilot seats ascended from the floor, their sizes distinct—the larger clearly meant for Bing, a nod to his unique stature.

With another fluid motion, Bing summoned two additional seats behind the pilot's area. These seats, echoing the design of familiar comfort, awaited Jen and Bucky, promising a secure vantage point for the journey ahead.

Bing indicated the left pilot seat to Marcus, his face alight with an eager smile. Marcus navigated past the newly formed seats, taking his place with an air of readiness. The seat, intuitive to his needs, adjusted for optimal interaction with the control array.

Bing's guiding hand next led Jen and Bucky to their seats. Bucky, intuitively choosing the position behind Bing, settled with a mix of curiosity and great anticipation. Jen, positioning herself behind Marcus, lightly squeezed his shoulder, her words laced with humor and caution, "Keep it under light speed, okay?"

Marcus smiled back at Jen and retorted with playful defiance, "I'll try, but no promises."

As Bing assumed his position, the control panel lit up, a holographic projection of their solar system materialized, hovering over the forward console with intricate detail. A solitary red beacon pulsated on Earth's representation, unmistakably marking their current location. This display, a stark reminder of their terrestrial origins, now served as the backdrop for their imminent departure from Earth.

As Bing's fingers danced across the panel, the spacecraft's interior plunged into darkness, save for the vibrant hues of the hologram that bathed the cabin in a soothing glow. The sudden shift to darkness struck Bucky with great unease, the panic of being trapped in an enclosed space reemerging. He leaned closer to Jen, whispering nervously, "It's pitch black in here. No windows or doors, how's anyone supposed to see outside?"

Bing seemed to catch the hint of apprehension in Bucky's voice. He offered a reassuring smile before returning his attention to the control panel. With a few deft touches, he initiated a transformation within the spacecraft. The walls and ceiling seemed to vanish, replaced by a panoramic view of their surroundings, as if the ship itself had become invisible.

"Wow!" Bucky exclaimed, jumping to his feet and extending his arms, exploring this new illusion. Touching the side walls, he felt the solid surface, despite the visual effect that made it seem otherwise. "That's the coolest thing ever!" he beamed, settling back into his seat, his earlier nerves forgotten.

Bing gestured towards the holographic Earth, then performed a motion that caused the planet to recede, bringing the vastness of the solar system into focus, Earth at its heart. "This interface," Bing explained, his voice a blend of warmth and mechanical precision, "serves as your navigational guide. As for me, my integration with the spacecraft negates the need for such visual aids."

Marcus, reached towards the glowing Earth, now outlined in white to indicate selection. Gently pulling back, he watched in fascination as Earth expanded within the holographic solar system. Experimenting further, he spun the display, orbiting the system around Earth with a touch.

After a brief tutorial from Bing, Marcus mastered the basics of the hologram. "This is beyond cool, Mr. Bing. I've got the hang of changing views and picking destinations. But how do we actually get moving?"

Bing dedicated a few moments to guide Marcus through the spacecraft's flight dynamics and control system.

Meanwhile, Bucky and Jen were captivated by the projected sunset, an experience in such high resolution they felt as though they were outdoors, witnessing the day's end sitting in the clearing.

Turning to his friends, Marcus announced confidently, "I think I've got it now. Thanks to Bing, steering this spaceship should be straightforward. So, what do you say? Bing has plotted a quick trip to the moon and back."

“The moon?” Jen echoed, her voice tinged with apprehension and a hint of excitement.

Bucky couldn’t help but chuckle, his optimism undimmed. “Hey, if this ship can cross galaxies, a hop to the moon’s a piece of cake, right?” He looked towards Bing, his question hanging in the air, a mix of jest and genuine curiosity.

“Do not worry. I believe Marcus understands the necessary controls,” Bing said.

“Yeah, you guys, don’t worry. This is simple,” Marcus said in a highly confident tone.

Jen and Bucky looked at each other with slight trepidation. Then Bing reassured them, “I have configured simple restraints in your seats. While you will only feel slight accelerations as we maneuver, the restraints are for maximum safety.”

They fastened their seatbelts and shoulder straps, then gave a thumbs-up to Bing and Marcus.

Bing pressed the control panel in several places while instructing Marcus. Just then, there was a slight vibration coming from behind the rear wall of the interior of the spacecraft. When Bucky looked around towards the back, all he could see was the clearing and the trees behind the craft, but there was a slight shimmer to the images.

The spacecraft began to rise and was quickly above the trees. Bucky gripped the side of his chair because it felt like they were in the open air, with the images on the walls reflecting the outside. The spacecraft continued to rise into the sky and quickly passed through the few clouds above them. He was in awe at the sensation of ascending vertically with his ability to see the ground, city, and even his school in the distance.

When they were high enough, they began to see the sunset again, with the amazing reddish hues and the reflection of the clouds below them. As they continued to rise, the sky darkened to almost a purple color. The stars became brighter and more distinct without the atmosphere to diffuse their light. He felt amazed at the detail of the Earth, the oceans, and clouds, and the transition between day and night, with the lights of the cities showing on the night side of the Earth.

Bing was still instructing Marcus, but Bucky could only focus on the stars above and the Earth now receding below. The giant sun shone so brightly in the distance, and he could almost see the surface boiling. He thought about Dr. Ron's lecture on the sun and wondered what he would say if he could see this now.

The spacecraft started accelerating forward and followed the curvature of the Earth until the moon came fully into view. Bing took his hands from the control panel and just gave Marcus instructions. Marcus was now interacting with the hologram and the instrument panel at the same time to accelerate the spacecraft toward the moon.

The Earth quickly receded from view as the moon became bigger and bigger in front of them. Bucky was amazed that he only felt the slightest acceleration when they began to travel very fast through space—only minutes had passed when they arrived at what looked like only miles above the moon. He had never seen pictures of the moon in this detail. He remembered the simple view through the telescope his father had given him when he was young.

He gazed at the barren and rocky landscape below them. The surface was covered in a layer of fine dust and rock fragments, and the bright sunlight illuminated the grayish-white color of the moonscape. He could see a number of craters of various sizes. Some were small and shallow, while others were large and deep. He also saw mountains and hills, as well as large, flat plains. The sky above them was black, and Earth appeared as a bright, blue-green disc in the distance.

"Oh my!" was all Jen could say.

"This is so unbelievable," Bucky added.

"I believe you understand enough about the spacecraft controls now, Marcus, that I will let you pilot us back to where we started," Bing said.

"Marcus..." Jen said, getting his attention. "You don't even have your driver's license yet, and now you're qualified to fly an alien spacecraft. That's amazing."

Marcus laughed and said, "I'll pick you guys up for school and park this in student parking. Wouldn't that be fun?"

"This is very important, Marcus," Bing said. "It may become necessary for you to pilot this ship if something happens to me."

"You keep saying that, Bing," Bucky said. "If something happens to you, what are we supposed to do?"

"My brother, we need to prepare for any possibility," Bing said. "The risk to your planet is too great. If we fail, your entire population will be enslaved."

"We won't fail," Marcus said confidently.

With several movements of his hands on the hologram and pressing areas of the panel, Marcus looked at Bing for approval before proceeding. The spacecraft pivoted and headed back toward Earth. Bucky turned around in his seat and watched the moon recede over the great distance. He then thought about the Apollo missions, how long it took them to reach the moon and back, and how dangerous it was. Again, within minutes, the spacecraft reentered Earth's atmosphere and descended slowly, touching down back in the clearing in the woods near Bucky's house.

They all stood up from their seating. Bing moved his hand over the panel, and everything in the interior returned to the way it had been when they first entered the spacecraft. The door opened, and they all walked out onto the ground outside the ship.

Bucky looked back at the nearly full moon in the sky and felt an amazing sense of wonder. "I can't believe we were just there," he said.

"Silent and serene, the moon shines above, guiding us through the night with its eternal love," Jen said. "I read that somewhere," she added. She then attempted to recite the poem in Bing's language.

Bing smiled and said, "Very good, Jen. My brother, you are very lucky to have such friends as these."

With a warm smile, he replied, "Yes, I'm very lucky to have you all."

"I must go now and continue to monitor the wormhole at the edge of your solar system for the Collectors," Bing said. "I believe we only have days before they will come. Tomorrow, we have the most important training, my brother. I cannot direct the immense energy of the Orb as a weapon. I know you can do it because you did it so long ago against the evil forces that attacked our home planet."

Bucky shuddered at the idea of fighting an army. *I couldn't even defend myself against a couple of bullies*, he thought. "Tomorrow, then, I'll do my best," he said in a not-so-confident tone.

"Jen and Marcus, I think it will be safest if just Bucky returns tomorrow. The next level of training will be dangerous."

"Good luck, Bucky," Jen said. "I know you can do it."

"Yeah, buddy," Marcus said. "Remember, we're your biggest supporters."

With that, they all said goodbye to Bing.

Back home in his bed that night, Bucky found it hard to sleep. When he closed his eyes, all he could see was the Earth and the moon from the trip in Bing's spacecraft. He was sensing many new things these days that he did not understand. Sounds and songs, like the entire galaxy, had a heartbeat. He knew the Orb was channeling energies from the galaxy like a radio receiver.

He tried to find Bing by somehow tuning Bing's soul song through the Orb the same way Bing had found him. He wondered what song his own soul made. Was it as beautiful and pleasing as Bing's? With that thought, Bucky drifted off to sleep.

Chapter Sixteen

The Explosion

The next day, Bucky returned to the clearing just before sunset. He saw Bing waiting for him, but something was not right. Bing wasn't smiling like he usually did when they would first meet. Worried, Bucky asked, "Are you ok?"

Bing stared past him with a stoic expression on his face. His eyes seemed lifeless and dark. Bucky waited for Bing to respond, and with every growing minute, he became more and more worried about his brother. His eyes caught burn marks on the side of Bing's spacecraft. There were black streaks across the side.

"Bing, what happened?" Bucky implored. Just then, life returned to Bing's eyes, and he slowly looked down at Bucky. A slight smile came across his face, and he whispered in a weak voice,

"I remember you had a small pet back home when we were growing up," Bing said. "Our father gave it to you. You loved it. You took such good care of it. I used to create these small carvings of our native birds, and that thing destroyed half of my collection. I was so angry with you. I remember I chased you while you were holding your pet."

Bucky looked on in silence.

"You were always faster than me. I remember you did not return home for a very long time. I became so worried you would never come home. When you did, you no longer had the creature. You said you set it free so it would not come between us. You were a good brother to me. I don't know why that memory has returned to me."

"I'm sorry it destroyed your collection, Bing," Bucky said, not knowing what else to say.

Still concerned about Bing, he asked, "What happened to your spacecraft?" pointing to the burn marks down the side of the ship.

Bing's eyes followed the direction of his brother's finger. "I was on the other side," he said in an exhausted tone. "They found me. They detected my programming had changed. They tried to reset my programming to make me the way I was before I found you."

Bucky gasped. "They found you? You were on the other side of the wormhole?"

“Yes,” he responded in a subdued voice. “They have ways of controlling this machine against any will I have. I fought it, my brother. I used my memories of us and our life before. I fought it, I fought it, and they did not succeed in controlling me or this machine.” He rubbed his chest with his robotic hand. “I am myself, but I felt pain for the first time since they enslaved me. I don’t know how it’s possible to feel pain, but it happened.”

“But you’re ok now, right?” he asked. “Do you still feel pain?”

“No. I am functioning well now without any pain. But I remember how it felt. For those moments, I remembered my life before this imprisonment, my life with you, the way we were.”

Bing knelt down, stretched his arms open, and beckoned Bucky over to him. Bucky stepped toward him, and he wrapped his large robotic arms around Bucky, hugging him.

As he felt the touch of the metallic arms against him, he imagined his long-lost brother and felt closer to him. He didn’t have a brother or sister in this lifetime, but he knew how it would feel because now he had Bing, such as he was. *Love transcends all things in space and time*, he thought.

Just then, he became aware of the Orb, and it translated Bing’s life energy as the song he was now familiar with. He heard it in his mind so clear and soothing. Bing had a beautiful soul song.

He felt a lump in his throat; he was on the verge of tears for him. The whole experience felt like family, like home.

He wiped a tear from his eye and asked, "Can you tell me what happened out there at the wormhole?"

Bing stood up, his one hand still resting on his brother's shoulder. "I will try. I returned to the wormhole and went through it. They discovered me, and I was scanned. It was determined that I was not in the correct configuration for my assigned mission as a scout, so they sent programming instructions to this machine to correct the condition. I fought it, my brother. I felt awareness of myself drifting away from me. My memories of you, and how we once used to be, saved me," Bing continued.

"I think they were not prepared for the resistance to the programming. I think they also detected I no longer had the Orb. That is when they attempted to destroy my ship. I only just escaped back through the wormhole. The wormhole was kept open by a probe that came from my ship. So, I was able to shut it down, collapsing the wormhole so that they could not follow."

"So, they won't be able to come to Earth now?" Bucky asked hopefully.

"They will still come. They will configure a new wormhole and use it to transit to this solar system," Bing informed. "But it will take some time to calculate the coordinates and configure another negative energy probe to open and maintain the wormhole."

Bucky felt anger building inside him. The idea of someone hurting his brother was unacceptable to him. He himself was surprised at the emotion. It was like how family should feel. He felt closer to Bing now, and he began to understand the essence of Bing's consciousness apart from the robot body.

"Bing," he said, hesitating. "What happened to our mother and father?" He wanted to learn more about himself and his brother, to try and understand his prior life experiences with another family on another planet. He knew this was the way to understand Bing better, at least who he was when they were together.

"I do not know," Bing responded. "What happened to us, our family, our people, was a tragedy. It was evil and wrong. I do not know how many survived after I was taken. Our weapons were no match against the Collectors and the others. We were able to resist, as long as we had you, and the Orb."

Bucky nodded. He knew the situation was, in some ways, the same. He had the Orb. He was with his brother, and they were about to fight the evil once again.

"It is time we prepare, for what I know will happen next. The Collectors will attack your world and try to destroy me. They will seek to retrieve the Orb, which means you will be in great danger. I could not bear to lose you again," Bing said in a sad voice.

"Show me," Bucky said. "Help me learn to use this Orb."

"You will unlock the powers of the Orb based on your ability to sync with it," Bing explained. "Your next training step is to generate a gravitational field that can move and manipulate larger objects." He scanned the surroundings and pointed to a substantial boulder at the edge of the clearing, near the tree line. The boulder, about five feet in diameter and two feet high, seemed half-buried in the earth.

"There," Bing directed, pointing at the boulder. "That rock will be your practice target."

"You want me to lift that boulder?" he asked incredulously.

"The power of the Orb is immense," Bing responded. "Manipulating physical objects, even those much larger and heavier than this rock, should be manageable with the Orb."

The two approached the boulder, stopping about thirty feet away. He glanced up at Bing, who wore a grave expression. "You have already mastered directing a negative energy field to manipulate small, low-mass objects. This larger mass should feel no different," Bing stated firmly.

He shook his head in disbelief. "It's hard for me to imagine lifting something so large and heavy."

"That's because you're thinking of lifting the boulder with your physical strength," Bing clarified. "Instead, try to channel and direct the Orb through your life energy."

Taking a deep breath, he closed his eyes and reached inward for the Orb. This time, he connected with it quickly. A chill rippled through him as the connection solidified, and he began to discern the distinct sensations of the connection. He felt the interplay of positive and negative energies, learning to differentiate and harness them.

It was like a deep physical push and a pull somewhere in the middle of his body. He knew the push sensation was the negative energy of the Orb. He knew he had to channel the negative energy to create, what he now understood was an anti-gravitational field.

Concentrating on the negative energy, which seemed to be on his left side, he noticed he could channel it through his entire body.

He pointed the fingers on his left hand toward the boulder and slowly lifted his palm. A shock of energy moved from the center of his body through his arm and hand. Immediately, the dirt and loose stones around the boulder flew into the air.

"Good," Bing complimented. "You are learning to direct the energy of the Orb."

He smiled. Perhaps he could do this. He focused again on increasing the energy directed at the boulder. He felt a much stronger vibration in his arm and hand. He then pointed with purpose at the boulder, and suddenly, it began to vibrate as if trying to free itself from the ground.

Slowly, the boulder began to rise, pushing through the dirt that covered it. There was a rushing sound, like the air itself around the rock was rising like a wind, carrying the loose dirt and leaves.

The boulder finally broke free from the ground and, in a cloud of wind and dirt, rose into the air, free from the force of Earth's gravity. The sheer size of it and the experience of doing such a thing scared Bucky, causing him to clench his fist and lower his arm by his side. The wind stopped, and the boulder fell back to the ground with a very loud thud that almost shook Bucky to the ground. The dust and dirt splashed back down around the rock.

"Whoa, Bing. Did you see that?" he said excitedly.

"I did," Bing replied. "You are making good progress."

"I felt it this time in my arm," he said, holding up his arm to show Bing. "I felt I could direct it where I wanted, at that rock," he added with excitement in his voice.

He looked around. "Can I do that to a tree?" he said as he easily summoned the negative energy down his arms to his hands and pointed, palms up, at a nearby tree. Immediately, the dirt around the tree started flying in the air, and the rush of wind raked the branches on the tree as it began to make cracking noises. The branches started to snap off and rapidly rise into the air.

"Do not use the energy of the Orb on living things," Bing said. "Not yet. You must have greater control."

He closed his hands to form fists and lowered his arms by his side. The wind and the cracking wood sounds stopped.

"Bucky, try again with the rock, and this time, raise it higher and hold it in place," Bing said.

He nodded. He turned towards his objective, summoned the negative energy through his arms and hands, and pointed to the boulder. Again, the dirt and rush of air rose around the boulder, and this time, it rose effortlessly and steadily. The boulder rose in line with the tallest trees around the clearing and then far above the trees, following his hands until it was almost out of sight.

Bucky had visited New York City and stood at the base of the Empire State Building, looking up. He figured the boulder was about as high as that building in New York.

"Good. Now, hold the rock in place there," Bing said.

The boulder stopped high in the air as Bucky stopped raising his pointed palms. It hovered in place and rotated slightly while he looked on at the surreal scene. He thought about how easily he was able to control the gravitational field associated with the boulder.

Holding the boulder aloft, he couldn't help but see it as a symbol of the enemy. Questions fluttered through his mind, pondering if such power would suffice to elevate the Collectors and their spacecraft into oblivion. A deeper desire stirred within him, not just to lift but to shatter and obliterate the threat.

At that moment, a distinct surge of energy cascaded down his right arm, pooling into his palm—a sensation starkly different from the one he used to manipulate the boulder. Instinctively, his palms turned towards each other, right parallel to left, as if ready to unleash a formidable force.

What followed happened in the blink of an eye. A minuscule, yet intensely luminous, orb of light spun into existence between his hands. His arms trembled violently, charged with an electrifying energy reminiscent of touching a live wire. Then, with no warning, the orb of light hurtled towards the boulder suspended so far above. Upon impact, the rock exploded in a blinding flash, vanishing without a trace.

The explosion's force mushroomed, sending a shockwave through the air. Bing, with swift decisiveness, shielded Bucky from the brunt of the blast, which carried a maelstrom of air and debris from the surrounding environment. Despite Bing's protection, Bucky found himself hurled to the ground, the roar of the explosion echoing in his ears, and the landscape around them changed irrevocably as trees were snapped from their roots and flattened from the concussion.

"Are you alright, my brother?" Bing's voice was laden with concern, cutting through the aftermath's shock wave, a thunderous clap moving away from their location.

"What happened? What was that?" Bucky's voice was barely above a whisper as he struggled to piece together the events that had just unfolded. His ears rang with a persistent, sharp pitch. Bing, ever the protector, helped him to his feet, dusting off the remnants of the forest that had settled upon him.

Standing proved to be a challenge; his legs quivered, barely supporting him. In an attempt to clear the ringing in his ears, he shook his head vigorously. Gazing upwards, where the boulder once hung suspended, all that remained was a dissipating cloud of dark smoke—a testament to the power he had unwittingly unleashed. Turning to Bing with a voice softened by disbelief, he confessed, "I didn't mean to do that. I wasn't even aiming at the rock."

He glanced down at his hands, a mix of awe and fear in his eyes. "I felt it—the push and pull of negative and positive energies.

It wasn't my fault to target the boulder. Just thinking about destroying it was enough," he murmured.

***

Meanwhile, at the LIGO Observatory in Hanford, Washington, alarms began to blare unexpectedly. The gravitational wave detection systems, usually dormant, were now flashing.

Chapter Seventeen

Miranda's Alarm

Miranda looked up at the main displays in the LIGO Operations Center as the alerts started flashing.

"Anomaly?" Miranda called out loudly, aiming to capture the attention of the other engineers in the operations room. Her call for urgency did not immediately produce a response as several engineers began furiously typing at their computer consoles. On the main screens, various graphs sprang to life, with amplitude and estimated distance calculations displayed prominently. Adjacent to these readings, images from the closed-circuit camera feeds of the laser interferometer tunnels flickered into view.

"No anomalies in the equipment detected, Dr. Richards," announced the telemetry engineer stationed nearest to Miranda. "The amplitude was notably low, but the wave frequency was elongated. It's possible we're looking at a seismic event," he speculated.

Another engineer chimed in, not bothering to divert his gaze from his console. "These readings were common when we first initiated the experiment, though I was under the impression we had recalibrated our equipment to avoid such false alarms." A nod of agreement followed from both engineers.

"Crosscheck with Livingston, just in case," Miranda commanded, her voice tinged with impatience.

"On it," the second engineer responded promptly. He glided on his chair to a neighboring computer and began his inquiries.

A brief moment passed before he stood, turning to address Miranda. "Livingston corroborated the signal, noting no anomalies on their end as well. They, too, attributed it to the characteristics of a seismic event," he reported.

"Seismic event, hmm," Miranda murmured, more to herself than to her colleagues. She approached the second engineer, peering over his shoulder at the display.

"Dr. Richards, we've also detected a very minute gravitational wave. Its amplitude was low, yet the wavelength persisted for several seconds," the engineer explained, pointing to a line graph that showcased a subtle spike coinciding with the signal's receipt. "Livingston confirmed this signal as well," he added.

Miranda pondered, "What could simultaneously trigger both a seismic and a gravitational wave detection? It would have to be something with common proximity to the detectors, must be an earthbound source. An explosion of some sort, possibly a nuclear test?"

"I can't fathom any alternative explanation for such a distinct signal," the engineer remarked, his shoulders lifting in a shrug.

"The military is obligated to notify us prior to conducting any significant ordnance testing," Miranda reflected aloud. She paused, considering her next steps. "I might know someone in Washington who could shed some light on this." With a thoughtful expression, she headed towards the door.

Halting momentarily before exiting, she turned back to address the room firmly, "Until we ascertain more about these signals, I expect no external communication, understood?" A chorus of agreement and nods from the engineers affirmed her directive.

Returning to her office, Miranda searched through her files for the contact details of an Air Force Colonel she met at the NSF conference in Washington, DC, the previous year. Colonel Martin Klena had approached her following her presentation on LIGO's initial observations. Although his initial inquiries were technical, his interest soon seemed to extend beyond the confines of LIGO's research. Offering his business card with a casual smile, he had said, "Call me anytime, for professional matters or otherwise."

Finding the card clipped to her conference presentation notes, Miranda contemplated the wisdom of reaching out. Colonel Klena's personal cell number was scribbled on the card. Hesitating briefly over which number to dial, she ultimately chose the personal line and waited for a response.

"Hello, this is Colonel Klena," came the answer from the other end.

"Hello, Colonel; this is Dr. Miranda Richards calling from the LIGO Observatory in Hanford, Washington. I believe we—"

"Yes, of course, I remember you, Dr. Richards," he interrupted her enthusiastically. "Your presentation on gravitational wave sources throughout our galaxy was captivating. I'm thrilled you've reached out. How may I assist you today?"

"Well, we've encountered an event that registered on our detectors, both here at Hanford and also at our sister facility—"

He interjected once more, "Livingston?"

She chuckled softly, amused by his eagerness. "Yes, Livingston, Colonel," Miranda replied, her tone warm.

"Please, call me Marty, Dr. Richards," he insisted.

"Um, alright, Marty," Miranda responded. She paused, sensing his attempt to steer the conversation toward a more personal tone, as if they were long-time acquaintances or perhaps something more. With a gentle sigh and a faint smile, she said, "And you can call me Miranda."

"Excellent, Miranda. Now, please share the details of the events at your observatories," Marty encouraged, clearly at ease with the shift toward a friendlier interaction.

"We detected a slight deflection in our lasers, indicative of a gravitational wave event or a seismic disturbance . However, what struck us as extraordinary was the wavelength, suggesting the source was alarmingly close to our detectors," Miranda explained.

"How close are we talking?" Marty inquired with interest.

"It's a preliminary calculation, but the source might have been within a few thousand kilometers. Ordinarily, we'd attribute this to a seismic event, but the Livingston facility recorded the same tension in their lasers at the identical frequency and, crucially, at the same moment as ours," Miranda noted, her concern evident.

"This is indeed atypical, considering our norm is to detect gravitational waves originating millions of light years away, usually from events like colliding black holes," she continued, pausing to ensure Marty grasped the significance.

"I recall from your presentation the intricate challenge of detecting gravitational waves," Marty responded.

"Yes," Miranda affirmed, her smile returning as it was clear he had not only paid attention during her presentation but had likely familiarized himself further with LIGO's work thereafter.

"I'm reaching out to inquire if you're aware of any significant ordnance tests or perhaps a nuclear test of some sort. Such an event is the only plausible explanation we can conceive that might produce a signature like what we've detected," Miranda posited.

"Miranda, even if I were privy to information about such tests, I wouldn't be at liberty to disclose that to you or anyone else. However, I can consult with my contacts at the National Nuclear Security Administration, NNSA," Marty offered.

"And the NNSA's role?" Miranda probed.

"The NNSA is chiefly responsible for overseeing the United States' infrasound monitoring system. Their Office of Non-proliferation and Arms Control manages our national in-frasound network, a key component of the IMS under the CTBT," Marty explained, his tone reflecting vast familiarity with the subject.

"Infrasonic detection?" she queried.

"Exactly. Infrasonic sound waves are low-frequency sounds generated by large explosions. The U.S. operates a global net-work of infrasound sensors capable of detecting these waves, pinpointing their origin, and assessing their magnitude," he continued. "Coincidentally, part of my duties involves liaison work with that agency here at the Pentagon."

"It seems I've indeed reached out to the right person," Miranda remarked, her smile persistent. "This anomaly felt distinct from our routine detections, potentially meriting scrutiny by a governmental body. I..." she trailed off, momentarily caught up in the personal undertone of their dialogue. "We at LIGO are ready to assist in any capacity. Our hope is for a mundane explanation, yet I deemed it prudent to consult with military expertise."

"I'll look into this and update you as soon as possible," Marty promised.

"Thank you, Colonel... I mean, Marty," Miranda said, her cheeks flushing slightly. "I look forward to hearing from you regarding your findings," she said as she ended the call. Only at that moment realizing she didn't give him a chance to respond.

Sitting on the edge of her desk, slightly embarrassed yet content, she whispered, "It was good speaking with you again, Marty."

Chapter Eighteen

Sirens

Bucky surveyed the aftermath intently. Many of the surrounding trees appeared to have borne the brunt of the blast, their trunks bent and twisted, roots exposed barely clinging to the earth.

"What happened, Bing?" he inquired, his voice tinged with awe and confusion.

"I believe you have discovered one of the many facets of the Orb's power. That is, to harness its energies as a weapon," Bing responded.

"But all I did was think about the rock's destruction, and then I felt the Orb's energies through my arms and hands, creating that ball of light," he reflected, his gaze fixed on his hands as if they were foreign objects.

"It appears you must first synchronize your life force, your very consciousness, with the Orb. Once achieved, you can wield it as we've just witnessed," Bing theorized. "This capability might be the key to stopping the Collectors. However, mastery and control are imperative before we confront them."

"How am I supposed to manage such power without causing widespread destruction?" he voiced his frustration. "The intensity of the explosion, the mess with the trees—I'm pretty sure the entire town noticed that," he remarked, his eyes scanning the disturbed landscape.

"It's likely that the local authorities will be alerted and could pinpoint this location imminently," Bing surmised.

"Perhaps I can fix the trees, put them all back, upright again," he suggested, a hint of hope coloring his words.

"It's a possibility," Bing concurred.

Bucky approached the nearest pine tree, a victim of the unintended havoc. Originally towering over twenty feet, it now lay on it's side, its roots gasping for earth. Connecting with the Orb had become second nature to him. This time, he channeled the Orb's positive energy, its distinct nature now recognizable to him.

As the energy flowed through him, he directed it towards the fallen giant. Miraculously, the tree righted itself, its roots reconnecting in the soil. His triumph was short-lived, however, as the tree continued its ascent, uprooted completely, and soared overhead past him and Bing, its departure marked by a cascade of dirt and debris. Its final descent disrupted a cluster of untouched trees, causing a domino effect of destruction.

"Maybe that wasn't a good idea," he conceded, a blend of disappointment and realization in his tone.

"Indeed. Your training is far from over," Bing responded, matter-of-factly.

"Can you fix this, Bing?" he pleaded, desperation evident in his voice.

Bing nodded affirmatively, approaching a tree that leaned as if in limbo. With ease, he nudged it upright, though some roots remained exposed, bare testament to the ordeal.

"Yes!" Bucky exclaimed, his spirits momentarily lifted, arms thrust into the air in a gesture of victory.

Bing methodically tended to several affected trees, realigning them with an effortless grace. Their task was interrupted by the distant wail of sirens, rapidly approaching.

"Oh no. What do I tell my mom?" Bucky pondered aloud, anxiety mounting.

"Now is not the moment for explanations," Bing advised. "You should make your way home."

After a brief embrace with Bing, Bucky dashed towards his home, the sound of sirens intensifying in his wake. Bing discreetly retreated to his ship, which ascended silently into the sky, vanishing amidst the clouds.

Back at his home, Bucky peered through the front window, watching emergency vehicles speed by.

"Bucky, what's going on?" his mother asked, concern evident as she approached, resting a hand on his shoulder. Surprised, he whirled around, guilt etched across his face, meeting his mother's inquisitive gaze.

"Whoa, I've seen that look before. What were you up to?" she inquired, her voice laden with suspicion.

"Nothing," he responded too hastily. "I mean, I didn't do anything."

"My goodness, what was that loud bang? Maybe that's what all the fuss is about," she mused. "Did you see anything, Bucky?"

"No. No, I didn't see anything," he replied, his tone betraying his nervousness.

"Did you hear it? There was also a very bright flash," his mom mentioned. "It shook the house and even knocked over one of my favorite vases."

"Maybe it was a meteor or something," he suggested. "Dr. Ron, our physics teacher, said these kinds of things happen all the time." He continued to gaze at his mother, offering a hopeful half-smile, wishing it would satisfy her curiosity.

He lingered by the window for some time, watching as more emergency vehicles sped by. Eventually, he joined his mother in the kitchen as she began dinner preparations.

"Are you okay?" his mother asked, noting his restless fidgeting at the table.

A loud knock at the door startled both Bucky and his mother. Visitors were rare, making the interruption unexpected. His mother approached the door with Bucky trailing behind. Upon opening it, they were greeted by a police officer on their doorstep. He was middle-aged with a noticeable belly, suggesting a lack of regular exercise.

"Good evening, ma'am. I'm Officer Jones," the officer announced, his tone overly official, as though he was trying a bit too hard to make an impression.

"Sorry to disturb you, but we're investigating some noise complaints from this and surrounding communities. Apparently, there was a significant explosion, and we're gathering statements from residents. Did you or your son witness anything unusual or suspicious in this area?"

"Yes, Officer, I did," his mom responded. "It was terrifying; the entire house shook. I thought the windows might shatter, but thankfully, only a vase was broken," she explained, gesturing toward a pile of debris neatly swept into a corner.

The officer glanced at the broken vase, then scanned the room. A smirk crossed his face, seemingly judging the modesty of their living conditions. He emitted a disapproving "hmmph" before taking out his notebook. Bucky noticed the disdainful look and immediately took a disliking to the officer, resenting the perceived judgment of his home.

"Would you like to come in, Officer?" his mother offered. The officer declined with a shake of his head.

"No, ma'am. That won't be necessary," he replied.

Bucky shot the officer a scathing look, which elicited another smirk from the officer. He then turned his attention back to Bucky's mother.

"Alright, please tell me exactly what you observed and heard," the officer prompted.

"It seemed to originate from over there," she indicated, pointing toward the clearing where Bing and Bucky had been earlier. "There was also an intense flash of light, brighter than the sun," she elaborated. "My son thought it might have been a meteor, Officer."

"Is that so, son?" the officer questioned, directing his gaze toward Bucky.

"Um, I just suggested it might be because I'm not really sure," Bucky replied, striving to sound assertive.

"We initially suspected a meteor as well, but found no evidence of an impact. Instead, we discovered numerous trees uprooted in the vicinity," the officer explained, gesturing in the direction of the clearing.

"Bucky, weren't you just over there? Near your treehouse?" his mother inquired, turning to face him.

Caught between the inquisitive stares of his mother and the officer, Bucky felt trapped. He was about to formulate a response when the officer interjected, "Your name's Bucky, right? Adams is your last name?"

Both Bucky and his mother exchanged surprised glances before she shot him a look of suspicion, wondering if he had somehow entangled himself with the law.

"My son attends your high school," the officer revealed, his focus sharpened on Bucky.

"He shared an unbelievable story about your antics with him and his friends. To be honest, I didn't believe him. Yet, each friend's account matched precisely. In our line of work, inconsistencies usually expose falsehoods, but their story held up after I talked to them."

Bucky's face lost its color as his mother's gaze fixed on him. *This officer had actually spoken to the bullies? What had they said to him?* Bucky thought.

"What did you do, Bucky? You never mentioned anything happening at school," she questioned, her tone laden with implications of impending trouble. Bucky was caught in a dilemma; admitting the truth about the bullies meant confessing to the altercation. Opting for the safer route, he chose to deny the accusations, despite knowing they had provoked him.

"I don't know what you're talking about. I didn't do anything to anyone," he asserted with as much conviction as he could muster. The officer's stare bore into him, unyielding and skeptical. His mother, catching the accusatory look, positioned herself protectively between her son and the officer.

"If my son says he didn't do anything, then we'll have to leave it at that. I believe our conversation here is concluded," she stated, her hand poised on the door, signaling their intent to end the discussion. The officer surveyed them both for a tense moment before reluctantly stowing his notepad.

"Perhaps you're involved with that explosion, huh, boy?" he speculated with a hint of accusation, turning to make his way back to his car, which was stationed conspicuously in front of their home. "We'll see about that," he muttered, his voice tinged with frustration and warning.

Chapter Nineteen

The Bat Phone

The following Monday, Miranda was sitting in her office reviewing the collected data from latest detection when her desk phone rang. "Dr. Richards, there is a Captain Reily from Fairchild Air Force Base who insists on meeting with you as soon as possible. He says he has orders from the Pentagon," the security guard at the front gate informed Miranda over her phone.

"Um, sure. Please direct him to my office in the Operations Center," Miranda instructed before ending the call. She glanced at Marty's business card and mused, "It's probably not a dinner invitation from you, huh, Marty?" Settling into her chair, she awaited the captain's arrival.

A few minutes later, a succinct knock at her office door preceded its opening. An engineer from the Operations Center gestured for the Air Force Captain to enter. The man stepped in and closed the door behind him.

He appeared to be around forty, clad in the standard Air Force uniform of dark blue pants and jacket, complemented by a white shirt and dark blue tie. His hat, which he removed upon entering, was tucked neatly under his arm, and he carried a black briefcase.

"Dr. Richards, my name is Captain George Riley, stationed at Fairchild Air Force Base. I've been briefed on the recent events at the LIGO Observatories following your conversation with Colonel Martin Klena at the Pentagon," he introduced himself.

"Good to meet you, Captain Riley," Miranda greeted, extending her hand for a handshake. "It's rather unusual for them to send someone to discuss a scientific matter."

"Dr. Richards, what I'm about to share is classified information that you cannot disclose to anyone. Is that understood?" George spoke in a firm and official tone.

"Uh, yes, of course," Miranda assured him. "Would you like to sit, Captain?" She indicated a chair across from her desk.

"No, thank you, ma'am," he declined, devoid of emotion. "I am here to brief you, provide you with a secure satellite phone for direct communications with Colonel Klena, and then return to my base as soon as possible."

"Excuse me, Captain, I think I need to sit down," Miranda said, moving to sit in her chair.

"Dr. Richards, you reached out to Colonel Klena, reporting a gravitational wave detection at your observatory, which was corroborated by the Livingston facility. Correct?" he inquired, maintaining his emotionless demeanor.

"Yes, that's correct," Miranda confirmed.

"You also suggested that the source of this event might be extraordinarily close to the detectors, possibly within the United States or a few thousand kilometers away. Is that accurate?"

"Yes, that's what our analysis suggested."

"Dr. Richards, the United States, in collaboration with various agencies and the Air Force, operates numerous systems designed to detect nuclear tests that would breach the Comprehensive Nuclear Test Ban Treaty, signed in 1996. This treaty bans all nuclear explosions, regardless of the environment—underground, underwater, or atmospheric," Captain Riley explained.

Miranda nodded, her expression betraying her concern. "We suspected the signal might have originated from a significant ordnance or a nuclear test, prompting me to contact Marty—Colonel Klena—to ascertain any military involvement," she elaborated.

"There was no test or any other activity from the United States military or any other government-related agency that would generate these types of signals," Captain Reily stated in a matter-of-fact tone.

"Dr. Richards, there are three primary systems used to detect any nuclear-type detonation: Seismic Monitoring, Infrasonic Detection, and Radionuclide Monitoring. Although all three detected an event of explosive nature, it is the Radionuclide aspect that concerns us the most," the captain explained solemnly. "Despite the radiation detected being very low, the signature indicated a nuclear type of detonation."

"Nuclear explosions release radioactive materials into the atmosphere. Our Radionuclide monitoring systems are capable of detecting and analyzing these radioactive materials. Our detectors here in the United States identified traces of radioactive signals, which we triangulated to approximately two thousand kilometers from this location," the captain elaborated, pausing to let the information sink in.

"This matches the approximate distance of the event calculated by your systems, correct?" he inquired.

"Yes, but our systems aren't designed to detect signals of such proximity; therefore, we suspected an anomaly," Miranda responded.

"I understand, Dr. Richards. It seems likely that you detected the same event as our systems, which also captured seismic and infrasonic signals," the captain asserted. "We were previously unaware that a nuclear detonation event would generate a signal detectable by the LIGO Observatories."

The captain placed his briefcase on Miranda's desk, extracting a folder marked 'TOP SECRET.' From it, he produced a single sheet of paper, handing it to Miranda. "We request you share all data related to the detected event with the entities listed on this document. Secure connections for data transfer will be established," he advised.

Next, he retrieved a small mobile phone with an stubby antenna from his briefcase, positioning it in front of Miranda.

"This secure satellite phone connects directly to our defense communications network. Colonel Klena, overseeing the Air Force's response alongside various agencies, insists you have this device for uninterrupted communication with him," he explained.

"The Colonel plans to involve you and your team in assessing and resolving this issue. Do you have any questions?" he concluded.

Miranda, visibly taken aback and somewhat daunted, examined the phone, noting its absence of numerical keys, featuring only an on-off switch along with connect and disconnect buttons. She looked up at the captain, her expression fraught with questions, yet she remained silent.

"Thank you for your cooperation, Dr. Richards. You'll receive further instructions soon," the captain said, as he tidied his briefcase and donned his hat. He then executed a crisp turn, exited her office, and softly closed the door behind him.

Miranda remained at her desk, poring over the sheet he had given her, noting the lack of any official markings that might hint at the document's origin. She then turned her attention to the satellite phone, its purpose and operation a mystery to her.

The phone's sudden ringing, indicated by a blinking red light, startled her. Reflexively, she pressed the 'Connect' button and cautiously greeted, "Hello?"

Chapter Twenty

The Military Comes To Town

Bucky boarded the school bus on Monday, the first day back since the explosion, and made his way to where Marcus and Jen were sitting. As he navigated through the bus, he couldn't help but overhear the excited chatter of other students recounting their experiences of the explosion. Their animated voices filled the bus with a buzz of curiosity. Reaching his friends, Bucky noticed their accusatory glances. He sank into the seat beside them with a heavy sigh.

"I… I don't know what happened," he whispered, leaning in so only Marcus and Jen could hear.

"Shhh," Jen cautioned, glancing nervously around. "Not now, Bucky. Not here. We'll talk later at school."

Suddenly, a commotion erupted at the front of the bus. Several students stood, craning their necks and pointing out the windows. The bus driver barked sternly, "Sit down, now!" but pulled over to the side of the road, stirring up a cloud of dust. Through the settling haze, Bucky, Jen, and Marcus saw the cause of the excitement: a convoy of military vehicles, camouflaged in dark green and black, sped past. Led by local police cars with flashing lights but silent sirens, the procession included large trucks with trailers and Humvees equipped with what appeared to be heavy machine guns. Antennas on many of the vehicles waved wildly as they zoomed by, pelting the bus with dust and tiny rocks. The spectacle held the bus captive by the roadside until the last vehicle had disappeared into the distance. Once the convoy was gone, the driver directed everyone to sit down and steered the bus back onto the road. Jen and Marcus exchanged worried glances with Bucky, who could only respond with a helpless shrug.

The morning's classes dragged on, heavily overshadowed by the recent events and the morning's military display. When lunch finally arrived, Bucky rushed to meet Jen and Marcus at their usual spot by the trees outside the school.

"Guys, you won't believe what happened," he burst out before they could even greet him.

"Try us," Marcus replied, his voice steady but his eyes reflecting a hint of concern.

Bucky recounted every detail of his training with Bing, his voice filled with a mix of awe and urgency. He didn't leave out the encounter with the police officer at his house—the same one who might be one of the bullies' father. As he spoke, the gravity of his story hung between them, marking the start of a deeper conversation yet to come.

"Bucky, I'm so afraid for you," Jen said, trying to comfort him.

"And all of us," Marcus added. "Those military vehicles looked like they were very serious. Did you see the guns?"

"I just wonder what they're going to do?" Bucky said.

Just then, a voice came over the school speakers that could be heard everywhere.

"Attention, please! Attention, please!" It was the High School principal. "Can I have everyone's attention? We need all students to assemble in the gym. The local authorities and the military have requested we assemble in the gym. Please proceed immediately to the gym in a calm and orderly fashion."

Then, several military vehicles and police cars from the morning entered the school parking lot next to the gym, lining up in an orderly fashion before coming to a stop. Teachers quickly ushered the students back inside, while soldiers and a few local police officers disembarked from the Humvees and police cars.

Among the military personnel, Bucky noticed a woman who stood out, not dressed in the standard camouflage uniform like the others. His attention was also caught by a familiar local police officer—the same one who had been at their house—joining the group walking toward the school.

"Hurry, please," a teacher urged him as he stood transfixed by the surreal scene unfolding at his school.

He walked into the gym with Marcus and Jen. Once seated in the bleachers near the top, Bucky surveyed the entire school packed into the space. The gym was warm and buzzing with the noise of numerous conversations. Soon, the principal emerged from a side door, accompanied by the military personnel, local police officers, and the blonde-haired woman. Bucky noted that all the military personnel had sidearms.

The principal raised a wireless microphone and tapped it with a finger, sending a muffled thump through the gym's speakers. "Quiet, please. Everyone, please settle down and be quiet," he called out, his voice echoing over the din. "Please, settle down. We have a very serious matter to discuss." Gradually, the chatter subsided into near silence.

"As you know, we had a very unusual incident several days ago," the principal began. "We have representatives from the military and a scientist here to evaluate and try to determine what exactly happened. Colonel Klena from the United States

Air Force is here, and he wishes to speak with you." He handed the microphone to a man in military camouflage who notably did not wear a sidearm. He was tall and he looked young for a colonel, Bucky thought.

"Thank you, Principal Smith," Colonel Klena said, after taking the microphone. "Thank you all for gathering at such short notice. As you are aware, there was an event here that may have involved an explosion. We have just begun our analysis and at this point, we don't have much information to share."

Both Marcus and Jen looked over at Bucky. He gave them a very weak smile. He could feel his hands become sweaty and he took a deep breath trying to calm himself. He knew they were all there because of him.

"We were hoping to reach out to all of you and determine if you have any information that might help us in our investigation," the Colonel said over the gym speakers. "We need to know if you saw or experienced anything unusual over the last few days and weeks. Anything that was out of the ordinary."

Again, the students started speaking to each other, causing a bit of commotion. Then, he noticed the bullies he had the Run-in with sitting in the front row, talking to each other in what appeared to be excited voices. Soon, the bullies started pointing back at Bucky and talking between themselves. In an instant, they all stood up and said almost together as loud as they could, "It was him. It was that kid there. Bucky Adams."

Suddenly, all the students stopped talking and looked toward Bucky, who was now trying to slump down so as not to be noticed.

One of the local police officers came over to the bullies and followed where they were pointing. Bucky noticed that one of the bullies had his hand on the police officer, and it was the man who had come to their house. He realized that this must be the policeman's son. He got a shock of fear as the policeman started making his way up through the bleachers toward him, shoving the students out of his way. He had a very angry look on his face.

When the policeman got to Bucky, Marcus stood up in front of him trying to shield him. The policeman shoved Marcus aside roughly. He reached to the back of his utility belt and pulled out a pair of handcuffs.

"Turn around with your hands on your head, boy," he ordered.

Bucky had a surreal sensation as he was roughly turned around, and the handcuffs placed on his wrists. He was then led by the arm back down the bleacher stairs. All the kids he saw were gawking at him and whispering to each other behind their hands. He looked back at Marcus and Jen. They looked helpless with Jen hugging Marcus with tears in her eyes. As Bucky was roughly guided past the bullies, they were all smiling wickedly and pointing at him.

“What are you going to do now, space boy? You should never have messed with us, you freak,” one of them said.

With the officer leading him back to where the Colonel and the Principal were standing, Bucky passed Doctor Ronald standing in the front row. Bucky looked at him, but quickly turned away seeing the shock and disappointment on his face.

The policeman holding his handcuffed arm, continued towards the principal and Colonel Klena. When he reached them, the blonde woman standing next to the Colonel, who had arrived with the military said, “Is that really necessary, Officer?” sounding very concerned.

“I spoke with this boy after the explosion, ma’am,” the police officer said. “I believe he knows something about what happened and may have actually been directly involved. My son...” the officer pointed at the bullies still standing in the front row of the bleachers, “said this boy attacked them... in a very unnatural way.”

“Unnatural way? What does that mean?” the Colonel asked, cutting off the blonde woman who looked like she was going to ask the same question.

"Let's just say I think you should restrain and interrogate him," the policeman said. "If you don't, I'll take him down to the station and do it myself."

"That won't be necessary," The Colonel said as he gestured to two of the soldiers behind him to move forward toward him. "Sergeant, can you take custody of, of... what is your name, son?" the Colonel asked.

Bucky was still in shock and his knees felt weak, as he looked at the Colonel and then the pretty blonde woman standing next to him. "Bucky," he answered shakily.

"Marty, can you have this officer remove those handcuffs immediately?" the blonde woman said in a serious tone.

"Of course," Marty responded. "Officer, can you please turn over Bucky to my men and, for God's sake, remove those handcuffs."

The officer reluctantly removed his handcuffs and shoved him toward the soldiers. "I know he had something to do with this. I just know it."

The blonde woman walked over to him, placing her hand on his shoulder as she bent over and said, "Don't worry, Bucky. It's going to be alright. My name is Dr. Miranda Richards, and I'm going to make sure you're ok."

He looked up at Miranda as he rubbed his wrists. He felt that she really did care about him, even as the soldiers led him out the side door of the gym. He could hear the Colonel continue speaking to the students in the gym as the soldiers led him out the gym door. But as they stepped outside, he could no longer make out what the Colonel was saying.

He looked up at the two soldiers walking with him and they had expressionless faces. He noticed they were taking him to one of the military Humvees lined up outside the gym. They opened the back door and helped him get in the back seat. As he settled in, they closed the door with a resounding thud and took their positions outside.

He began to feel a little panicked. It was hot inside the Humvee. The seats were not comfortable, and it smelled a little like metal and diesel fuel. He looked around the interior and noticed it was all drab green—a lighter green color than the outside of the Humvee. There were green-colored wires along the top of both sides of the vehicle and a thin black metal steering wheel in front. There were several green metal boxes toward the back.

He began to breathe in short breaths and noticed his hands and feet started to tingle like pins and needles. He felt he should escape. What were they going to do with him? What would his mother say? Then he thought about the Orb. *Should I try to use it now?*

They would really know he had something to do with the explosion if he used the Orb in any way. He concentrated on connecting with the Orb. The overwhelming sense of power came to him immediately. As he connected with the Orb, the Humvee shook like it had just run over a big rock, but it was not moving. The soldiers standing alongside the vehicle were startled and took several steps back from the Humvee, looking in at him with surprised expressions.

He immediately broke the connection with the Orb, not wanting to draw any more attention and trouble to himself. The soldiers both had their hands on their sidearms. They did not remove the weapons from the holsters, but looked ready if needed.

Just then, he could see Colonel Klena and Miranda come out the side door of the gym and walk over toward the Humvee. The Colonel noticed the soldiers had their hands on their sidearms and said, "Sergeant, is there a problem?"

The soldier standing on the left beside the Humvee said as he saluted the Colonel, "Sir, no issue, sir. We're just securing the boy."

The soldier that answered Colonel Klena looked at the other soldier in a way that said neither of them wanted to explain what had just happened. The Colonel opened the front door of the Humvee and looked back at Bucky.

"We need to speak with you about what happened here. The local authorities and several of the students at your school believe you had something to do with the incident. We're going to take you back to our base camp and ask you a few questions, ok? We'll notify your parents from there," he said, trying to sound reassuring but still with an assertive tone. He didn't wait for a reply from Bucky before backing out of the front seat to be replaced by one of the soldiers standing guard.

The other soldier got into the driver's seat and started the Humvee, which made a loud rumbling engine sound. The Colonel walked to the driver's side and said, "Follow us back to base camp. We didn't get any other leads from the rest of the students."

He then returned to the other Humvee in front of Bucky's vehicle. He noticed Miranda getting into the back of the same vehicle. She paused, looking back at him. She had a very concerned look on her face before she entered and shut the door.

Chapter Twenty-One

Bucky And Miranda

As the Humvee rolled through the center of town, Bucky peered out the window at the bystanders lining the sidewalks, their gazes fixed on the convoy with intense curiosity. They continued through town, and soon he recognized they were approaching a small park surrounded by trees in his neighborhood near the familiar clearing where he first encountered Bing. The park was now transformed into a makeshift military camp, with about a dozen large trailers linked by green canvas overhangs and circled by Humvees, each manned by a soldier in the top gun turret.

His stomach hurt to the point of wanting to vomit as he pondered what awaited him. Would they interrogate him about his involvement? How could he possibly explain the last few days and weeks, or convey the grave danger threatening Earth from a distant force? And how could he reveal the existence of the powerful Orb, created from the black hole at the galaxy's center?

The convoy halted just outside one of the larger green military trailers adorned with numerous antennas and communication dishes. Bucky watched as the Colonel and Miranda entered the trailer through a rear door.

Inside the now stationary Humvee, the engine turned off, and the stifling heat began to build with the windows rolled up. As he sat with the two soldiers, the dryness in his mouth worsened from both the heat and his growing nervousness. Experimentally, he tugged at the door handle only to find it locked, his heart racing as he realized he was trapped. His breathing became shallow, and a wave of panic set in, his hands and feet tingling with anxiety.

Just then, movement at the edge of the clearing caught his eye. About thirty meters away, at the tree line, he spotted Marcus and Jen dismounting bicycles. A wave of hope washed over him as they paused in the shadows, offering him a discreet wave. Careful not to draw the soldiers' attention, Bucky refrained from waving back, but his spirits lifted, comforted by the knowledge that he wasn't completely alone.

Colonel Klena emerged from the trailer's back door and approached Bucky's Humvee. He opened the door and said, "Bucky, please come with me."

Relieved to escape the stifling heat of the Humvee, Bucky followed Colonel Klena with a sense of apprehension . He noticed two soldiers positioning themselves behind him as they walked toward the trailer. Casting a quick glance towards the woods, Bucky saw Jen and Marcus who offered him a subtle wave of encouragement again.

The colonel opened the trailer door and gestured for Bucky to enter. Inside, the trailer was sparsely furnished, illuminated by stark fluorescent lighting and devoid of windows. It measured about twenty feet in length and ten feet in width. A small metal desk was positioned midway towards the back, flanked by simple, all-metal chairs on each side and several more against the walls toward the entrance.

The interior was noticeably cooler, thanks to an air conditioning vent in the ceiling that expelled a steady stream of cold air. Colonel Klena motioned for Bucky to sit behind the desk, taking a seat opposite him. The soldiers entered next, seating themselves in chairs along the sides. The door shut with a heavy clank, the sound of a robust lock sealing them inside.

"First, I want to apologize for these accommodations, Bucky," Colonel Klena began, his tone formal yet apologetic. "This is standard procedure. We are here only to question witnesses in private."

Bucky nodded faintly, looking around at the windowless interior and again feeling a little panicked at the confinement.

"My name is Martin, and I want you to relax as best you can and tell us what you know about the explosion that took place two days ago," Colonel Klena said in as comforting a voice as he could muster.

Bucky took a dry swallow and thought about how he should respond. He had to stall for time to think of a way to answer the question.

"“Sir... can I have some water, please?" He asked.

"Sure, Bucky," the colonel said as he gestured to one of the soldiers sitting close by. "I'm sorry, Bucky. We should have had water for you here."

As the soldier walked out the door of the trailer, Colonel Klena smiled weakly at him, and he returned his own, uncomfortable smile. One minute later, the soldier reentered the trailer and locked the door behind him. He carried a small plastic bottle of water and handed it to the colonel, who twisted the top off and gave it to Bucky.

He took the water and raised it to his mouth slowly, taking several small gulps. The water was cold and felt good. He put the water bottle down on the table and gave the colonel a sheepish smile.

"I'm sorry, Sir. I really don't know anything about what happened," he said, trying to sound as convincing as possible.

Colonel Klena appeared convinced Bucky was not ready to explain anything. He frowned at Bucky and looked looked like he was deciding his approach.

"Where were you at the time of the event?" the colonel finally asked.

"Sir, I really don't know anything about what happened," he repeated. He realized it would have been impossible for him not to have heard or seen something if he was anywhere within ten miles of the town, like everyone else. He just shrugged his shoulders and said, "I'm sorry, Sir. I can't help you. Can I please go home now?"

Colonel Klena leaned back in his chair, his expression marked by visible frustration. It was clear to Bucky that the colonel did not believe his account.

"I see," Colonel Klena finally said. He rose from his seat, signaling to the two soldiers to follow him. Using a key, he unlocked the door, and they exited, securing the door behind them with a definitive click.

Left alone, Bucky sat in silence. Several minutes trickled by until the sound of the lock clicking heralded the arrival of Dr. Miranda Richards. She stepped through the doorway, closing the door which locked automatically behind her. Dr. Richards approached, setting her backpack down beside the table.

"Well, isn't this a positively dreadful room," she commented, surveying the sparse surroundings as she moved towards him. Rather than taking the chair across the table, she walked around to Bucky's side and knelt next to him. Placing a comforting hand on his shoulder, she spoke in a soothing tone, "Bucky, I'm so sorry you have to go through this. This is a military operation, and they tend to handle things in a very particular way..."

"Prisoners?" he said, finishing her statement.

"No, Bucky, you're not a prisoner," she said in a reassuring tone. "I'm sure they only want to get help from anyone who witnessed or knew something about what happened. The local police and those boys seem to think you had something to do with it. Did you?"

He was a little surprised at her direct approach. He thought maybe she would be nicer than the military people. He remembered one way to test the good in people. Perhaps the Orb could help him. He closed his eyes and took a deep breath. He immediately connected with the Orb. The electric shock shuttered his body for just a moment.

He searched for Miranda's soul song. The vibrations given off by her life energy. He immediately sensed her. It started as a few beautiful musical-like notes in his head. Then, the notes continued in sequence to form a very beautiful song. What he found interesting was the fact he could search for her energy, like looking for something visually, and he just knew it was her instinctively. That thought answered a question he had about Bing finding him across an entire galaxy.

He knew she could be trusted. He opened his eyes and smiled at her. "I did have something to do with it," he revealed.

"I only want to help, Bucky," Miranda assured.

"I know," he said with an innocent smile.

"What kind of scientist are you?" he asked trying to formulate an organized response.

"I'm an Astrophysicist."

Bucky felt a little confused, so she added, "an Astrophysicist specializes in the study of celestial objects and phenomena in the universe. We investigate the formation and evolution of stars and galaxies, the nature of dark matter and dark energy, cosmic radiation, and the structure of the universe itself."

"Nice," he responded. "I think you're the right person to talk to. Maybe you can help us."

"Us?" Miranda asked.

"My friends and Bing."

"Tell me about them," she continued.

"There is life out there in our galaxy—other civilizations with beings somewhat like us," Bucky said slowly, ensuring his tone was serious. He was aware of the myriad alien conspiracy theories, often splashed across tabloid headlines at the grocery store checkout. It was crucial to him that he didn't come across as just another fanciful kid.

"Go on," Miranda encouraged, her voice patient.

"Well, I have two very good friends from high school who have been supporting me a lot. And Bing—he's a robot from another planet," Bucky stated matter-of-factly.

Miranda's eyebrows lifted slightly as she replied with a cautious, "Okay."

"I think the best place to start is when I first met Bing, a few days ago." He paused, organizing his thoughts. He was hesitant to describe Bing as his long-lost brother from another time and place—such a claim might be too much for even an astrophysicist to digest at first. Nevertheless, he continued, "Bing landed near my tree fort in the woods close to where I live."

"Landed?" Miranda interjected, her interest piqued.

"Yes. In his spaceship," Bucky confirmed.

"He had a spaceship?" Miranda asked, her skepticism evident.

"Yes. He said he traveled from the center of the galaxy through a wormhole."

Bucky paused upon noticing the change in Miranda's expression. She seemed to be contemplating his words deeply. She then stood up and sat on the edge of the table next to him. As he waited for her response, Miranda took a deep breath and said,

"It just so happens that around the time you said you met Bing, we observed a gravitational wave event at LIGO that was unlike anything we've previously detected. In fact, one of our physicists described it as a potential wormhole. Do you know what a wormhole is, Bucky?"

"I think so," he replied. "It connects two locations in space like they were right next to each other."

"Yes, that's a good description," she said. "We've never actually observed or detected one before. We theorize that it would take a tremendous amount of negative energy to keep it from collapsing."

"Like the negative energy from a black hole?" he questioned.

Miranda looked at him surprised. "Well, Bucky, negative energy in black holes is just a concept related to the mathematics of general relativity. It's just a theory since we have no way to test it."

"Negative energy does exist. And when combined with positive energy, it can even blow up rocks... apparently," he said confidently.

Miranda's eyebrows lifted slightly in intrigue.

"Well," he continued, "I'm not exactly sure how I caused the rock to explode. I have an energy inside me that apparently comes from a black hole." He paused, watching for Miranda's reaction.

Just as Miranda was about to respond, the door flew open. Colonel Klena stormed into the trailer, his urgency evident, causing both Bucky and Miranda to turn toward him in surprise.

"We have orders to return to base immediately," Colonel Klena announced. "I also have direct orders to take the boy into custody."

Two soldiers entered behind him, each carrying large black machine guns.

"What? Are you sure?" Miranda exclaimed, standing up and stepping in front of Bucky as a shield from the soldiers.

"I'm sure, Dr. Richards," the colonel affirmed, using a formal tone.

Miranda, taken aback by his formality, pressed for more information, "What is it? What's happening?"

The colonel seemed torn between professional discretion and the urgency of the situation. "Miranda," he began in a gentler tone, "NORAD has tracked an unidentified object entering Earth's atmosphere at high speed. It appears to be maneuvering independently and has landed in the center of Los Angeles. Local authorities have confirmed the sighting."

"A UFO?" Miranda asked, her voice a mix of skepticism and alarm.

"I don't have any more information at this time," Colonel Klena explained. "The Air Force, along with other units, is still assessing the situation. My men will secure Bucky here until we are ready to depart."

"Can I at least stay with him?" Miranda asked, her concern evident.

The colonel paused, weighing her request. Finally, he nodded. "Yes, that would be okay," he conceded, signaling to the soldiers who acknowledged with a nod before exiting the trailer. They took positions outside the door, which was then closed and locked from the outside. Miranda turned to Bucky, offering a reassuring smile amidst the uncertainty.

"It's going to be alright, Bucky," Miranda reassured him gently.

"Bing warned me they would come," Bucky replied somberly. "He called them Collectors. We're all in great danger."

"We have the military to protect us," Miranda countered, trying to inject a note of confidence into her voice.

"It won't make any difference," Bucky said, shaking his head slowly. "Dr. Richards, I can't go with them. I need to find Bing and my friends," he insisted, his voice tinged with urgency.

Just then, a commotion erupted outside the trailer. The air filled with shouts, quickly followed by a deafening crack of gunfire. Instinctively, Miranda moved toward Bucky, draping her arm around him as they both stepped back from the door to seek cover. The shouting grew louder, and the gunfire intensified, sounding like a barrage from multiple machine guns.

Suddenly, the lights in the trailer flickered out, and the cool air from the vents ceased. Darkness enveloped them, and the air grew warm and stale almost instantly. Miranda pulled Bucky closer and whispered, "My god, what is happening?"

The trailer began to tremble violently, as if being hoisted upward like an elevator. The vibrations intensified, causing metal chairs to clatter and clang against the floor. Miranda couldn't suppress a small scream. Clinging to each other, they knelt on the floor, struggling to maintain balance as the trailer unmistakably lifted off the ground.

The gunfire and shouts outside faded, receding into the distance. The trailer shook once more, this time with a sideways force that seemed to accelerate them further.

“What is happening?” Miranda asked, her voice filled with desperation, still clinging to him.

“I think it’s going to be ok,” Bucky replied calmly.

After several minutes of violent vibrations and the sound of the wind outside against the trailer, they could feel a sensation of descending, again, like an elevator. They felt the trailer contact something hard and come to a stop. Then, there was only silence.

“Are you ok?” Miranda whispered in the dark.

“Yes. I’m ok,” he replied.

They heard something contact what they knew was the door of the trailer at the other end. Suddenly, with a very loud bang, followed by the bending and tearing of metal, the door of the trailer was ripped off, and bright sunlight shone through the opening. A large figure leaned into the opening where the door was. Miranda gasped and moved in front of Bucky, trying to shield him.

“My brother, are you hurt?” came a deep and concerned voice.

Bucky stood up and moved in front of Miranda despite her protest to keep him behind her. "Miranda, meet Bing," he said, looking at Miranda and gesturing to Bing.

Chapter Twenty-Two

Bing And Miranda

Bucky navigated around the fallen chairs and the table, stepping out into the bright sunlight. Bing enveloped him in a brief, firm embrace with his large metallic arms before stepping back. With a grave expression, he said, "My brother, the Collectors have arrived."

"I know," he responded.

Marcus and Jen, who had been anxiously waiting behind Bing, rushed to Bucky and embraced him tightly.

"I was so worried after they took you from the gym," Jen said, her voice trembling with emotion.

"When the soldiers escorted you to their camp, we were clueless about how to help," added Marcus, his tone laden with concern. "We found some bikes and followed you. After they led you into that trailer, we headed to the clearing where we first met Bing, and thankfully, he was there. We explained everything, and then we flew here in the spacecraft."

"Thanks, guys," Bucky replied with a smile. "I saw you at the edge of the trees. It really helped."

"Bing detected the Collectors, and we knew we had to come get you," Marcus said, his voice laced with excitement. "When we flew over your trailer, they actually started shooting at us. It was surreal, seeing everything from the spaceship with the external view enabled."

Turning to Miranda, who was still inside the trailer, appearing both shocked and surprised, Bucky reassured her, "Miranda, it's okay. These are my friends." He stepped back inside, picked up her backpack, and handed it to her. Taking her hand, he gently guided her out of the trailer.

Marcus and Jen promptly introduced themselves. Bing approached with his large robotic hand extended and said, "I am Bing."

Miranda managed a small smile and cautiously grasped his mechanical hand, her eyes wide as she inspected him. "You are amazing. Are... are you a machine?" she inquired, examining his human-like facial features.

"I am a machine, but this form contains my life energy," Bing responded analytically.

Miranda released his hand, her gaze shifting between Bucky and Bing, her curiosity piqued. "You existed in another form... before?" she asked.

"Yes," Bing answered. "Our people resemble humans, with very similar biological structures. This projection," he gestured to his head, "is programmed from what I remember of my own likeness."

Bucky had grown accustomed to seeing Bing almost as a person, so it was slightly jarring to be reminded that he was still a machine, his face merely an approximation of his former self.

"Fascinating," Miranda murmured, stepping closer to examine him. Her voice softened with sympathy as she added, "I can't imagine how difficult this must be for you." Her gaze shifted between Bing's spacecraft and his robotic form, her expression turning serious. "How is it that you are here now?"

"My function was to act as a scout for the one who seeks to collect and control all sentient life energies in this galaxy," Bing explained. "The Orb, was integrated within this machine and used to detect and locate that energy. Each sentient being has a unique energy, a frequency that the Orb can detect. Scouts like me travel to the source of these energies to evaluate them for collection."

"Like Earth?" Miranda asked.

"Yes, like Earth," Bing confirmed.

"That's terrifying," Miranda commented. "I suppose physicists and scientists always hoped our first encounter with alien life would be benevolent."

"How do we know you can be trusted? You said you guided the Collectors here?" Miranda pressed, looking over at Bucky and his friends, then back to Bing.

"I trust him, Dr. Richards," Bucky interjected.

Miranda turned to him and said firmly, "He's a machine, Bucky. An alien technology. A programmed machine."

"Dr. Richards, there are things I have learned about our existence, our place in this galaxy, that I still struggle to believe," Bucky responded. "The Orb that Bing mentioned is now a part of me. With it, I can... sort of hear people's life energy as a song. Each song is distinct for good and bad. I can't completely explain it, but I know. It's how I knew I could trust you. It's how I know I can trust Bing."

Miranda's face was inscrutable as she stared at him, clearly wrestling with the enormity of the situation.

"It has other powers," Bucky continued, watching her reaction closely. "The Orb possesses both negative and positive energies that can be directed at objects."

After several moments, Miranda finally spoke, "Let me see if I understand. This thing you called an Orb, can detect life energy across the galaxy, and you can use it like a weapon by combining negative and positive energy?"

"Yes," Bucky responded. "And... apparently, I used it on those bullies at school, and on the rock that exploded. I guess that's what you detected."

"And you traveled here through a worm hole? Using some form of negative energy?" Miranda asked turning towards Bing.

"Yes." Bing replied.

Miranda paused, looked down and walked a few steps away from them. "The possibilities," she said to herself. "This is amazing." She turned and walked back to the group and said "As a physicist, we study the energy of the very large and the very small in our universe. We study the effects of positive energy and make hypotheses and calculations regarding the existence of negative energy. But so far, negative energy only exists as a theoretical model in physics." she paused before turning to Bing again.

"But here we have proof of alien life in our galaxy," she said gesturing to Bing. "So, I suppose anything and everything is possible. What I'm struggling with," she paused looking back at Bing. "What seems to be most important right now is we have aliens, I assume that look like you..." she said pointing again to Bing, here right now to steal our souls? Really?" Miranda asked in a slightly desperate tone.

"Why?"

Bing paused before responding, his facial features composed yet hinting at a depth of unresolved complexity. "I cannot fully explain the motives of the entity that collects life energy," he began slowly, his voice tinged with a mix of frustration and resignation, "It is vast and its intentions are not disclosed to those like me"

He looked directly at Miranda, then at Bucky, his gaze steadying. "What I do understand now is the value of an existence with free will, the bonds we have to each other that transcend time and space. My purpose is now my choice. Saving my brother, protecting him and his world. That is what is important now."

His voice carried a newfound determination, a robotic yet profoundly human resolve that resonated with Miranda and Bucky alike.

Bucky turned to Miranda and stated with a sense of urgency, "You're a scientist, an astrophysicist, Can you help us? Help us figure out a way to stop the Collectors?"

Miranda took some time apparently trying to take in, what was a completely surreal situation. With a deep sigh, she began,

"And save the earth?" Miranda asked, again in a rising tone. She put her hands on either side of her head. "You've got to be kidding me."

"The Collectors are here now," Bing said. "We are all that stand between the destruction of sentient life on this planet and saving all humans from a terrible fate, such as mine, or worse."

Before Miranda could say anything else, the sound of approaching helicopters thumping the air caught their attention.

"We must go now," Bing said, gesturing towards his spaceship. A door appeared in the side, and without hesitating, they all ran towards the spacecraft. All except Miranda. She stood, looking back toward the approaching helicopters and then over at the spaceship.

Bucky stopped just short of the spaceship. His eyes widened as he spotted three imposing helicopters approaching. From their distinctive appearance, he guessed they were Black Hawks. But these were different, more menacing, with large machine guns ominously mounted in their open doors.

The helicopters thumped over the trees and hovered about thirty feet above the clearing. The noise, wind, and dust were overwhelming. They all descended, and as they touched down,

Colonel Klena leaped from the one closest to Miranda, about 100 meters away. He was followed by a formidable squad of six heavily armed soldiers. Each was outfitted in black combat fatigues and black helmets, their faces obscured by dark goggles and face coverings. They were armed with fearsome looking machine guns.

Soon after, additional helicopters landed, disgorging more soldiers who quickly fell in line with Colonel Klena's forces. Clad in his combat gear, the colonel raised a clenched fist, a signal for his troops to hold their positions.

With an authoritative gesture, he beckoned Miranda to approach him. When she did not immediately move towards him, he gestured again, with more urgency to Miranda.

The dust and wind from the still-rotating helicopter blades whipped Miranda's hair. She again looked between the colonel and the spaceship where Bucky and his friends stood just outside the entrance, gesturing to her to come with them.

Miranda lingered for just a moment longer, her gaze locked on the colonel and his troops. Then, with resolve, she turned and sprinted towards the spacecraft. As she reached the entry, Bucky and his friends extended their hands to help her aboard.

"So glad you're with us, Miranda," Bucky said, his smile reassuring as he guided her away from the opening.

Just then, the satellite phone in her backpack began to ring. Without hesitation, she pulled it out and quickly switched it off.

“I really had no choice,” Miranda confessed, her eyes scanning the faces around her. “I don’t think I’ll ever sleep again without nightmares of soul-sucking aliens. Here, with you all, I believe I can make a real difference.”

As she finished speaking, the spaceship’s door sealed shut. Moments later, the craft ascended smoothly, piercing through the clouds and vanishing into the sky.

Chapter Twenty-Three

The Collectors

Miranda peered around at the interior of the spacecraft with a look of obvious wonder. Bing had fashioned a chair for her to sit in, similar to the others and behind Jen and Bucky. Marcus was sitting next to Bing at the front. Marcus was actually controlling the spacecraft now, manipulating the controls and interacting with the 3-D hologram. The interior was lit only by the soft light from the interior walls. Jen turned around to face Miranda.

"We're so happy you're with us, Dr. Richards," she said. Marcus repeated similar sentiments.

"I'm a little overwhelmed right now," Miranda confessed. "This technology is incredibly advanced, and imagining what a violent advanced civilization could do is daunting." She glanced around the spaceship's interior and at the three-dimensional image floating above the control panel. Suddenly, the walls seemed to vanish, replaced by a projection of the outside view. Miranda gasped and clutched the edges of her chair.

"This is amazing," she murmured, awe coloring her voice. After a moment to collect herself, she turned her attention back to the urgent matters at hand. "Bing, where are the Collectors now? Do you have any idea what they are doing?"

"Dr. Richards, once the Collectors arrive on a planet, I no longer track their movements directly," Bing explained. "What I can tell you is there are two of them and there is a pattern to the collection process. They travel in a spacecraft similar to this one but equipped with weaponry and capabilities our vessel lacks, including advanced energy collection and storage facilities."

"Collection and storage?" Miranda echoed, her tone sharpening with concern. "Is that what they use to harvest sentient life energy?"

"Yes," Bing confirmed.

Miranda paused, processing the information. "Is there any way we can observe them or gather more information on their activities?" she asked.

"Maybe it's on the news," Marcus said without turning around from the control panel.

"Hey, Bing, can you intercept broadcast signals from..." Bucky said, trying to think of all the ways television signals are broadcast.

"How about satellites or microwave signals?" Marcus suggested.

"Yes," Bing said. "Receiving and processing signals from all the transmissions from your primitive orbiting machines allowed me to learn your language. I can scan for signals that will allow us to observe."

Bing placed his hand on his side of the control panel, which was devoid of any conventional dials or outputs, and initiated another three-dimensional display. This display, flat and several feet wide, flickered with static initially. It then started cycling through images rapidly, resembling a channel changer operating at high speed. Various scenes flashed across the screen until it finally settled on a live news broadcast. The news ticker at the bottom of the screen announced, "Craft of unknown origin has landed in central Los Angeles. Authorities request calm."

"That's it!" Bucky exclaimed, pointing at the screen.

Bing adjusted his hand over the console to stabilize the channel. The broadcast shifted from the reporter to focus on the spacecraft. This craft, while resembling Bing's, was noticeably larger and equipped with several protrusions. It also featured a round, turret-like structure on top, resembling a gun turret with twin barrels each about ten feet long. Initially filled with static, the audio from the news channel soon cleared up, revealing the strained voice of the announcer.

"I'm here at Pershing Square, downtown Los Angeles, where an extraordinary event has unfolded. An object, which appears to be an alien spacecraft, has made a landing in the park's open grassy area," the announcer reported, his voice laden with tension. The camera zoomed in once more on the spacecraft, providing a closer view of its intricate details.

"The authorities have not yet been able to set up any kind of barrier to prevent people from approaching." As he spoke, the camera also captured several hundred people gathering close to the spacecraft, with many more running in the same direction. They were creating a packed concert-like crowd in the park.

They continued to observe the news feed as the image showed the authorities attempting to assert control of the growing mass of people. The police and several firetrucks were slowly working their way through the gathering crowds, with lights flashing and sirens blaring.

The image focused again on the news reporter as he continued to talk about the arriving authorities and the crowd size, which he mentioned was in the thousands now.

Just then, something seemed to be happening behind the reporter. He stopped talking and turned to face the spaceship. He directed the camera toward it, and the picture zoomed in.

"It appears something is happening now. I think there seems to be an opening in the side of the spaceship," the reporter said in an excited, higher-pitched voice. Then, the sound from the projected image included many screams and people shouting and pointing.

"Yes, there definitely is what appears to be a door opening now. We can only hope the authorities can get this crowd back... to... keep everyone... Oh, my god!" he said suddenly, as the image shook and many of the gathered crowd started screaming and running and pushing past the news reporter. He and the cameraman were bumped and knocked around, making the projected image distorted.

Bucky and his friends gasped at what they saw on the projected news cast.

"Incredible!" Miranda exclaimed, her eyes wide as she and the others watched the broadcast intently. A figure emerged from the spacecraft, stepping out through an opening in the side. It resembled Bing but differed in the head, which was a long cylinder. Soon, a second figure appeared, identical to the first, both clad in dark, advanced battle-like armor. They stood tall and imposing, positioned side by side ten feet from the ship, facing the camera directly. The crowd reacted with screams, recoiling from the sight.

The alien on the right extended its metallic arm, pointing to the turret atop the spacecraft. The two long black tubes at the top of the turret began to rise, eventually pointing straight upward and forming a V shape, still connected to the turret at the base.

With another sweeping motion of its large robotic arm, the first alien caused the turret to detach and float gently down to land on the ground in front of them. Simultaneously, another turret appeared on top of the spacecraft, its two tubes extending outward.

On the ground, the circular structure at the base of the tubes, began to spin in front of the two aliens. It accelerated rapidly, the tubes on top blurring into a whirl of motion, emitting a loud buzzing sound that resembled an impossibly large bee.

The news reporter and his crew started backing away, still recording the scene. The picture became unstable as the news crew was close to running.

The footage from the news broadcast became chaotic for a few moments, marred by an unstable video feed. Suddenly, there was a brilliant flash of white light followed by a deafening sound akin to thunder, and the camera operator halted and redirected the camera towards the spaceship.

From about fifty meters away, the camera captured a disturbing scene—20 to 30 people were sprawled on the ground around the spacecraft. These were individuals who hadn't fled when the aliens appeared. Their bodies were strewn across the ground in unnatural positions, as if they had collapsed instantly and without control.

"Oh, my god! Are they dead?" Jen exclaimed, her voice filled with shock.

"Their biological systems are still functioning," Bing explained. "However, they are not the same. Their bodies are now devoid of their life energy."

"Isn't that the same as being dead?" Bucky questioned, trying to understand the grim reality.

As the camera continued to roll, the broadcast showed one or two of the fallen beginning to move. They awkwardly pushed themselves up with their arms, but something was clearly wrong. Their heads drooped unnaturally as they struggled to stand. Soon, all the bodies began to stir, each mimicking the same unsettling attempt to rise, their heads all sagging in a similar eerie manner. A voice, presumably the cameraman's, could be heard over the newscast, adding to the tense atmosphere.

"Someone needs to help them. Wait, what the ..."

The bodies that were all on the ground were now all standing and still. Altogether, their heads raised slowly as if they were all hearing the same instruction. Each had their mouth wide open with an unnatural expression. They looked like they could be screaming, but no sound came from them.

They all slowly turned away from the spaceship, each facing a different direction. Then, in perfect synchronization, they began to move together, stepping away from the spacecraft like choreographed puppets. Suddenly, they broke into a run, their movements appearing oddly disjointed as their arms swung loosely by their sides while they moved with almost unnatural speed.

As the camera remained trained on the spaceship, one of the affected individuals, a man in his late thirties clad in a dark business suit and tie, staggered towards the camera. His gait was so abnormal it was baffling how he remained upright—his head drooped, mouth hung open, and his arms flailed oddly at his sides.

As he neared the camera, his face showed no hint of emotion; his expression was vacant, his eyes lifeless. Abruptly, he reached the cameraman. The microphone picked up the cameraman's scream as the man raised his arms and made contact, followed by a sharp, double cracking sound, reminiscent of electrical discharges. Suddenly, the camera tumbled to the ground, capturing only the grass and dirt before the feed cut out.

The silence in Bing's spaceship was intense as the projected image faded to black, but the audio continued to relay screams and more crackling sounds until the transmission abruptly ceased.

Bing lowered his head, then slowly shook it. “The collection has begun,” he murmured somberly.

Miranda leapt from her seat, moving quickly to stand beside Bing. “What was that initial burst of light? What does it do?” she demanded, urgency in her voice. “Bing, what was that?”

“The Collectors have a technology that extracts and stores life energy. We just witnessed the beginning of the extraction process,” Bing explained, raising his head.

“But why did they... how did they re-animate?” Miranda pressed. “And those two popping sounds after the touch—what were those?” she continued, her tone shifting to that of a scientist piecing together a puzzle.

“Bing. We must go there,” Miranda stated emphatically. “I need to examine that collection device up close to understand how they extract the energy. It’s the only way we might devise a strategy to stop them.”

Chapter Twenty-Four

The Collection

As their spacecraft descended toward downtown Los Angeles, Bucky, and his friends gazed in awe at the sprawling cityscape before them, observing the 360-degree scene projected on the interior walls of the spacecraft.

From their vantage point, the skyline of Los Angeles was a breathtaking sight to behold. The city's architecture boasted an array of towering buildings that blended the best of contemporary design with hints of the past. Glass and steel monoliths shimmered in the late afternoon sunlight, their surfaces reflecting the vibrant colors of holographic billboards and pulsing advertisements. Among the modern buildings were older, more nostalgic structures, telling the story of a city that had grown and evolved over time.

But the beauty of the skyline was marred by the sight of several large fires raging throughout downtown. Plumes of thick, black smoke billowed into the sky, casting shadows over the city, creating a stark contrast to the otherwise pristine structures.

The fires illuminated the late-day sky with an eerie orange glow, painting a grim portrait of the unfolding chaos and destruction below.

"What happened?" Bucky asked.

"The power may have been disrupted. Maybe gas line breaks," Miranda said. "Many bad things usually happen when people are panicked."

As the spacecraft neared the park, they could see the rotating sphere about ten meters across. A dazzling display of light and electrical discharges burst from it, streaking across the sky in all directions. The phenomenon was accompanied by a cacophony of sound that intensified as they drew closer, resembling the sharp crack of hundreds of whips snapping in unison. As their spacecraft drew closer, they could see the frantic movements of people in the streets below, desperately trying to escape the infernos and the menace of their fellow humans.

"I don't see the Collector spaceship," Marcus said, looking around the interior of their spaceship, which was projecting the outside view.

"They have moved to another large, populated area to continue deploying the collection mechanisms," Bing said. "The collection process will continue until all are taken."

Bucky looked startled. "My mom," he said with a note of desperation. Marcus and Jen looked at each other, and each looked frightened at the thought of losing their families.

"It will take some time for the collection process to reach all the smaller populated areas," Bing said, attempting to comfort Bucky and his friends.

"How does that mechanism work? What are those electrical discharges?" Miranda asked Bing, pointing to the image of the rotating sphere below them in the park.

"I do not know the exact mechanics," Bing said.

"We must get closer," Miranda said forcefully. "I need to observe the human interactions to get some idea of the physics."

"We can land on top of one of those buildings around the park," Marcus said, again scanning the area for a clear rooftop next to the park.

"I agree with you, Marcus," Jen said. "I think landing in the park would be too dangerous."

"I agree," Bing said.

"Ok, how about that building that looks like a hotel? It looks like it has a heliport," Marcus said, pointing to a brown brick building across the street from the park.

"Yes. Can you land there, Marcus?" Bing asked.

Marcus took a deep breath and skillfully manipulated the controls, bringing the spacecraft to a soft landing on top of the building's helipad. The outside images projected inside went off, replaced by the soft light. Bing stood up and faced them.

"This will be very dangerous," he warned. "It would be best if only Dr. Richards proceeds down to the collection device and observes the collection process."

Bucky and his friends immediately protested the idea of staying behind.

"Please don't leave us here," Jen pleaded. "I think we all have something to offer, something we can do to help Dr. Richards."

After pausing to consider the options, Bing finally said, "This ship would be attacked if the Collectors came back. Perhaps it would be safest for you to be with me," he said in an accommodating tone. "But do not let anyone touch you. Stay behind me and stay close together."

"And maybe I could use the Orb to protect us," Bucky said emphatically.

"The energy signature using the Orb would be detected by the Collectors, and they could attack us," Bing said as he turned to the others. "But now we must help Miranda make the observations that will help her determine the collection mechanism, and perhaps help Bucky understand the required energies from the Orb."

Bing faced the side wall, and an opening appeared large enough for them to leave the spaceship. The first thing Bucky noticed was warm air rushing through the opening and the acrid smell of something burning. There was also a very loud buzzing noise coming from the rotating sphere in the park. There was also a continuous and almost constant popping noise like an electrical arc emitting from the collection sphere.

One at a time, they stepped through the opening and gathered just outside the spaceship. Bucky and the others had to cover their ears from the terrible sounds of the collection device.

Bing guided them cautiously away from the heliport, leading them down a flight of stairs to the rooftop. From there, they inched their way towards a door situated at the edge of the building. One by one, they entered the dimly lit passageway, finding themselves in a narrow hallway that opened up to a metal staircase.

As they gathered, they closed the door behind them, which helped mute the noise from the outside. However, with the door shut, they were now reliant on the faint glow of emergency lighting to navigate their path. The eerie red light cast an unsettling ambiance.

"The power seems to be off," Marcus stated as he tried a light switch against the wall with no effect.

As the group cautiously traversed the stairs to the lower levels, the tension was extreme. Bucky's heart was racing with the fear that, at any moment, they could be ambushed by humans-turned-zombies, whose mere touch could transform them into one of the soulless. He remembered the scenes of terror Bing shared with him from his prior life.

They slowly descended the stairs to finally come out to a great hall. With the electricity cut off, the once resplendent hall and soaring ceiling were plunged into an eerie darkness, illuminated only by the faint beams of the various emergency lighting.

The once-glistening chandeliers were shrouded in darkness. The hotel's frescoes and elaborate plaster moldings seemed to loom ominously overhead, casting sinister shadows on the walls. They pressed onward, unsure of what horrors lay ahead.

"Millennium Biltmore Hotel," Marcus said, reading the words stenciled in gold along one of the walls.

"What?" Bucky asked.

"That's where we are. That's the name of this hotel," Jen said adding, "Where is everyone?"

"There are no bodies," Miranda said in a whisper.

Suddenly, they heard screaming coming from the far end of the great hall opposite of where they stood. They could hear running footsteps approaching. A young woman dressed in a white shirt and a dark business dress came running around the corner. She had blood on the white shirt and no shoes. She stumbled and fell. From the floor, she looked back in terror for whatever was chasing her.

Bing gestured quietly for them to enter a large, recessed doorway set back far enough so they would not be seen.

They heard the woman regain her feet and continue running towards them. She had ragged breaths and muffled screams as she struggled to get away from the unseen pursuer. Then they heard other running footsteps.

At that moment, the woman appeared in front of them in the middle of the great hall. She stopped and looked over at them. The look on her face turned from great fear to what can only be described as hope. She smiled and reached her hand out to them.

The next moment, the pursuer reached her and ran clumsily into her, knocking her down. At the first contact, there was a popping sound, like an electrical arc, and a small white flash.

Just as quickly, there was another pop, again sounding electrical.

She fell awkwardly, completely limp, and hit the floor with a smack. Her attacker was an elderly balding man. He, too, looked like he might be an employee of the hotel. He had on a white shirt that also had blood on it, and he wore pants with a red cloth stripe down the sides similar to a doorman.

The doorman jumped up immediately, as he did, he immediately spotted all of them standing in the shadow of the doorway. His head was tilted down, and his eyes peered up at them. His face was inhuman, unnatural. His mouth was wide open as if to scream, but no sound came out. His expression was like no expression at all. No fear, no emotion, nothing.

He moved so quickly toward them, running without moving his arms. They were all stunned and frozen in place, except for Bing.

With even more speed than the doorman, Bing moved toward him and placed himself between the zombie doorman and his friends, who were still frozen in place. He caught the old man by his arm and leg at the same time and lifted him easily off the floor. It was such a strange, surreal sight as they looked on.

Bing held him up in the air. The old man's expression did not change, but his legs kept working like he was trying to run in the air. Jen let out a scream as Bing flung the man across the hall until he hit the floor hard and slid headfirst into the opposite wall. The old man did not move after that.

Then, the young woman, who was sprawled on the floor in a very awkward position, started to twitch and push herself off the floor in an almost inhuman manner. She got to her feet and faced them. The expression on her face was now gone. She, too, tilted her head down and looked at them with her eyes rolled up in their sockets and mouth agape. She started moving towards them quickly with her arms dangling by her side.

Bing again moved in front of her and picked her up the same way he did the doorman, and looked like he would throw her the same way.

"Wait!" Miranda shouted at Bing.

Bing stood there holding the woman, who was also running in the air.

"Can you restrain her without hurting her?" Miranda yelled at Bing.

"Yes, Dr. Richards," Bing replied. He put her down on her feet but held her by both arms. He then lifted her slightly so that her feet did not touch the floor. Her legs kept moving in a strange running motion. Miranda came closer to the suspended woman.

"Can you hear me? What happened here?" she asked in a loud voice that might break through to her.

The woman Bing held in place made no sound or gesture of recognition. Miranda tried one more time to communicate and then backed away.

"Please don't hurt her, Bing," Miranda said with concern in her voice.

"I will not," Bing replied. "But she must be restrained somehow. Her touch will collect your life energy."

Miranda observed the struggling woman for a few moments and finally said, "My god. It's like a virus. What an efficient mechanism. To use us against each other. Very little physical destruction. Two collectors with that technology can probably wipe out all life on a planet in a matter of just days.

"But what energy powers them now?" Miranda continued. "If their life energy is extracted, they should be dead. But they seem to be stronger and faster with whatever is controlling them now."

"What do we do with her?" Marcus asked as he gestured toward the still-struggling woman.

"I can render her unconscious in a way that will not harm her," Bing said. He released his grip on the woman with one mechanical hand. He moved it to the back of her neck, where a very small electrical arc contacted her neck, and she immediately went limp. Bing lifted her easily in his arms and placed her gently on the floor. She was still breathing heavily, but was still.

"I still need to get a closer look at that mechanism in the park, and then we can get out of here," Miranda said.

"I will take you to the front of this building, but any closer will be too dangerous," Bing said. "The rest of you stay here."

Bing and Miranda headed down the great hallway and turned the corner towards what looked like the front entrance to the hotel. Jen went over to the woman lying on the floor and knelt beside her.

"I wonder what her name is," she said.

Marcus moved behind Jen and lifted her gently by her arm.

"Jen, I think it would be very bad if you touched her. You saw what that old man did and what happened."

"I know. It's like a horror movie. It's so hard to believe this is all happening," Jen said. "And what about our families? What can we really do to save them?" she said with some desperation in her voice as she embraced Marcus and started sobbing.

Bucky walked over to them and said, "There has to be something I can do with this Orb that will help, or fight back, or something."

"We'll figure it out, Bucky," Marcus said. "I believe in you. We all believe in you."

Chapter Twenty-Five

Bucky Loses A Friend

Just then, they heard a scream that sounded like Miranda. It came from around the corner where they had gone to the front of the hotel. Then Miranda bolted around the corner, running as fast as she could, shouting, “Go! Go! Go!” She waved her hands toward the end of the hallway behind them.

Jen and Marcus joined Miranda as she sprinted by them, but Bucky stood in the hallway, looking back towards the entrance.

“Where is Bing? Is he all right?” he shouted back towards Miranda.

“He’s coming,” she yelled back to Bucky.

Miranda, Marcus, and Jen stopped at the door at the end of the hall that led to the great dining room, and all looked back towards Bucky.

“I can’t leave without Bing,” he shouted.

Then, a cacophony of footsteps echoed across the hotel's tiled entrance, punctuated by the heavy, metallic thud of what could only be Bing's armored footsteps. He rounded the corner at high speed, pursued by a horde of zombie-like creatures. With powerful sweeps of his robotic arms, he flung them against the walls, but they were relentless. Despite his efforts to repel them, more of the creatures clung to him, threatening to overwhelm him.

Bucky knew it was time to act—to make a difference, to save his friends. Closing his eyes, he took a deep breath and connected with the Orb. Channeling the negative energy through his arms, he extended his palms towards the advancing mob and unleashed a powerful blast of energy. The force surged down his arms and erupted from his palms, hurtling the soulless creatures into the air where they struck the ceiling and remained pinned.

As Bing regained his balance, he quickly swept aside the few creatures that Bucky's blast hadn't reached and hurled them to the far end of the hallway, where they lay motionless. Sprinting towards Bucky, Bing wore a grateful smile. "Thank you, my brother. I see you're mastering the Orb. That's good—we're going to need much more before this is over," he said, his face then clouding with concern. "The Collectors know we are here now."

Releasing the negative energy with his hand gesture, Bucky watched as the soulless creatures previously stuck to the ceiling crumpled to the floor. “Ouch,” he muttered, turning to sprint towards his friends who were gathered at the door at the end of the hall. Together, they hurried inside.

They found themselves in the great dining room of the Millennium Biltmore, a once-opulent space now shrouded in darkness due to the power outage. The only light in the room came from the feeble glow of emergency lights, casting ominous shadows that shown across the walls and floor. The grandeur of the space seemed to be swallowed up by the darkness. The dining tables and chairs were displaced, and many were turned over.

As they moved cautiously through the room, they couldn’t help but notice the elegant balconies lining the perimeter, their intricate railings barely visible in the dim light. It was not hard to imagine a time when these balconies had been filled with laughter and conversation. Now they stood empty, serving as a grim reminder of the chaos that had taken over the city.

Suddenly, the sound of shuffling footsteps echoed through the room, growing louder and more frantic by the second. The group realized, with a jolt of terror, that they were being pursued once again by the horde of zombie-like humans running down the hallway leading to the great dining room.

They broke into a desperate sprint, dodging overturned chairs and debris as they raced through the dining room. The relentless horde of zombies pursuing them, entering through the door, their unnatural forms illuminated by the flickering emergency lights. As they sprinted, the room seemed to transform into a nightmarish landscape.

As the group neared the far side of the dining room, Bing pointed to swinging double doors that led to the kitchen. They hurried through the doorway as they tried to catch their breath. Bing entered and braced himself against the double doors, holding them with each of his large mechanical hands. He turned around and said, "Find the stairs back to the roof. I will catch up with you."

They could hear the zombies colliding with the chairs and tables and finally crashing against the door. Bing was able to absorb the shock with his robot arms.

"Go!" he shouted to them as they all stood there looking shocked.

Startled, they ran out the door on the other side of the kitchen. Bucky paused, looking back at Bing holding the doors closed against the weight of the of soulless creatures.

"Go," Bing said, looking back at him. "I will be alright."

Bucky turned and followed the others out of the kitchen to a stairwell across the hall. As they began their ascent up the stairway of the hotel, making their way back to the rooftop and the waiting spaceship, the dim glow of the emergency lights again cast an eerie and foreboding atmosphere around them. Shadows flickered and danced on the walls, making it difficult to discern what was real and what was just shadows.

He experienced a mix of adrenaline and dread coursing through his veins as he climbed the stairs, the weight of their mission pressing down on him. The anxiety of not knowing what lay ahead, combined with the haunting, low-lit environment, filled his thoughts with ominous possibilities. The silence was only broken by their own heavy breathing and the echoing sound of footsteps as they hurried upward.

As they reached the top floor and prepared to cross the threshold onto the heliport, they were confronted by a lone zombie. It was the young woman they had seen earlier in the main hallway, her features now twisted and grotesque. She lunged at them from a shadowy doorway, her eyes locked on Jen with a predatory hunger.

Reacting with lightning-fast athletic reflexes, Marcus threw himself between Jen and the zombie girl, determined to protect his friend. In the chaos of the moment, the young woman crashed into Marcus, and the now too-familiar double-popping sound rang out in the cramped hallway. Marcus' eyes widened in horror as the realization set in. He had been infected. He fell to the floor with an awful thud. Jen let out a horrified scream,

"Nooooo! Marcus, Nooooo!"

She moved toward Marcus, strewn on the floor, but Miranda grabbed her arm and pulled her back away. The woman who had infected Marcus now came for the others, quickly closing the distance between them. Just as she was about to touch Jen and Miranda, she was lifted off her feet and hit the ceiling of the hallway. Miranda and Jen turned to see Bucky with his arm and hand extended toward the kicking girl pinned to the ceiling.

"The Orb?" Miranda shouted to Bucky. He nodded in response.

As if the surreal scene could not get any worse, the body that was Marcus twitched and lurched to its feet. It had the same macabre wide-open mouth and expressionless face.

Jen screamed again and held on to Miranda as Marcus' body rushed toward them. Just as he was close enough to make contact with them, Bing appeared and, with unnatural speed, gripped Marcus by wrapping his arms around him. He lifted him gently as Marcus' body squirmed like the other soulless.

Bucky, still holding the girl to the ceiling with the power from the Orb, started crying and, with a sweeping gesture of his hand, caused the girl to crash against the far wall and slump to the floor motionless.

Wiping tears from his eyes, he went to Jen, who was crying intensely, and wrapped his arms around her and Miranda.

"We have to go," he said sobbing.

They made their way back to the spaceship and entered through the door that had opened in the side. Bing trailed behind them, still holding the struggling body of Marcus.

Once they were inside, Bing entered and moved to the rear section of the interior and morphed a chair from the floor. But this chair had restraints to hold Marcus' body in place.

Jen's tears flowed uncontrollably as Miranda wrapped a comforting arm around her, offering what solace she could in this moment of despair. On her other side, Bucky placed his hand gently on Jen's shoulder, his own eyes glistening with unshed tears.

Chapter Twenty-Six

Back To LIGO

Bing assumed control of the spacecraft, directing it to ascend from the hotel rooftop and suspend itself above the frenzied spectacle below. Bucky remained alongside Miranda and Jen, unable to muster the strength to glance back at Marcus' soulless form that was still writhing in its desperate attempt to break free.

A suffocating wave of guilt washed over Bucky, for he had failed to protect his friend despite possessing the formidable power of the Orb. "How can I possibly save the earth?" he brooded as if the weight of the world bore down on him.

"Bing, if I give you latitude and longitude coordinates, can you take us to that location?" Miranda asked in a low voice.

"Yes," Bing responded, also in a low voice.

Miranda recited the coordinates, and the ship set off away from the collection point and the smoke and chaos. They moved along the California coast, witnessing the chaos spreading out from Los Angeles. Several towns had lost electricity, and columns of thick black smoke rose across the landscape.

Miranda turned to Bucky and said, "I need to understand more about this Orb if I am to be of any help. I've given the coordinates of my lab in Hanford, Washington, to Bing. The lab is somewhat isolated, so we may have some time to try to figure this out."

"Can you help us save Marcus?" Jen asked in a still, soft, and desperate voice.

Miranda turned toward Jen and, with a sad look, answered, "I don't know. His body is still functioning, so that should give us some hope."

The journey to Miranda's Lab was solemn. As they approached the site, the spacecraft descending through the clouds above the Hanford Washington laboratory. The expanse of the LIGO facility came into view on the vast patchwork of Eastern Washington's desert landscape.

The scrubland below gave way to the scientific oasis. The long, straight arms of the LIGO facility stretched out beneath the spacecraft like enormous rulers laid out on a dusty parchment. The laser tunnels, concealed beneath their protective earthen covers, trace two perfect lines in an L-shape, each reaching out towards the horizon for four kilometers. Their audacious length and rigid straightness clashed against the otherwise random, gentle undulations of the surrounding terrain.

They began to make out the central station, the beating heart of the facility where the two arms met. It was populated with a collection of anonymous-looking buildings with metallic surfaces gleaming under the now-setting high-desert sun.

Near the intersection of the two arms, a dome-shaped structure stood apart. Inside, a complex of ultra-sensitive detectors lay ready to receive and decode the subtle whispers of the universe captured by the facility's long arms. The spacecraft continued its descent, and the LIGO facility grew larger in the interior projected image.

"Bing, can you land there?" Miranda asked as they pointed to a small stretch of grass in front of the main central building.

There was no one to be seen. No one outside. There were still a few cars in the parking lot next to the grassy area where they landed, the spacecraft settling softly on the grass.

"I am sure some of the staff is still in the facility," Miranda said. "I recognize some cars in the lot. Let me speak with them before any of you enter the facility."

They all nodded in agreement. The opening door in the side appeared, and she stepped out onto the ground. Bucky watched as she walked quickly toward the main building. As she approached, three men and one woman came out of the facility's main door.

One of the figures, a security officer, had a firm grip on what was unmistakably a handgun. His posture was tense, ready to use the weapon at a moment's notice. The arrival of the alien spacecraft had clearly rattled everyone.

The group quickly gathered around Miranda, with several members embracing her in relief. Bucky observed as she spoke urgently to them, using broad gestures towards the spacecraft as she attempted to explain their extraordinary situation.

Miranda beckoned Bucky and the others to follow, and they disembarked from the spacecraft to join her on the ground. Bucky and Jen quickly traversed the twenty-meter gap to reach Miranda. Bing's exit from the spacecraft, however, elicited a very different response. His distinctly alien appearance sparked a wave of fear among the four co-workers, their faces turning pale.

The security guard, reacting instinctively to the sight of Bing, raised his weapon and aimed it at the alien. Miranda acted quickly, soothing the guard and gently pushing his arms down so that the gun was no longer directed at Bing. Approaching Miranda, Bucky could see the fear etched on the faces of the other engineers.

"It's ok. He's friendly," he said.

Miranda walked over to Bing, turned around to face her colleagues, and assured them saying, “He is here to help us.”

In the following minutes, Miranda described what they had seen in Los Angeles and their flight back to the LIGO facility to the clearly shocked members of her team, who mostly were just staring at Bing as she spoke.

“We were watching the news before the broadcast was cut off,” Lori Johnson said.

She was the only other woman of the engineers at the facility.

“There are reports of some alien virus spreading around many locations across the planet,” she added, with a note of despair.

“We still have power here. Not sure for how long, though,” said Mike Jones. A young graduate assistant with unkept brown hair wearing a dark t-shirt, jeans and sandals. He walked cautiously over to Bing with a look of wonder on his face.

“I assume he has something to do with what is happening to us,” Mike said, pointing to Bing and looking back at Miranda and the others.

“Yes,” Bing said, causing Mike to startle and jump back a step. “They are called Collectors. They have come to your planet for the energy that animates your biological units,” Bing said.

"What energy would that be?" Mike asked out loud for anyone to answer. "Wait..." he said, the reality appearing to dawn on him. "Our souls? Is that the energy you're talking about?"

"You mean there is actually a specific energy associated with humans?" Bob Brown, the eldest of the engineers, said with a note of scientific curiosity. "And now we've been attacked by..." Bob looked at Bing, "Alien robots that look like you? You're a robot, right?"

"My name is Bing. I was once humanoid, like you, before we were attacked."

A look of horror came over Bob's face as he slowly looked around at everyone gathered there.

"You were like us? What does that mean?" he asked. Mike walked a few steps to get a closer look at Bing.

"Where are you from? Why are you here if you are not one of those Collectors? And why on earth do you have a human-looking head if you're a robot?"

Bucky rushed to stand between Mike and Bing. Jen and Miranda moved likewise to join him.

"He saved our lives more than once today," Jen said firmly, crossing her arms.

"That's right," Bucky said emphatically.

"We have a more immediate challenge," Miranda said, trying to redirect her team from Bing.

"One of our team was affected by the alien virus. He is restrained in the spacecraft."

"You brought one of them here?" Bob and Mike said in unison.

"We couldn't leave him," Miranda said at once, trying to calm them.

"He sacrificed himself for me," Jen added emphatically.

Miranda started walking towards the front door to the main building but then stopped and turned to face the group.

"We all need to get inside now. It will be dark soon. Secure the doors," she ordered, looking at the security guard. He nodded and said,

"Ok. You heard the doctor. Everyone inside."

Miranda turned to Bing. "Can you secure your ship and make sure Marcus will be ok in there?"

"Yes, Dr. Richards." He turned toward the spacecraft as the door sealed itself.

They all moved quickly inside the main building. Once inside, Miranda turned again to the security guard. "Do whatever you can to secure these doors and windows. We have no idea when the collection virus will spread to this area," she pointed to the main door and then the windows on either side.

The other engineers joined the security guard and started moving the lobby furniture, which consisted of several exhibit tables, chairs, and a lobby couch.

Miranda gestured for them all to go into the main control room. The screens were still lit with streams of data displayed on top of the laser tunnel images. She moved to the center of the room as the engineers gathered around her, along with Bucky and Jen. Bing, an imposing sight, stood just inside the doorway.

"I don't know how long we have before we're attacked either by the virus-infected or the Collectors," Miranda said. "One thing we do know is whoever or whatever is behind this is integrating life energy into the robotic systems like Bing here," Miranda said, gesturing to Bing. "Bing said he was human-like before they were attacked. Is this our fate? Is there nothing we can do to protect ourselves?" Miranda finished in a frustrated tone.

Bucky thought hard about what to say next. He had a vivid memory of the scene Bing showed him back on their home planet of the attack. The galaxy Orb that he used to defend their planet so long ago was now a part of him again. He thought about the bullies, the exploding rock, and how he had protected his friends from the attack in the Los Angeles hotel. Would any of that help them now? It was something. Perhaps there was more to discover about the Orb. Maybe he had greater power that he could direct and control. To save his friends.

He looked up at Bing. He wondered why Bing didn't say something to this group about the Orb, but then he realized it really was up to him since he was most affected. Maybe the only one who could help fight the Collectors, and perhaps the creator of all this chaos.

"I may be able to help," He said loudly, drawing everyone's attention.

Chapter Twenty-Seven

Tracking The Collectors

The group's response was a mixture of skepticism and curiosity.

"Help us? How?" Bob asked, his tone balancing professional skepticism with a genuine interest.

Another scientist, perhaps a bit more cynical, chuckled softly, shaking his head. "Are you suggesting you have some sort of special knowledge or technology that we don't?" he questioned, not unkindly, but with an edge of doubt.

Bucky took a deep breath, gauging the mixed reactions from the LIGO scientists before he spoke. His voice steady, reflecting a newfound confidence mixed with the gravity of the situation.

"I've come into contact with technology that's not from our world," he began, capturing the group's full attention. "It's an object, an Orb, that interacts with gravitational fields. I can move objects and even cause explosions."

Seeing the interest and skepticism on their faces, Miranda joined in. "I know it sounds incredible, but I've witnessed its capabilities firsthand. With this technology, we could potentially fight back. We have to come up with some sort of plan," Miranda continued, looking around at the small LIGO team.

"The brief look I got of the energy collector in the park back in Los Angeles, I observed it wasn't just collecting but also transmitting some peculiar form of energy," Miranda said. "It seems to function as a conduit for a two-way process - an exchange of energies, if you will."

She paused, deep in thought, then continued. "Hypothetically, if this so-called 'life energy' is siphoned from our bodies, it's logical to assume that our biological systems would cease to function. But there appears to be an alternative energy — a substitute — that perpetuates animation within the body."

Miranda furrowed her brow, her face a mask of concentration. "What confounds me is the mechanism by which this parasitic energy morphs our biology into a conduit for further energy extraction. It seems to spread with a virulence-like contagion."

"A contagion?" Bucky questioned.

"Like a virus, Bucky," Jen said as she shook her head in disbelief.

"We witnessed the process with that woman in the hotel hallway and..." Miranda looked over at Jen, "and your friend, Marcus," she finished in a sad tone.

"Bucky, you never did tell me exactly how you caused that explosion. You said something about it involving negative and positive energy," Miranda said.

"Yes," he answered.

"Does the Orb allows you to project negative or positive energy at an object?" she asked.

"The combination of negative and positive energy, together they caused the rock to explode and disappear," he answered.

"Matter anti-matter annihilation. Fascinating. How is it possible for an Orb or anything to contain negative and positive energy without itself being destroyed?" she said as she tapped her finger on her chin.

"Bing, is your spacecraft powered by negative energy?" she asked.

"Yes, Dr. Richards. Directed negative energy fields that allow the spacecraft to move from one location to another either by warping space or the creation of what you call a wormhole."

"A real warp drive. Fascinating," Miranda said, still tapping her finger against her chin.

"And I assume the Collectors use the same technology?" she asked.

"Yes," Bing replied.

Miranda looked slowly around at her staff and said, "A warping of spacetime by compressing space in front while expanding spacetime behind it..." She looked at her team expectantly.

"Would create gravitational waves!" Lori shouted excitedly.

Miranda pointed, acknowledging her, then moved over to one of the large whiteboards on the side wall of the control room. She picked up one of the erasers, cleared the writing, and began to draw.

"Well, more likely a gravitational wake, like a boat traveling through water," Miranda responded.

"So, we have earth," She drew a large circle and then added curved longitudinal lines to provide a more sphere-like representation. "Say we're here," she added as she continued drawing a small circle toward the left middle of the earth figure.

"And say the Collectors start by traveling to the largest population centers first and then on to less populated parts of the planet in order to capture as much or all the energy possible," she continued.

"So, these Collectors are using their warp drive to almost instantaneously move around our planet, disturbing spacetime and creating gravitational wakes," Miranda said, sounding a little more hopeful.

"We should be able to track their movement using data from our gravitational wave detectors. The good news is no matter where they are on the planet," she said, drawing a crude flying saucer on the far right of her earth figure, "even the other side of the planet, the gravitational wake will move through Earth and tense our lasers."

"Yes!" Mike said with excitement. "They're probably creating waves with very high frequency given their proximity to the detectors."

"Not sure what the amplitude would be, given the spacecraft does not have significant mass compared with the stellar high-energy events we've been tracking up until now," Miranda continued.

"I would bet that their gravitational wake can be detected if we know what to look for in the data. They have been moving around for the last couple of hours or so. We need to analyze the data for a pattern that might indicate their movement. It may look like noise, but it should definitely have a unique frequency and amplitude signatures."

With excitement, Mike raised his hand, "I know exactly how to pull that type of pattern from the data. In order to triangulate, to get their location, we're going to need the data from Livingston as well. Maybe we can rig something to display the telemetry in real-time," he finished.

"That's great, Mike," Miranda said, sounding more upbeat. "We may not have a lot of time. Perhaps we can work out an algorithm that estimates how long it will take them to travel first from LA to all the other major cities around the globe," she drew several red marker curved lines around her earth picture.

"It will probably take them only a couple of days to allow the collection virus to propagate across the entire planet. Eight billion people, including us," she concluded with a serious expression.

"If we can find them, perhaps we can stop them somehow. Maybe Bucky can blast them with his superpowers," Miranda said, looking over a Bucky and Bing.

Bucky stood with his mouth agape, unable to speak at that moment. He realized what she was saying. It was up to him, Bing, and the Orb to save the planet. At that moment, the Orb seemed to connect with him, and he felt the now familiar surge of energy shake his body. He was somewhat reassured, at least he could still make the connection.

Miranda followed several of the engineers to their workstations. She began the process of evaluating the recently stored data for the Collector spacecraft gravitational wakes. Jen walked over to Bing and Bucky and said,

"I wish Marcus was with us. He could really help with these types of problems."

"I know. I miss him too," Bucky said, trying to reassure her. "We will figure out how to save him. We have to," he added, looking up at Bing.

"Yes. I am very fond of Marcus," Bing said.

Several hours passed, during which Miranda and her coworkers managed to filter the signal data to isolate what was clearly a repeating pattern from the detectors. With some additional testing, they were now tracking the Collectors' spacecraft gravitational wakes.

They programmed the real-time data monitors to generate the triangulated position at each observation, cross-referencing the data from Livingston. They developed a geospatial representation using software and displayed the results on the main screen. In addition to recent movements over time, they could now detect, almost in real time, the movements of the Collectors' spacecraft.

What they saw when they connected the transit points on the screen over time was a pattern almost like a spider web covering the bottom half of the earth and working upward. It was now just south of the equator.

"Can we predict how long until that pattern completes? I assume around the last inhabited areas of the northern hemisphere," Miranda asked Mike and Lori.

"Let me try this predictive algorithm against the data," Lori said. She pulled out one of the large software documentation binders used to program the software and systems used for their facility computers. She thumbed through it until she found the section she was looking for. She transcribed the commands and executed the run against the data. After several minutes, frustrated by several output errors, she said, "I think I got it. Let me output the pattern to the main display screen."

The large screen displayed the earth with red dots, marking each point the alien spacecraft came to a stop. Next, the display connected the points based on the time sequence.

"We've lost the Livingston data feed!" Mike shouted, and then he turned to Miranda. "I think we have enough triangulation data to predict their next geolocation, though. Based on the algorithm, in exactly twenty-one minutes and twenty-four seconds, they will be here," Mike said, pointing at his screen with a map of the northern hemisphere.

Miranda walked over to Mike's workstation, wrote down the coordinates and the estimated time on a pad, and tore the sheet. She then set a timer on her watch. She looked up at the small team and said forcefully, "If we don't do something before these Collectors complete their mission, billions of people will be enslaved, and their bodies will ultimately die." She desperately looked over to Bing and Bucky.

Bing knelt down in front of Bucky and placed his large mechanical hands on his shoulders. "My brother, only together can we stop the Collectors. I will help you in any way I can, but it is up to you, using the Orb. That is our only real chance."

Bucky felt fear run through him. For a moment, he wanted to run away to where he would be safe from this nightmare. But that feeling passed quickly as he realized there was nowhere safe to run. He was in possession of a unique and powerful force from the natural world, and he could help save his friends. He looked around at the expectant faces in the control room.

The Orb, as if anticipating him, nudged a small bolt of energy down his arms, causing them to vibrate slightly. *Ok, ok,* he thought to himself. He took a deep breath and said, "Together."

Bing smiled and hugged him gently. Jen and Miranda walked over to Bing and Bucky and joined the hug.

Suddenly, there was a loud bang and crash of breaking glass from the hallway outside the control room, like the front door had given way. The inner door burst open, and at least ten transformed human creatures, shambled quickly toward them. They rushed into the room and overwhelmed the guard, immediately knocking him to the floor with a loud, familiar, electrical double-popping sound.

Bing swept up Miranda, Bucky, and Jen in one arm and held them as high as he could. With his other arm, he brushed aside the attackers; a group of three went sprawling across the room, crashing into the desks and knocking over computer monitors. Dozens more rushed into the room, mouths agape in the awful un-scream, with their arms dangling by their sides in an unnatural running motion, they attacked Bing.

Miranda screamed, "NO!" as she watched her colleagues immediately run down by the now increasing number of zombies, before they could even flee or protect themselves. Again, the loud popping noise echoed in the control room as each was trampled by the possessed mob. The look of fear and terror on their faces quickly gave way to the empty, blank look of the Collected.

Chapter Twenty-Eight

Escape From LIGO

The situation became desperate. The chaos unfolded so rapidly that Bucky had no time to use the Orb to defend them. The control room quickly filled up with dozens of zombie-like creatures now turning their attention to the only un-collected life energy sources. Even Miranda's colleagues had joined the melee.

Bing shielded Bucky, Jen, and Miranda from the attackers, hoisting them high onto his shoulders. With his free arm, he swept back and forth in powerful arcs, sending the soulless creatures flying in all directions. He then surged forward, taking several swift and massive strides toward the door, momentarily bewildering the attacking horde. As the creatures regained their focus, they collectively shambled after him, their relentless pursuit echoing through the hall.

As Bing neared the front door, he carefully lowered his friends, cradling them securely against his metallic chest with both arms. Lowering his shoulder, he charged through the remnants of the door, effortlessly brushing aside the barricade of furniture. With a series of powerful leaps, he propelled them into the open, sprinting toward the spaceship with unwavering speed.

Bing managed to create a gap between himself and the attacking mob. As he approached the spaceship, an opening appeared in its side. With the attackers closing in, he carefully set Bucky, Jen, and Miranda inside the spacecraft. Bing turned to block the door, bracing himself as the zombie mob crashed into him. The spaceship door quickly sealed shut, leaving Bing outside to face the relentless horde.

Bucky moved to what use to be the door inside, but now was a solid wall; he yelled, "NO! Bing!" Just then, Bing's large robotic arm and hand morphed through the wall of the spaceship and snapped into a thumbs-up.

"Yes!" Bucky said, relieved. The remaining parts of Bing morphed through the side of the spaceship until he was completely in and standing before them. Bucky rushed over to Bing and embraced him. He looked up at him and said, "Thank you for saving us. I'm... I'm sorry I couldn't save the others. It happened so fast."

"Yes, Bucky," Bing replied. "You may save them all yet. We must prepare to meet the Collectors now. Remember the training as best you can." Then, he turned to Miranda and asked,

"Dr. Richards, do you have the calculated position for the Collectors?"

Miranda nodded and retrieved a piece of paper from her pocket. "These are the coordinates," she said as she held the paper out for him to read. "I believe this is in the Northeast United States. Maybe even New York City." She glanced at her watch and added, "We only have about eighteen minutes to get there."

Bing swiftly moved to the front of the spaceship and took his position at the guidance console. A holographic projection of Earth materialized before him, rapidly zooming in on the Northeast. The image halted over New York City, glowing with pinpoint precision.

"About nine million people live in New York City," Jen informed, looking at the hologram. "I have many relatives there. We would visit them during the holidays when I was little. I remember the lights crossing the George Washington Bridge late at night in my parent's station wagon."

Jen turned to face the body of Marcus, still restrained in the back. "And I'll take you there someday, Marcus. After this is all over," she said. The body of Marcus still had the blank expression, but the mouth was closed, and it was no longer trying to escape its bonds.

"Remember, Marcus is still dangerous," Bing warned Jen. She turned to Bing and gave him a determined look, "I know."

The projection of the outside covered the interior of the spacecraft, and immediately, Bucky stepped back at the sight of the dozens of ragged people pressed against the exterior of their ship. They were brushed back and then watched the spacecraft with their open-mouthed blank faces as it lifted off.

Bucky watched as they flew into the clouds and headed toward his unknown fate. He closed his eyes. With his heart racing, he practiced connecting with the Orb. He was getting good at this. The Orb was really a part of him now. Something that he could control like any other part of his body. He practiced energizing his arms with positive and negative energy, forming a tiny ball of energy between his hands. He adjusted its size with little conscious effort.

When he looked up, he noticed Jen and Miranda staring at him with astonishment as the tiny ball of energy illuminated the spacecraft's interior. He smiled at them, and they nodded back.

Miranda turned to Bing and asked, "How long before we arrive?"

"I cannot engage maximum power because of the damaged propulsion engine. But I calculate fourteen minutes thirty-two seconds until we touch down in the park at the center of the city. That's where they will likely set up the collection device," Bing responded.

Bing stood up from his seat at the console and moved to kneel in front of Bucky. He gestured for the other two to join him. "We have two challenges before us," Bing started. "We need to stop them from setting up any more energy collection devices. We must also stop the collection processing of the existing systems. The storage and central control of the energy collector is contained within their spacecraft. If we disable the central machine, it will disable all the devices around the planet."

"What about the storage?" Miranda asked.

"That's why we cannot destroy their spacecraft," Bing responded. He turned to Bucky. "You will need to be very careful not to damage or destroy both the spacecraft and the internal systems."

"Then we need to draw them out, away from their ship," Bucky said. "You also said they want the Orb back, right?" He directed the question at Bing.

"Yes," Bing replied.

"That also means that they won't try and destroy us until they have secured the Orb," Bucky added.

He thought for a moment then said, "Can you get them to land and leave their ship?"

"I can communicate with them. Offer the Orb in exchange for your lives," Bing proposed. "But of course, we will never give them the Orb. Jen, if something happens to me you must try to communicate with them. Give Bucky time to position himself to attack them."

"Yes, I will do what I can to help," Jen said firmly.

Bing placed his large robotic hand on Bucky's shoulder.

"I do not know about the energy storage," Bing said.

"I've been thinking about that," Miranda said. Everyone turned their attention to her expectantly.

"Of course," Bucky said excitedly. "You're a physicist, the best!"

"I'm not sure about that, Bucky, but analyzing the potential science associated with the collection devices, it seems to behave like a two-way communications network. This is what we saw with the collection device in Los Angeles. First, extracting life as energy and then pushing energy that animates the body and modifies the biology to act something like a terminal. All linked to the central systems on board the Collector spacecraft." Miranda paused, appearing deep in thought.

"I believe the energies between the people that were collected and the false energy inserted into their biology are entangled. This would explain how they can be controlled remotely from the Collectors' spacecraft," Miranda continued. "The false energy on the spacecraft is instantaneously switched with the life energy, and the life energy is then contained on board their spaceship. The collection devices are spread all over the world. Perhaps the energy extraction can be reversed using the same devices."

"How can we do that?" Jen asked.

"The system that holds the collected energies is completely enclosed and sealed," Bing said. "Only the Entity can remove the life energies from the containment system."

Bing turned back to the console. "We are approaching the coordinates, Dr. Richards," he said as he sat back down at the control console.

As the craft descended toward New York, Bucky gazed at the projected images of the great city. He looked over the sprawling metropolis stretching out beneath them—a mix of towering grey skyscrapers and grid-like streets. The distinctive silhouette of the iconic skyline was dominated by the majestic Empire State Building, the spire of One World Trade Center, and other architectural marvels.

The spacecraft maneuvered gracefully between the labyrinthine and corridors formed by the skyscrapers, weaving through the urban canyons. Bucky marveled at the precision and agility of the alien spacecraft technology, contrasting starkly with the typical chaotic flow of human traffic.

As they approached Central Park, Bucky's eyes widened with awe. The park, an oasis in the middle of the concrete jungle, sprawled beneath them like a mesmerizing emerald tapestry. Their spaceship lowered, gently skimming over the treetops, causing leaves to rustle in its wake.

The few remaining people in the park had scattered and sought shelter behind trees or huddled together in small groups. Fear was etched across their faces as their gazes were fixated on the extraterrestrial arrival.

Chapter Twenty-Nine

The Fight

"Jen, do you have the translation device?" Bing asked.

"Yes, Mr. Bing," Jen responded. She reached into her pocket and held up the small device for Bing to see.

"Good, I will communicate with the Collectors using our common language. It is important that you follow what is said and translate for the others as necessary."

"I will, Bing," Jen replied as she placed the device in her ear.

Miranda checked her watch again. "We have ninety seconds," she announced.

As fear surged through him once again, Bucky realized this was his defining moment—the time to face his fears head-on. He glanced around at his friends and at his long-lost brother, now trapped within the metallic confines of a robotic body. The world around him seemed infinitely larger, his senses attuned to the vast expanse of space. He felt a deep connection to the energies of the galaxy, energies drawn from the supermassive black hole at its heart, Sagittarius A—a name he now knew well. Touching his chest, he struggled to grasp the reality of his transformation, the profound changes affecting his friends, and the looming threat to humanity. Suddenly, he felt a large metallic hand rest reassuringly on his shoulder.

"My Brother," Bing said, his voice steady. "We fight side-by-side once more. Stay behind me when we confront them."

Bucky noticed the most human expression on Bing's synthetically perfect face.

"They possess the life energy collected so far in a special containment on board their spacecraft," Bing continued. "We must be very careful not to damage the ship or the containment. Our first objective is to stop them. You will use the Orb the best you know how. From the experience you have so far."

"Am I supposed to… to… kill them?" Bucky asked.

"They must be stopped, if we have any chance to save the billions of human souls that have been collected from this planet. We are their only chance. You are their only hope," Bing said with grave concern in his voice.

"There!" Jen shouted as she pointed to the hologram displaying their location in New York Central Park.

An object appeared as a red blinking dot on the 3-D display over lower Manhattan. Just then, there were two very loud booms, one quickly followed by another, that shook the spacecraft.

"Sonic booms?" Bucky questioned, looking at Bing.

"They are decelerating into the atmosphere from the warp transit," Bing responded. "They have no need to hide."

They all watched as the red blinking dot approached their location from the south. The ship slowed as it approached them. The interior of Bing's spaceship still projected everything from the outside. They all looked in the direction of the Collectors, and then they saw it.

It was much larger than Bing's spacecraft. Its angular design featured sleek lines and sharp edges, giving it an unmistakably otherworldly appearance. The vessel's metallic surface glimmered under the city lights. As the spacecraft hovered above Manhattan, strange appendages emerged from its hull. These protrusions revealed an array of what looked like advanced weaponry, bristling with menacing energy.

It came to a stop just about one hundred meters above and to the side of Bing's spaceship. Suddenly, there was a bright flash from one of the Collector's spaceship protrusions. At the same instant, Bing's spaceship was rocked, and a loud bang echoed inside. The projection of the outside flickered but did not go away.

They all looked at Bing with fear on their faces.

"They could have destroyed us if they desired," Bing said in a calculated voice. "They know we have the Orb, so they won't risk losing it. The Entity will have programmed them with instructions to retrieve the Orb. I will speak to them to arrange an exchange." Bing's gaze shifted to Bucky, then he shook his head silently, his lips forming the word "no."

Bing moved to the control panel, his fingers gliding over the surface. With his hand held over the panel, he began to speak in a language none of them could understand, except Jen. She put her hand to the ear with the translation device and listened intently.

"Not all the words are in understandable English," she said, "but I think Bing is telling them to land, and he will meet them to give them the Orb."

Then, Jen's eyes widened in surprise, and she exchanged a quick, worried glance with Bucky and Miranda. "I can hear the Collectors!" she exclaimed. "There are two voices. They sound angry. They keep demanding something... something that sounds like 'small dark sun,' in English."

"The Orb," Miranda said, looking at Bucky.

Bing stopped speaking in the alien language and turned away from the console. He moved toward the side of the spacecraft as an opening appeared large enough for him to exit. He stopped before he exited and turned to the Others. "Leave now and move away from this ship and find cover in the trees. Try not to let them see you."

He then turned his attention to Bucky. "My brother, you will come with me and stay behind me until they exit their spacecraft. When they are far enough away from their ship, you must summon the energy of the Orb and attack them. It must be quick and leave no chance for them to strike back. They expect me to have the Orb, so their focus will be on me."

Bing then gestured to Miranda and Jen, signaling them towards the doorway.

Miranda kissed Bucky on the cheek and gave him a quick hug as she said, "I know you'll be ok, Bucky." She put her hand on Bing's arm and gave him a weak smile as she exited the spacecraft.

Jen also stopped to give Bucky a hug. "For Marcus," she said softly before following Miranda outside.

Bing and Bucky stood together for a moment, in silence. Bucky nodded that he was ready, and they both walked slowly outside the spacecraft.

Bucky felt the cool breeze of the early fall air as he stepped onto the grass and noticed the hint of fall color in the leaves. It was late in the day, and the streetlights were just beginning to illuminate. Under normal circumstances, he would be looking forward to Halloween and then Thanksgiving and Christmas. It was his favorite time of year.

He was snapped back to reality when he saw the Collector spacecraft descend from the sky to land about 50 meters from them. Bing took a few steps toward the menacing alien ship and check to make sure Bucky remained behind him.

Bucky realized this would be the moment to prepare. He attempted to connect with the Orb. To his horror, his worst fear was realized as he could not. Concurrently, an opening appeared in the Collector spacecraft, and slowly, two Collectors stepped out. They had dark-colored, advanced-looking armor. Their heads were cylindrical, and they each had what looked like a weapon attached to their forearm.

Bucky attempted to connect to the Orb once more, but again, he was met with failure. Meanwhile, Bing advanced toward the Collectors, who had already raised their weaponized arms, aiming them at him. They began to speak loudly in their alien language, their voices echoing with a sense of urgency. Bing halted and raised his arms slightly, striving to appear non-threatening in the tense standoff.

They shouted again and held out a round container about eight inches in diameter that pulsed with a faint white light. They gestured toward Bing, holding up the container.

Bucky knew this had to be the storage mechanism for the Galaxy Orb. The Collectors yelled one more time, gesturing for Bing to hand them the Orb.

Bucky's hands trembled uncontrollably as beads of sweat trickled down his forehead. His breath came in shallow, rapid gasps, and his eyes darted frantically around the scene. His mind raced with the horrifying possibility that Bing would be killed and his friends would be collected and enslaved like Bing. He clenched his fists, desperately trying to think of a way to prevent the impending disaster.

Bing lowered his hands to his side and turned slowly to look at Bucky, expectantly.

Suddenly, there was a very loud cracking sound and a bright red flash. Bing was struck in the chest, and he was flung backward to the ground with a great crash. He looked up at Bucky in shock as his head morphed back into the familiar cylinder shape. Then he didn't move.

"No!" Bucky shouted as he turned to the Collector, who had raised its weapon to shoot Bing.

He instinctively raised his arms and hands and directed them at the Collector. He felt the energy of the Orb surge through his arms and create a focused field of negative energy that sent the Collector instantly flying into the air and out of sight.

The second Collector advanced toward Bucky, raising his weapon. As he fired, Bucky instinctively directed a surge of negative energy toward his attacker. The Collector's energy blast collided with Bucky's field, deflecting and striking a nearby tree. The tree erupted in a fiery explosion, sending splintered wood and burning leaves into the air. The Collector hesitated, momentarily distracted by the blazing tree that illuminated the surroundings. Seizing the opportunity, Bucky unleashed another blast of negative energy. The force catapulted the Collector into the sky, where it disappeared, joining its colleague in Earth's outer atmosphere.

Bucky quickly turned his attention back to Bing, who was sprawled on the ground, unmoving. Jen and Miranda left the cover of the trees to join them. They all bent over Bing, trying to detect life.

"Is he dead?" Jen asked desperately.

"Not sure," Miranda said, looking for a way to help Bing. "Bucky, can you find him?"

Bucky knew what she meant. He was still connected to the Orb; he could feel it. He concentrated inward and searched for Bing's soul song. At first, he sensed only the energies around him and even nearby in the Collector containment device.

Bucky suddenly felt a profound and hollowing sense of loss. Bing was his family. He loved him. Bing had sacrificed for him. He placed his right hand on Bing's chest and closed his eyes, fighting back tears.

"Bing," he said in his mind. "Don't leave me. I need you. We all need you."

Just then, he felt a slight shock in his hand touching Bing's chest. He knew it did not come from the Orb. Then he heard it. Very faint, but unmistakably there. Bing's soul song. The vibrations he received were the most unique he ever heard in the entire universe. Sweet and simple. Soothing and familiar. Bucky's gaze lifted to Miranda, and a wide smile crossed his face.

"I found him," he exclaimed.

Jen and Miranda together exhaled a sigh of relief. Miranda moved quickly to Bucky and said,

"We have to examine the Collectors' spacecraft to find the life energy storage containment system."

Miranda and Bucky moved quickly to the Collectors' spacecraft. There was still an opening in the side. They cautiously stepped in. The inside of the alien spacecraft was very sparse, except for a large sphere suspended in the middle. It was clearly the collection storage device that Bing spoke of. Bucky glanced and thought, *the life energies of humanity.*

The containment chamber glowed with radiant light as countless tiny dots shimmered within its confines, representing the souls of Earth's inhabitants. Bucky and Miranda stood amidst the ethereal display, their eyes scanned inside of the spacecraft and the complex patterns that were etched on the collection chamber's surface.

There was a smaller sphere hovering just above the larger one. There were small continuous bolts of what looked like lightning, extending out of the smaller sphere contacting the other, each bolt generating a popping sound. Because there were so many at once, the sound was more like a loud buzz.

Miranda and Bucky looked on in amazement. "Those are people's souls, Bucky," Miranda said in a loud voice over the sound of the continuous buzz.

Bucky held his hand over his chest and at once was overwhelmed with the soul songs. Each had a unique tone and frequency, but together was the sum total of billions of human beings harvested for the essence that made them human. Miranda scanned the interior of the spacecraft as if looking for some way to disrupt the machine.

"I don't see any way to stop the collection," she said above the din of popping noise.

Just then, some sort of alarm sounded, and the interior of the spacecraft glowed bright red and started pulsing. A very loud, mechanical-sounding voice in the alien language seemed to be broadcast inside and outside.

Miranda and Bucky glanced at each other with a confused and frightened look. After a few seconds, Jen came to the entrance with her hand held over her ear containing the translation device and yelled above all the noise, "It's a warning! This spacecraft will self-destruct unless the pilots return and disengage the alert."

"No! Everyone will die!" Bucky said with an absolute sense of panic.

Miranda stood still for a few moments, looking at the collection sphere. At the same time, Jen ran to Bucky and screamed, "Marcus. We have to save Marcus."

"Jen!" Miranda yelled. "Does the warning say anything about how much time until it self-destructs?" she asked.

"I think there is a countdown, but I don't understand the numbers if that's what they are," Jen replied.

"Jen, get back to Bing's ship and stay inside. Don't go near Marcus yet," Miranda commanded. Jen nodded and left through the opening.

"Bucky, we don't know how much time we have. Listen carefully," Miranda said urgently. "I don't think there is any way we can stop the destruction of this spaceship. There don't seem to be any physical controls. So we have to find another way to save the collected soul energy."

She paused, watching the fear in his eyes. She knelt down in front of him and put her hands on his shoulders as the alien voice sounded the warning. "From everything we've observed about the life energy collection, it seems to be an entangled exchange. Life energy is extracted, and false life energy takes its place. I believe all the individual souls collected here are still connected at the quantum level with the false energy animating their bodies. We have to find a way to reverse the collection process."

"What can I do, Dr. Richards?" Bucky asked, more focused now.

"Bucky, I believe the collection uses some sort of positive energy to draw the collected life energies to it. I believe we might reverse the process by applying negative energy. Can you try to give a blast of negative energy towards the containment system?"

"I'll try," Bucky replied.

He turned to face the large circular vessel, raised his arms, and, with his palms outstretched, willed a blast of negative energy toward the sphere. The energy blast rebounded on them, and both were violently knocked against the side of the spaceship. Bucky struggled to clear his head as he rose from the floor. He quickly moved to Miranda and extended a hand to help her up. She was holding her head where it had made contact with the wall.

"Dr. Richards, are you ok?" he said above the still buzzing noise.

"I think so," she replied as she stood, still a little shaky. "Bucky, I still think the negative energy is the way to reverse the process," she said, looking around at the interior again. "If we could only get inside somehow."

"Inside?" Bucky said, looking at her intently.

She looked back at him. "It's our only chance."

"You mean to apply the negative energy from inside that thing?" Bucky said, pointing to the large containment sphere.

"Yes," Miranda replied with a look, like a doctor telling a patient they didn't have long to live.

Bucky looked down, thinking hard. He could still feel the Orb. Perhaps connected to his soul. His life energy and the Orb were as one. He looked back up at Miranda and said in a strong voice,

“I have to be collected.”

Miranda gave him a sympathetic look. “Yes, Bucky. I think that’s the only way. It may mean you will die,” she said matter-of-factly. “But I think the energy of the Orb may protect you and your consciousness in there.” She pointed again at the sphere.

“Marcus can do it,” Bucky said as he ran to the opening of the alien spacecraft. He stopped and turned to Miranda. “Come with me, please, Dr. Richards. I don’t want to be alone right now.”

“Of course, Bucky,” Miranda responded.

Together, they exited and ran to Bing’s spaceship. Jen was sitting at the opposite end of Marcus, looking at him with an incredibly sad expression. Marcus still had a blank, empty look. His arms were outstretched toward Jen in an inhuman gesture. Bucky moved quickly to stand in front of him.

“No, Bucky, what are you doing?” Jen yelled.

Miranda moved quickly to Jen’s side and put an arm around her. “Jen, Bucky may be the only chance we have. This is the only way,” she said.

"But Bucky will turn into one of them. Like Marcus," Jen said in a desperate voice.

Just then, Bing appeared at the entrance. He looked damaged, his left arm dangled uselessly at his side. He did, however, have his human head and face again. He smiled weakly and said in a rough, mechanical voice, "My brother, I will protect your body and your friends while you do what you must do."

Bucky felt a renewed sense of strength when he caught sight of Bing. He looked at everyone around him and said, "It will be ok." Then, he took two steps toward Marcus' outstretched arms and touched him.

Chapter Thirty

Bucky's Soul

An excruciating pain surged through Bucky's entire being. It felt as if every fiber of his existence was being stretched to its limits, threatening to tear apart. With a blinding flash of light, his soul was violently torn from his physical body, leaving him in a state of weightless disarray.

Time and space blurred.

As his consciousness awakened in the void, his full awareness remained intact, his thoughts and memories swirling within him. Floating weightlessly in the void. He now existed as a pure, ethereal entity. He sensed the Orb as part of him, the physical energy from his spacetime anchoring him to his current existence.

Time ceased to be linear. Moments stretched and contracted, blurring into a surreal combination of past, present, and future.

Visions emerged around him, shimmering and elusive, as if projected onto a translucent screen. He witnessed places he had never been, worlds he had never imagined, and creatures whose forms defied conventional understanding. There were flashes of his prior life with Bing. It was from his perspective looking at Bing before he was enslaved by a robot. Flashes of his family with Bing.

He sensed the life energies spread across the galaxy, even prior lifetimes, like a radio tuned to all life frequencies in the galaxy simultaneously. He felt ultimately connected through the Orb.

Then, his awareness was consumed by the absence of any light. Infinite, ultimate darkness. He was suspended in this state for how long his consciousness did not know. There was no sense of time. Then there was a light. Distant as if at the end of a tunnel. It was as pure as the sun's rays. It embraced him with an indescribable warmth, permeating every fiber of his consciousness. It was a light that seemed to possess an inherent intelligence. This essence understood him intimately, welcoming him with open arms.

As he immersed himself in the light, he experienced an overwhelming sense of emotion. Waves of joy, serenity, and unconditional love washed over him. Dissolving any remnants of fear or pain that may have lingered from his earthly existence. He felt a profound connection to a universal consciousness. This collective presence embraced him as part of something greater than his single consciousness. He sensed he could just give in to the light. Let it take him away from all that troubled him in this life. He hesitated.

He remembered at that infinite moment that he had a purpose to fulfill, a reason not to give in to the light. He sensed the energy of the Orb that surrounded his being. Its power anchored his spirit to this spacetime.

Then, all that he was, in this ethereal state, his consciousness and soul energy, was pulled violently, unnaturally from the light, from the sense of serenity and ultimate peace. He had no control to resist this force. He sensed an evil purpose to it. Then he sensed he was trapped. It was all enclosing darkness. He sensed a force that constrained his essence, a controlling energy.

He sensed the bounding energy. A cosmic prison. He was not alone. There were countless tiny, glowing, forever sparks floating in suspension, radiating a haunting aura. These were the captured souls of billions of humans imprisoned within this extraterrestrial device.

Awareness flooded his disembodied form, a profound understanding of his purpose. He knew he couldn't allow the souls of his fellow humans to remain captive.

His consciousness focused on the Orb. He asserted its power to regain control. The energy of the Orb encircled him, shielding his soul energy from the energy of alien control, granting him autonomy amidst this cosmic prison. Miranda was right, his free-form consciousness thought.

He had to harness the galaxy Orb's unique properties to create a negative energy field, a force capable of disrupting the alien containment sphere. He started channeling his own energy merged with the Orb's enigmatic power.

Like a distant memory, his consciousness remembered It was a race against time. If the alien ship was destroyed, all would be lost. The earth and all its inhabitants. He needed to create a powerful negative energy field that would counteract the forces binding the human life energies, setting them free.

He focused his consciousness on the galaxy Orb. With every ounce of willpower, he summoned the energy within himself, drawing upon the knowledge and strength he had accumulated. A brilliant surge of negative energy emanated from his essence, rippling through the containment sphere.

There was a brilliant flash. The negative energy field spread across the expanse of the alien containment. As it flashed over the trapped life energies, the quantum entanglement, the connection between the human souls and the false energies, reversed. The entrapped souls returned to their physical forms all over the earth in an explosion that rippled through the fabric of spacetime.

The souls were set free. They dispersed, instantly replacing the false energy controlling their original bodies. Each soul was reunited with its earthly body. Their liberation was not only a matter of physical release but also a restoration of their voices, their individual soul songs reaching out to rejoin the grand cosmic symphony. Each note, each cadence, soared through the ethereal realm.

The sensation to his consciousness was an abrupt shock, where all the physical sensations returned at once. The effect was almost disappointing compared to the ultimate peace he had experienced.

He was released from his ethereal state, and his consciousness regained control of his physical body.

Chapter Thirty-One

Saving Earth

Bucky opened his eyes, gasping for breath, as he once again inhabited the realm of the living. He looked up at Bing's smiling face. Bing was holding him in his large robotic arms.

"Welcome back, my brother. You did it. You showed so much courage," Bing said with heartfelt emotion.

"You saved me, Bucky," Marcus said, standing over him and smiling broadly. Bucky got to his feet, still a little shaky from the experience, and put a reassuring hand on Marcus' shoulder.

"Marcus. So good to see you. We all missed you," Bucky confessed.

Jen joined them. "Yes. Marcus, we were so worried we lost you forever," she said.

"We have to deal with the Collector spacecraft," Miranda spoke up with some urgency.

Miranda and Marcus helped Bucky walk as quickly as they could to Bing's spaceship opening. They supported him outside, where he assured them he could stand on his own. Bing followed them outside, not looking so good himself, followed by Jen.

The Collector spaceship was in front of them and was still making alarm noises with the alien message repeating.

"What time are they describing until self-destruct?" Jen asked Bing. "I know it's a countdown, but I don't understand the time increments."

Bing paused to listen to the alien language. "It will self-destruct in one minute and thirty-two seconds, earth time," Bing said in a calm and calculated voice.

"What?" Marcus shouted. "What do we do? What can we do?"

Bing turned calmly to Bucky and said, "You know what you have to do."

Bucky hesitated for only a brief moment, and then, with a faint smile on his face, he shifted his focus toward the alien spacecraft. Raising his arms, palms facing downward, he shut his eyes and took a deep breath to confirm his connection with the Orb. He could feel the energy surging within him. Lifting his palms upwards, he directed them at the Collector spacecraft and willed a surge of negative energy towards it.

The air around the alien ship swirled in violent tornado-like vortexes. Rocks and dirt immediately started flying skyward around the ship. Then it began to shake and vibrate, on the verge of breaking into a thousand pieces.

"Twenty-two seconds," Bing said calmly.

Bucky opened his eyes and turned towards Bing with a slight smile across his lips. He then pushed his palms toward the Collector ship, and a ripple of negative energy field pulsed out from him and hit the ship. It immediately vaulted into the sky with a booming sound, like thunder, after a great lighting strike. Bucky followed the spacecraft with his palms until it was only a distant speck in the night sky.

"Three, two, one," Bing said calmly.

There was a blinding flash in the sky where the Collector spacecraft was. For a moment, it looked like a small sun. The flash subsided, the dark, night sky returned, and the shock wave and thunder from the explosion rippled through the atmosphere. It passed over them with a great boom and rush of air that knocked them all to the ground, except Bing. Bucky got up quickly and looked around at his friends.

"Is everyone okay?" he asked.

"That was amazing!" Marcus beamed, rising to his feet. He extended a hand to help Jen up, brushing dirt and leaves from her clothes. One by one, they all reassured each other they were okay and unhurt from the ordeal.

Bucky walked quickly over to Bing and said,

"Bing, are you okay? I thought they killed you back there." He noticed the odd, limp position of his left arm. "Is your arm okay?"

Bing smiled. "I am well, my brother. This can be repaired," he said, gesturing to his arm.

"Man, that was a crazy experience," Marcus said. "I don't remember much, but the pain I experienced when that thing touched me was not like anything I've ever felt before."

"Thank you for saving me, Marcus," Jen said as she kissed his cheek and wrapped her arms around his neck in a tight hug, which he returned.

"It's okay, Jen. I know you would have done the same for me," Marcus said, a little embarrassed by the attention.

"You were right, Dr. Richards," Bucky said, addressing Miranda. "It was the negative energy that reversed the collection process."

"It was quite a light show when all the life energy reversed," Miranda replied.

Just then, they all noticed a crowd slowly moving towards them from all directions in the park. This time, none had the horrifying looks on their faces and the strange shuffling walk. Although, they did look quite disheveled and exhausted. Several of them were pointing toward Bucky and his friends and smiling like they knew they were in no danger.

An older-looking woman in a torn business suit walked slowly up to Bucky and stopped just a few feet from him. "Thank you, young man. I don't know quite how you did it, but you saved us," she said, finally coming close enough to shake his hand. Bucky smiled and returned her handshake.

Several of the other onlookers gathered around Bucky, and a larger number circled Bing, but stayed well back from him, looking like they were not quite sure if it was safe.

Miranda approached Bing and said, "Perhaps it would be better for us to get a safe distance from here. The authorities may show up with a lot of questions we can't answer right now."

"You are right, Dr. Richards," Bing replied. He looked around at his team and gestured with his good arm towards his spacecraft.

They all moved quickly towards the ship and entered through the opening in the side. The crowd, which had grown even larger, was now following but still keeping their distance. Just as Bucky entered the Spaceship, the last one in, they all heard sirens in the distance. They were getting louder, indicating the authorities were coming.

The spaceship door was sealed after Bing was inside. Marcus looked at Bing with a smile and asked, "Can I take control?"

"Of course, Marcus," Bing replied, returning his smile.

Marcus took his position at the command console and cracked his knuckles. He then started manipulating the controls to bring up the 3-D hologram above the console. Jen walked up behind him and put her hand on his shoulder. Marcus looked at her, and the two smiled at each other.

With a few hand gestures, Marcus activated the internal view of the outside environment. They all looked around as there were now hundreds of New Yorkers gathered around them, pointing and speaking to each other. With a few simple gestures from Marcus, the Spaceship rose slowly from the grass and began to move forward, just clearing some of the trees surrounding the park.

Marcus elevated them to about half the height of the surrounding skyscrapers hovering above Fifth Avenue. He looked around at Bing and, with a sly smile, said, "If I promise not to go too fast?"

"Marcus, no," Jen breathed out, sounding a little frightened.

"You are the pilot, Marcus. I believe you are skilled enough," Bing said.

The view was spectacular. With the projected images of the surrounding buildings, Marcus moved the spacecraft gracefully down Fifth Avenue. Its eerie silence contrasted with the usual cacophony of the city. The towering skyscrapers now seemed even more majestic as they passed by. The glass facades reflected the now bright moonlight in dazzling arrays, creating mesmerizing patterns that danced across the interior of the spacecraft.

The spacecraft accelerated to a high speed, and the world outside became a blur of lights and colors. The familiar cityscape of Manhattan transformed into streaks of multicolor lights. Racing through the sky, the spacecraft shot past the iconic Empire State Building several blocks over from Fifth Avenue. In the blink of an eye, the monumental structure was reduced to a mere flash of silver and glass as the Spaceship shot straight up and away from the city. With the amazing alien technology, none inside felt the acceleration as the ship shot through the clouds, breaking through to a star-filled sky with the now illuminated Manhattan streets stretched out like threads, interwoven with the dark patches of Central Park.

The dark night sky was full of bright stars, with the northeast coast of the United States receding quickly below them. Marcus brought the Spaceship to a halt about one hundred miles above the earth.

"Wow!" Bucky, Miranda, and Jen said in unison.

"Nice," Jen said, lightly punching Marcus in the arm.

They were all silent for several minutes, admiring the amazing view of the beautiful earth. Eventually, Miranda broke the silence, her tone serious as she turned to Bing and asked,

"When will they send more Collectors or worse?"

Bing shifted his gaze towards Miranda, his joyful expression giving way to seriousness. After a contemplative pause, he responded,

"They will come again, that is certain. But when? That I do not know."

Chapter Thirty-Two

The Plan

Bing moved to his seat at the controls, and with a wave of his hand over the console, a snaking tendril emerged from the side wall, and its finger-like extensions started working on his damaged arm.

"I must repair myself and this ship," Bing said. "And we need to evaluate our course of action."

"Before we talk about the next steps, I need to understand more about what we're up against," Miranda said, sounding a little frustrated.

"What exactly is this Entity, and why is it collecting sentient energy?"

"I do not know what the Entity is, Dr. Richards," Bing responded.

"Before we were taken, our scientists suggested it may be something that has existed for many thousands of your years before our civilization evolved. Perhaps a technology that grew beyond the control of its creators."

"The concept and technology behind enslaving life energy, our souls, is terrifying," Miranda said with a shudder.

Bucky was still not used to seeing the outside as if there were no walls, like they were floating free near outer space. The stars shone so much clearer and brighter this high up. He looked at all these stars and sensed the civilizations and life in the galaxy. The Orb was humming gently within him. It was connected with the galaxy's life energies somehow. The infinite soul songs of the abundant, and now very real, life in the galaxy.

"You ok, Bucky?" Jen asked as she knelt next to him.

"Pretty crazy," he replied. "So much has happened. It's still really hard for me to believe."

"I know what you mean, Bucky," Jen responded.

"We had no idea you lived with Bing in a prior life. You didn't mention that in Speech Class," she added, laughing a little.

"Yea. That would have been a lot more interesting than my speech on what I did last summer," Bucky said.

They both shared a welcome laugh after all they had been through. The mechanical arm that had been working on Bing retracted into the wall. He stood up and rotated his shoulder joint, testing the results.

"Dr. Richards, Bucky, Jen, and Marcus, we must speak regarding a plan to prevent another attack against your planet," Bing said in a serious tone. "Bucky possesses the one weapon that gives us a chance against the evil Entity," he added.

"Will the power of the Orb be enough?" Miranda asked. "I do not know, Dr. Richards," Bing responded.

"I believe we have not yet discovered all of its powers. The creator used the black hole as a forge to create objects such as the Orb. Even on my planet, we had those who only sought power and control. There was never enough of either to satisfy them. I believe this Entity seeks ultimate control of this galaxy and perhaps other galaxies."

"Are there others in this galaxy that fought against it?" Miranda asked.

"Of all the worlds that have been attacked, none have survived. It sent only Collectors to Earth, believing that there would be no resistance given the lack of technology to defend against the collection virus. It is building forces meant to conquer this galaxy. If we have any chance to save your planet and perhaps other civilizations in this galaxy, we must go to the source of its power. The black hole at the center of this galaxy," Bing said with finality.

The others looked at each other with some trepidation. Then they all looked at Bucky with deeply concerned expressions. Once again, Bucky was overwhelmed with the responsibility and expectations of his friends and Bing.

He took a deep breath and calmed himself. He wondered what else this Orb could do under his control. Would it be enough to take on an entire army? He knew he had to face his fears and protect his friends. He trusted Bing, and now they had Miranda, a physicist, to help them. *Wait, Do Miranda, Marcus, and Jen even want to be a part of this potential suicide mission?* He thought to himself. He looked around at them.

"Bing, you said we need to go to our galaxy's supermassive black hole?" Bucky asked.

"Yes," Bing replied

"Are all of you on board with that?" Bucky asked, looking for their reactions.

Marcus and Jen looked at each other and nodded. Bucky looked over at Miranda and saw her smiling face as she said, "You know I wouldn't miss the opportunity to study a black hole up close. And I also want to do what I can to help you and Bing. So, yes. Of course, I'm in."

Bucky felt a knot of emotion welling in his throat. He coughed a little to cover the fact that he felt like crying. These people were his family now. Whatever happened to them, at least they would all be together. He looked over at Bing, and the smiling expression on his face told him everything about dedication and love. At that moment, he felt he could take on the galaxy. He knew they would eventually figure out some way to fight back, to stop this evil. They were a team, his team. He knew they were his biggest supporters, and now they would fight together. Bing walked over to Bucky and placed his hand on his shoulder, reassuring him, and then returned to the console to take his position.

"Marcus, we need to take this ship to a location where we will not be disturbed while I initiate the repairs necessary for transport to the wormhole," Bing said.

"We will also need provisions," Miranda said, looking around at the spacecraft interior, possibly for someplace to store them.

"I will need to take on water and acquire sustenance for you all," Bing said. "Perhaps you can help me with the specifics, Dr. Richards."

"Sure, Bing. How long do you think we'll be away?" Miranda asked, her voice trailing off a bit as she spoke, like she realized, along with the others, they may never come back if they failed.

After a brief discussion, they agreed to search for a food source in a less conspicuous, rural area of New York. They still had no idea how long it would take for life to return to normal after the Collector ordeal.

“I need to see my mother,” Bucky said. “I need to know she’s ok.”

“Me too,” both Jen and Marcus said.

Bing took each of them to their respective homes. Miranda returned to her brothers and the others to their homes in Bucky’s town. They all planned to have brief reunions with their families before embarking on their journey to the center of the galaxy.

“I will repair the ship and return to get you,” Bing said to Bucky as they landed in the field near Bucky’s house.

Bucky ran to his home and burst in, shouting, “Mom, I’m home!”

“Bucky!” his mother screamed as she ran into the room to greet him. She hugged him as if he had just returned from war.

Bucky sat her down and, with great difficulty and long explanations, which did not include how his soul had left his body, explained what had happened. He determined that the virus had not reached his small town, so his mother was spared the collection.

She made every effort to understand, and in the end, they spent an hour discussing their entire life together and their family experiences. There were many tears shed, and when it was time to leave, he gave her one final hug before returning to the clearing to reunite with Bing and his friends.

Once they were all back together, Marcus brought the spacecraft back down towards what appeared to be a well-lit area just outside a small town. They followed a main road that had streetlights lit to what was clearly a shopping center with a large, well-lit food store. He gracefully landed the spacecraft in the parking lot, well clear of any cars.

The area appeared devoid of people at the moment. Clearly, not everything had returned to normal yet. They all exited the spacecraft and walked through the parking lot toward the entrance. Once inside, the store also seemed empty of people, but the lights were on. They collected what they thought was appropriate to survive for some time. They bagged what they had gathered, and without an attendant to pay, they exited the store and started back towards the spacecraft.

They were immediately shocked by what they saw when they left the store. There were several police cars with about half a dozen well-armed officers surrounding the spaceship. When the officers saw them standing in front of the store, especially with Bing's imposing presence, they turned their weapons on them.

"Stop where you are!" came a booming voice amplified by a megaphone.

Bing moved in front of the group, followed by Bucky standing next to him.

"I said freeze, or we will fire!" came another booming command.

Just when Bucky thought things could not get worse, two Army Humvees came racing into the parking lot. They had large machine guns mounted on the top, with soldiers holding them and pointing the ominous weapons at Bing as they came to a stop about 25 meters from them, blocking their path to the spaceship.

"You've got to be kidding me," Marcus said in a frustrated voice. "We survived the Collectors to now face our own people threatening us like this?"

"They don't know any better, Marcus," Jen said, trying to comfort him.

"Well, Bucky," Miranda said, "we can try to talk our way out of this, which we clearly don't have time for, or you can use that Orb of yours to get us out of this."

"Caution, my brother," Bing said, looking at Bucky.

"I know, I know," Bucky reassured as he thought hard about what he needed to do.

Whatever it was, it would be a new way to utilize the Orb. He didn't want to hurt them, and for sure, he didn't want any of his friends to get hurt. He thought he'd try the direct approach first.

"Um, gentlemen," Bucky spoke. "We have a very important mission to save all mankind from a further attack like what we've just experienced. So, if you could just let us pass, we'll continue on that mission."

Several officers snorted a laugh at Buckys' fictional statement. The gunners on top of the Humvees pulled the loading handles on the large machine guns that made a loud, ominous chunking sound as the guns were prepared to fire.

"I don't think they believe you, Bucky," Marcus said as he stepped closer to Jen and put his arm around her to shield her.

One of the soldiers in the Humvee stepped out, put a walkie-talkie to his ear, and started speaking into the mouthpiece. Bucky knew he was calling for backup, and very soon, their situation would get much worse. He had to think of a way to use the Orb to get past them and to the spaceship. *Some sort of shield,* he thought. Something that would not hurt the police or soldiers and, at the same time, protect them against possible gunfire. How would that work exactly? What hand movements would be required to create a protective energy field around them?

He connected with the Orb and felt the surge of potential energies jolt his body. He started his hand movements slowly, willing the negative energy through his hands, limiting the field to just around himself. He noticed the loose stones and dirt move around him. This time, he managed to hold the loose stones and dirt suspended around him without sending them into the sky. Gradually, he extended the energy field away from himself and was even able to leave gaps to allow Bing and his friends inside the protective energy bubble. The effect was interesting. All their hair was standing straight out, and if the situation was not so serious, they could all have a good laugh at how they looked.

With the energy field around them now, Bucky started moving slowly toward the Humvees and the spacecraft. The others stayed close to him, also sensing the energy field around them. The effect prevented them from hearing the police and soldiers yelling, which they were clearly doing, as well as raising their weapons and pointing at them.

Bucky thought about whether this energy field would deflect bullets. Then he remembered deflecting the Collectors' weapon and felt surer that bullets would react the same way. He walked slowly towards the Humvees, noticing that the soldiers were not shooting at them, yet.

Bing and his friends stayed close as he walked. When he was about eight meters from the nearest Humvee, he felt the energy field would contact the vehicle with the next step he took.

He hesitated only slightly before moving closer. To his astonishment, when the energy field contacted the Humvee, it moved it, dragging across the pavement, pushed by the negative energy field. The soldier on top had to grab the side of the turret to brace himself from the jolt. Within the next few steps, the other Humvee was pushed aside like a weightless plastic toy.

"Very good, my brother," Bing admired as he smiled at Bucky. "You are learning the control dimensions of the Orb."

"If that means I'm figuring it out, then yes," Bucky smiled back at Bing.

As Bucky and his friends pushed past the Humvees and police vehicles, they noticed the look of surprise on the officers and soldiers. They were also not shooting at them, and Bucky was very relieved they were not testing the energy field.

Once they were all back inside the spacecraft and the opening secured, they stored the supplies and took their seats. Marcus returned to his position at the control console and activated the navigation. With the others taking their seats, the spacecraft rose into the air. Bucky noticed the continued surprised expressions on the officials' faces as they lowered their weapons.

The spacecraft rose quickly through the atmosphere, and soon, the Earth looked smaller and smaller. They all looked longingly at the Earth and, for some time, did not speak, surely thinking of the dangers and challenges that awaited them.

Chapter Thirty-Three

Through The Wormhole

As the spacecraft accelerated through the solar system, Bing provided coordinates to the navigation systems to the wormhole awaiting them some billions of kilometers away. The negative energy drive created an expanding space behind the spaceship and compressed it in front, creating a spatial distortion. It formed a hyperspace tunnel as they entered the realm of faster-than-light travel.

Bucky marveled at the scene of the tunnel in front of them that appeared like a swirling kaleidoscopic corridor with streaks of colors and patterns bending and shifting around the spacecraft. It seemed to stretch and warp.

Stars and celestial objects stretched into elongated streaks, becoming smeared across their field of view due to the relativistic effects. This was not the same as looking at a star-filled sky where the stars were streaks of light passing them like in the movies. The light from the stars and galaxies appeared to shift toward the blue end of the spectrum in front and red-shifted looking behind.

Miranda was in awe of the sight. Astrophysics was her passion, and she continuously and excitedly described the scientific basis for what they were witnessing.

Bing pulled Bucky aside and began to tell him about what they were in for.

"There is much that is still unknown to me. As a scout, I have limited knowledge and programming about the mechanisms of the Entity. I do know that it uses the black hole as a source of destructive energy. I do not know how we will stop it. I know we must try. The Orb is the key because it gives us a chance."

Bucky looked overwhelmed. Once again, he thought about the fact he was just a sixteen-year-old boy thrust into an impossible situation of ultimate life and death.

"Bing, I don't know what I'm supposed to do," he said, sounding a little desperate.

"There is a central control ship that guides the construction of a great structure around the black hole. I believe it is key to the collection of energy from the black hole," Bing said.

"If we can board it and find a way to destroy it, perhaps we can at least disrupt the energy transfer from the black hole. We must try. If we do nothing, more worlds like your earth will be attacked, and all life will be extinguished in this galaxy and perhaps others."

"I will do my best," Bucky said, trying to reassure himself.

"And so will we," Marcus said as he approached Bing and Bucky, obviously overhearing their conversation.

"Yes, Bucky," Jen said, coming to stand next to Marcus.

Miranda joined them and said, "Perhaps we can learn about some of the technologies used to extract energy from the black hole. Learn about those responsible for the powerful objects such as the Orb."

"Together," Marcus said as he extended his hand forward, palm facing down.

"Together," they each said as they placed their hands on top of Marcus'.

"We are approaching the wormhole now," Bing announced as he returned to the console.

The images outside began to change, to return to normal as they decelerated from faster-than-light speed. The stars were no longer red and blue streaks and the blurred star clusters and gas clouds returned to their normal-looking state.

"There!" Marcus shouted, pointing toward the front of the spacecraft, which projected the outside space.

There appeared before them a vast, swirling tunnel of shimmering light that looked like an iridescent cosmic whirlpool. The colors of the wormhole shifted and changed, ranging from brilliant blues and purples to vibrant greens and pinks, with occasional flashes of intense white light dancing along its edges. It looked several miles in diameter.

"Please be seated and secure your restraints," Bing announced as the spacecraft neared the wormhole. "The transition may be a bit rough."

When they entered the wormhole and studied its contours, the spacecraft felt like it was riding on an invisible roller coaster. Gravity within it fluctuated, which caused moments of near weightlessness that were followed by sudden pulls in different directions. Bucky and the others gripped their seats and the restraints as their senses heightened by the intensity of the transit.

As the spacecraft penetrated deeper into the wormhole, the visuals intensified, and for a few moments, time and space became even more distorted. The projected external images flickered on and off. The moments the external images were off, there was complete darkness inside the spacecraft. Bucky was reminded again of his basic fears, the nightmare he experienced. The unknown darkness, trapped with no ability to escape.

He fought hard against his panic. He looked around at the others, and they seemed to be feeling the same way. Fear on their faces as they all plunged headlong into the unknown. He was comforted by the fact he was not alone. If they all survived, he thought, what an amazing story they would have to tell.

Every moment felt like an eternity, and yet, in the blink of an eye, they emerged into the heart of their galaxy.

They all gasped at once at the sight before them. The black hole dominated the internal projected image and the entire space in front of them, a colossal swirling light vortex surrounding the ultimate darkness. Its event horizon loomed like a voracious maw, emitting an eerie glow at its edges as it devoured light and matter alike. The space around the black hole was peppered with bright stars and nebulae glimmering with vibrant colors, providing a stark contrast to the gravitational monster at the center.

Around the black hole's light ring, they observed what Miranda described as the phenomenon of gravitational lensing – the bending of light due to the immense gravitational field. Stars and galaxies from behind the black hole were visible, their light distorted into peculiar arcs and rings, like celestial jewels scattered around its dark heart.

"Over four million times the size of our Sun," Miranda said in an awed voice.

"And look at that!" She pointed out towards the massive accretion disk.

A cosmic maelstrom of luminous gas, dust, and stellar debris orbiting the black hole, caught in its immense gravitational pull.

"It's the accretion disk surrounding the black hole. It's super-heated gas and dust," Miranda said with great wonder in her voice.

They were still millions of miles away from the supermassive black hole. Still outside of the full relativistic effects of its gravity.

As they drew closer, they saw something that turned their wonder to fear. They saw before them thousands of alien spacecraft in orbit around the black hole. What appeared to be tiny dots but moving with some purpose. They seemed to be constructing a massive but partially completed frame-like structure, a web of curved metallic beams that extended dangerously close to the event horizon of the black hole.

"That seems to be some sort of energy-collecting device. They seem to be siphoning energy from the black hole," Miranda said, more analytically now.

"This structure has been under construction for hundreds of years," Bing stated. "When completed, it will represent the most powerful weapon in this galaxy and perhaps this region of the universe," Bing said as he zoomed the internal image onto another structure.

There was a disk-like shape hovering menacingly near the supermassive black hole that appeared as a colossal metallic saucer of ominous proportions. Its surface was an iridescent black that reflected the faint glow of the surrounding accretion disk. The dish was immense which stretched thousands of kilometers in diameter, and it rotated slowly around its central axis. Along the surface of the dish, intricate and menacing symbols were etched. The symbols seem to come alive, undulating and shifting as if they held a deep and sinister sentience of their own.

Suddenly, an ominous transformation began to unfold before their eyes. The structural rings, which once appeared inert and lifeless, started to emit an eerie glow. Growing brighter with each passing moment. They watched in awe and horror as the energy beams among the partially completed structure aligned in perfect synchronization. As if guided by a sinister intelligence, the beams converged toward the circular dish where all the gathered energy was focused with terrifying precision.

In a cataclysmic display, the beams discharge all at once, unleashing a blinding torrent of light and energy toward the disk. Another massive beam of focused energy shot out into the galaxy, leaving a trail of brilliance in its wake. The light from the beam was so intense they had to shield their eyes. The sheer power and scale of the unleashed energy was overwhelming, causing their spaceship to shudder, even from their great distance from the event.

As the destructive beam cut through space, it carved a path of devastation in its wake. Celestial bodies in its trajectory were instantly incinerated, reduced to nothingness by the overwhelming power of the black hole supplied energy weapon.

"Oh, my god," Miranda gasped, almost breathless. "I had no idea."

She turned to Bing to ask him about what they had just witnessed and was shocked to see that his head had returned to the cylinder shape. He did not move.

"Bing!" Bucky yelled, getting up from his seat.

Bing did not respond. Then, some words came from him, broadcast into the small enclosure of the spaceship. Alien words.

Jen screamed.

"What is it, Jen? What did he say?" Marcus shouted to Jen.

"He said his mission was completed. He said, 'I have done your will,'" Jen said in a shaky voice.

More alien words came from the robot, which used to be Bing.

"No!" Jen yelled as she looked over at Bucky, tears starting to run down her face.

"What, what did he say?" Bucky yelled, near panic now.

"He said his mission was to bring you here to be destroyed," Jen said.

"Something about your power with the Orb, something like when you returned, it would find you and destroy you."

Marcus held Jen and helped her over to stand with Bucky. Miranda followed quickly to join them, and together, they all gazed at Bing with his robotic cylinder head and body sitting at the console, unmoving.

"Bucky, I don't think that's Bing saying those things," Miranda said desperately. "I think he is being controlled somehow by the thing responsible for all of this."

Bucky held on to his friends, not sure what to do so far from home in this unimaginable circumstance. How could the Orb help him? How could he save his friends and now himself?

Just then, the robot that was Bing stood up and turned around to face them. Then he started slowly stepping towards Bucky and his friends.

Chapter Thirty-Four

Home Again

Suddenly, the interior of the spacecraft became completely dark. Bucky had never experienced anything like it before. He lost all sense of up and down. He felt overwhelmed with panic, trapped so far from home. All the things he took for granted about home. Beautiful earth he missed so much now. The air became cold and stale. He felt sure there would be no oxygen to breathe soon.

A small light pierced the darkness inside the spacecraft. Bucky looked over and saw Miranda holding a small flashlight, which was now shining on Bing.

“Bucky!” Miranda yelled. “Can you do something?”

Bucky heard panic in her voice, which unnerved him. He could see, however, that the robot that was Bing had taken a step towards him.

Just then, Jen moved between him and Bing. She held up her hands to stop him and yelled something Bucky knew was Bing’s native language. Bing stopped moving. The voice, that was not Bing's, boomed from the robot. The robot that was not Bing swept Jen aside with its right arm. Jen crashed against the side of the spacecraft. Miranda showed the flashlight on the heap that was Jen and ran to her side.

Marcus rushed at Bing and was caught across the chest and flung against the chairs behind the control console. Jen regained her feet, stood up, and yelled something again to Bing in the alien language. Bucky could see a trickle of blood down her face from a gash in her forehead.

Miranda again trained the small flashlight on Bing. Again, there was a booming voice response. This time, Bing stopped moving towards Bucky and faced Jen. Its arm slowly raised until his hand, with one finger pointed at Jen.

"Bucky, I have its attention. Can you use the Orb?" Jen yelled desperately. "Whatever is controlling Bing is saying we will all die," Jen yelled. "And it will take back that which belongs to it."

Marcus again rushed toward Bing, but this time, instead of being struck, Bing put up his right hand towards Marcus as if to say stop. Bing then slowly pointed to the control panel and Marcus's chair. In the dim light of the flashlight, Bucky could see Bing's right hand move over the control panel while his left arm was reaching for him.

Jen continued to engage whatever force was controlling Bing. Only now it seemed it did not have complete control of Bing. Even the volume of the voice seemed a little diminished.

Bucky knew that his time was now. He saw in the dim light that Jen was still bleeding from her head as she continued to shout the alien language. He felt enraged and quickly connected with the Orb. The entity seemed to realize that Bucky was now in control of the Orb, and it gave a horrible shrieking sound through Bing.

Bucky felt an overwhelming sense of anger and focus and began to project what he knew now was the energy from the Orb as a shield. He pushed it past all his friends and outwards outside the spacecraft. As the energy shield swept over Bing, the cylinder head immediately reformed into his familiar young man's head. Bing turned quickly and began many rapid movements over the control panel.

Warm air started to fill the inside again. The control panel lit up, and the outside projection was now shown on the inside walls of the spacecraft. Bucky, Miranda, Jen, and Marcus all screamed at once when they saw the image outside the spacecraft. It was a horrible undulating smoke-like mass that was as big as a large planet. It had thousands of tendrils, each moving independently like each had its own will. It was moving towards the spacecraft. It was the most evil and unnatural thing Bucky could ever imagine. At that moment, he chose to fight.

He was going to save his friends. He concentrated his focus on holding the Orb energy shield and even strengthening it.

"Let's go," Bing said in a loud voice as he made a gesture over the control panel, and the spacecraft shot away from the evil cloud and the great black hole. The outside view became a mass of color streaks that Bucky was now familiar with as faster than light speed.

Bucky released the energy shield and collapsed onto his knees. The others rushed to him and also went to their knees, where they just held each other.

After several moments, Bucky stood up and faced Bing, saying. "Are we going home?"

"Yes, my brother. To our home".

Printed in the USA
CPSIA information can be obtained
at www.ICGtesting.com
LVHW090358021024
792702LV00007B/556